SPECIAL MESSAGE TO READERS

THE ULVERSCROFT FOUNDATION
(registered UK charity number 264873)

res | Hyland | | Sou | or
ses.

Eye

WITHDRAWN

reat
and
logy,

up,

tern

Books should be returned or renewed by the last date above. Renew by phone **03000 41 31 31** or online *www.kent.gov.uk/libs*

oyal

You _____ tion

E\ _____ ou
w   or

THE ULVERSCROFT FOUNDATION
The Green, Bradgate Road, Anstey
Leicester LE7 7FU, England
Tel: (0116) 236 4325

website: www.foundation.ulverscroft.com

C161019422

After graduating from the University of Leicester, Linda Priestley spent several years in clinical research before starting a family. Once her children were at school, she started writing mysteries under the name of Linda Gruchy. The author of numerous short stories and non-fiction articles for magazines, she is also a keen amateur photographer and gardener.

Visit her website at:
www.lindagruchy.wordpress.com

BOOK LOVERS

Amy moves into her aunt Debbie's house to study and to help her aunt through chemotherapy. The last thing on Amy's mind is romance — she's been hurt before — but when a charming stranger wanders into the house, mistaking it for its former incarnation as a second-hand book shop, Debbie is irresistibly drawn to him, despite her uncertainty as to whether he is a burglar or a genuine book lover. To complicate matters, Uncle Bernard, Debbie's dubious ex, suddenly appears on the scene, inveigling his way into the household and back into Debbie's heart. What are Bernard's real motives, and can Amy really trust the new object of her affections?

Books by Linda M. Priestley
Published by Ulverscroft:

EARTH MAGIC

LINDA M. PRIESTLEY

---◆---

BOOK LOVERS

Complete and Unabridged

ULVERSCROFT
Leicester

First published in Great Britain in 2012

First Large Print Edition
published 2015

A catalogue record for this book is available
from the British Library.

ISBN 978–1–4448–2401–8

Published by
F. A. Thorpe (Publishing)
Anstey, Leicestershire

Set by Words & Graphics Ltd.
Anstey, Leicestershire
Printed and bound in Great Britain by
T. J. International Ltd., Padstow, Cornwall

This book is printed on acid-free paper

Dedication

For my mother Veronica and my mother-in-law Hilda who both enjoy a love story

And for Dave, Jo and Alex, as always.

Acknowledgements

I now have so many writing friends it's hard to thank everyone who has helped in some small way, but I would like to thank in particular Nicola Slade for her very helpful comments when reading through the manuscript, Elizabeth Lord and Paula Readman for their comments, Ju Stacey for scrutinising what I'd thought was the polished book, and Sally Zigmond and Jo Frith for their faith in my writing.

1

'Who on earth are you and what are you doing in here?' demanded Amy as she stepped back inside her aunt Debbie's house. She clutched the cheesecake she'd just bought to her chest defensively, trying to quell the wild beating of her heart. A burglar was standing in the large hallway, looking at one of her books.

The man stared at her and frowned, looking perplexed. 'What d'you think I'm doing? I want to buy a book, of course. Looks like Mr Murray's doing second-hand books now. If you're Mr Murray's assistant, your customer care needs attention, if you ask me.'

'How dare you? I live here. Mr Murray doesn't, not anymore. The bookshop closed down ages ago. You're trespassing.'

The man's mouth opened so wide he could almost have swallowed the book he was holding. He flushed a dark crimson, which clashed horribly with his toffee-blond hair. He still managed to look attractive though, in his neat charcoal suit and tie, but that just added to Amy's anger. 'I'm so sorry — the door was open. I just assumed — whatever must you think? But the books . . . ' He swept his arm round to indicate the shelves full of Amy's books, all sorts of books just shoved any-old-how onto the old bookshelves left from when Amy's uncle ran the bookshop. The large hallway and front room were entirely fitted out with bookshelves and Amy had made good use of them.

Not a burglar after all, and her greeting must have sounded very rude. Amy giggled. 'There are rather a lot, aren't there? I can see why it looks like a second-hand bookshop to you. I've just moved in with my aunt and I haven't had time to sort them out. You knew my uncle when he ran the bookshop, then?'

'Knew? I hope he hasn't passed on?' The man's face fell.

'No. He's — gone.'

He looked relieved. 'Oops, looks like another foot-in-mouth moment. I'm so sorry. I knew Mr Murray very well. I used to buy at least one book a fortnight from him. We'd spend ages chatting about books. So is your aunt Mrs Murray, then?' Not waiting for her answer, the man babbled on, 'I missed my train, and there isn't another one for an hour, and I fancied a book so I came to the old bookshop. I used to live in Runworthy years ago. Went to school here. In fact, I've just had an interview for a teaching post at my old school . . . ' His voice tailed off; perhaps he thought that she wasn't really interested. A job interview explained his suit, then, which looked oddly out of place when everyone else was wearing light summer dresses or slacks or shorts. He looked very good in it: broad across the shoulders, trim waist, narrow hips. The cut looked expensive, not exactly from the local supermarket, and a gold watch gleamed on his wrist. He had a leather briefcase by his feet. He looked like a very well-to-do businessman. How could she have thought him a burglar?

His ferocious blush had diminished to a soft glow. 'I'll, er . . . I'd better leave you in peace then. I can't apologise strongly enough for the intrusion.'

'Take the book if you like.'

'Pardon?' His face was so expressive — sensitive, yet with underlying strength written into his bone structure. His eyes were as grey as smoky quartz, his nose finely modelled above lips that invited kisses.

Stop it, Amy told herself. *You sound like a slushy romance.* He had a good, strong chin, her mind continued. She started to blush, wondering if her admiration was obvious. 'You said you wanted a book to read . . . take that one.'

'I couldn't possibly . . . ' He shook his

3

head, lips parting into an embarrassed grin.

'Yes you can. I've read that one over and over. I ought to cull some of them; it's getting ridiculous, don't you think?' She looked round at the full shelves. 'This isn't the half of it. The front room is pretty full too. I have far too many, haven't I?'

The man followed her glance around. 'Not really. You've plenty of accommodation for them, after all. I don't think I could bear to part with any of my books.'

'I can bear to part with that one.'

'Well, if you're sure. It's very kind. I'd better get to the station. I don't want to miss the next train.' He slid past Amy with a fluid movement and she caught a faint, almost subliminal, whiff of expensive aftershave. He flashed her a shy grin, closing the door gently behind him. The large hallway seemed bereft when he'd gone.

Amy stood still for a few heartbeats, cheesecake still clutched to her chest, fingers digging into the paper bag, then exhaled. Wow. What a fright that man had given her. She was slightly shivery and her throat hurt from her heart's pounding. Still, an honest mistake, easy to make.

She locked the front door and went upstairs to the kitchen to put her cheesecake in the fridge. She'd gone off the idea of eating

4

it and would save it for later. It wasn't much of a supper, but she didn't like to eat much in front of Aunty Debbie at the moment, and cooking anything was a no-no because of the smell, let alone the heat — late July and sweltering. A stab of worry hit her and she blinked back tears. Everyone was putting on a brave front, and so must she.

'Who was that?' Debbie called from her bedroom, voice feeble with fatigue.

Amy poured a small tomato juice and took it through to her aunt. Debbie was propped up in bed. A handsome, capable-looking and amply covered woman, she looked diminished against the pillows, though her smile was as ready as ever.

Amy grinned at Debbie's question. 'This rather hot man was standing in the middle of the hall snooping over my books, wanting to buy one from Uncle Bernard. Idiot hadn't even noticed that the bookshop sign's gone. I'd only popped across the way to the deli for five minutes.'

'As in 'Murray's Bookshop', eh?' Debbie laughed. 'We used to get a lot of people assuming it was still a bookshop when it first closed down; just walked in or even hammered on the door wondering why we were shut. But we took to locking the iron gates across the cobbled private lane for a few days, and that sort of broke the habit since they couldn't get to the front door anymore. But it was a bit inconvenient having to open the gates every time we needed to go out, or Alison from the deli wanted access to the garages, so we keep it open during the day now and hope the 'private property' sign is enough to stop people wandering down the lane. If people are going to walk into the house like that, maybe we should think about locking it again. I'll have a word with Alison when I feel a bit better.'

Debbie took the proffered juice, sipped, then placed the glass on the bedside table. 'It's best to always keep the front door locked, though, Amy love,' she continued, 'even if you're popping out just for a minute, even just across to the deli. You can't trust anyone. We used to get well-dressed people nicking books, or people wandering around the garden, not realising the lane is private. Our local bobby, PC Bishop, often comes round to say there's a spate of purse-dipping or a gang of shoplifters working the town. You can't be too careful.'

Her aunt took another sip of juice. 'So . . . this bloke was hot, was he? You should have offered him a glass of water.' Debbie's expression was serious, almost reproving.

Amy opened her mouth for an indignant

6

reply and saw Debbie struggle to hide a smile, eyes twinkling. 'Oh you . . . '

'Did he give a name, or did he run away screaming with embarrassment?' added Debbie.

'The latter. Sort of.'

Though the windows were wide open, the sounds of the town seemed muted, as if wearied by the soaring temperatures outside. The bedroom looked out over the back of the property, so was quieter than Amy's room, the guest room at the front, though the clatter of passing trains could be a bit intrusive. Amy moved over to the window and looked out across the back garden. It was level at first, a brick terrace leading onto a lawn, then dropped away in terraces towards the railway line. In the distance, across the line, she could see the station platform. The man was sitting on a platform bench, one leg cocked over his other knee, head bent over, reading. He was so far away he looked tiny, but as if he felt her gaze, he looked up exactly in her direction. She couldn't see his eyes, or even see if his mouth was smiling. She waved but he didn't respond. 'I was a fool. He's really hot, best looking bloke I've seen since beastly Gareth, and I didn't even get his phone number. I wish I'd dashed after him and given him mine or something.'

'That would have been a bit unseemly, don't you think? You panting after him like a blushing schoolgirl?'

'Unseemly? What an old-fashioned word. This is the twenty-first century, not Victorian England. For goodness sake, Aunty, why must you be so, so proper?'

'Unseemly and unwise,' said Debbie with a grim nod. 'I thought you'd learned your lesson after that situation with Gareth. Handsome is as handsome does. Men are not trustworthy. My mum, your gran, used to say they were only After One Thing. I was deeply, desperately in love with your Uncle Bernard — still am a little bit, truth be told — but he was a prize rat for all his verve and charm.' She blinked a couple of times. 'Don't fall for some stranger just because he's a dashing and charming young man, especially a stranger who walks uninvited into houses. And don't get caught on the rebound.'

Crumbs, thought Amy. *Uncle Bernard walked out on her seven years ago, she's divorced and everything, and she still feels sore about it. You'd think she'd be over him by now.*

Just like you're over Gareth? she continued to herself dryly. A wave of anger, hurt and bitter resentment broke over her. She shivered and turned back to the window,

8

grabbing the windowsill with white-knuckled hands and leaning into the sill for support. She could feel her aunt's eyes boring into her tight shoulder muscles. Amy gave a sigh. Debbie was right.

'I think we should forswear all men,' quipped her aunt. 'Amy, love, Gareth's not worth the angst, really he isn't. He's history. Time to move on.'

'I know,' Amy told the window. 'I know it in my mind, but my heart still says different. This is the first time since Gareth that I can actually bear to think of a man in that way. He broke my heart, you know, even though it was I who dumped him.'

'Hearts are unreliable creatures, just like men,' said Debbie. Amy detected a bitter undertone to the straightforward way Debbie spoke.

Amy turned back, eyes flicking wide. 'I know. The weird thing was, my heart kept telling me what a gorgeous man he was, when all the time my head was telling me to be careful, telling me he was very dodgy.'

'Gareth is a cad and a liar.'

'I meant the man just now — the book-burglar. There we were in the hallway, with me furious and thinking him a burglar, and at the same time thinking how good-looking he was, despite deciding men

9

just aren't worth it. He was pretty cool.'

'First he's hot, now he's cool,' laughed Debbie. 'You don't really have to forswear all men, Amy, I was joking. Where would we be without them? But tread carefully, that's all I'm saying. Look with your head and ignore that capricious idiot called the heart. Stop being so impulsive.'

'I know; you're right as usual, Aunty Debbie.' *I'm not impulsive, am I? Just muddled. Scared, maybe. I just want things to settle down a bit.*

'I've said to stop calling me 'Aunty' now you're twenty-one. It makes me feel old, fat and frumpy.'

'Sorry, Debbie. Are you feeling any better?' Debbie had just started chemo-therapy treatment for breast cancer. She looked translucent as porcelain, with dark smudges below her eyes, her face slightly puffy from the steroids and other drugs she'd been given to keep the sickness at bay during the first round of chemo. But her eyes were as kind and twinkling as always.

'To be honest, I'm not sure how I feel just now. It's like I've all the nasty effects of getting drunk without drinking anything. Like a mad carousel that I can't get off. Ugh. And I have this vile metallic taste in my mouth. It's sore, too. I know I was warned, but it's still a bit of a shock. Everything's happened so fast, I've hardly caught breath. I wish I could fast-forward over the next few days and get over the worst effects of the chemo. How's your unpacking going? Sorry I'm in no fit state to help at the moment.'

Amy's family had just moved to the States for her father's work, and let their home out, so Amy had come to live with Debbie. Amy had thought she'd have plenty of time to sort her belongings out and pack carefully, but time had run out, and in the end much of her stuff was bunged in boxes willy-nilly and moved to her aunt's capacious home to be sorted at leisure. 'Apart from the odd tall, fair, handsome man walking off with one of my books, it's going OK. Everything's still an awful muddle, but I'd rather sort things out slowly. It's been such an upheaval.'

'The stranger actually stole one of your books?' Debbie frowned and sat herself up in bed.

'No, I let him have it. He looked utterly mortified over his mistake and it's one I've read several times. I let him have it to show him I'd forgiven him.'

'Hmm, so long as it was a genuine mistake and he didn't just come in to burgle the place after all.'

'I think it was a genuine mistake.'

'Seriously, I know you jokingly called him the book-burglar, but he could have just wandered in on the off-chance of grabbing something valuable. Doesn't take very long, you know . . . just a minute or two to grab a few things and walk off with them, like a laptop or a handbag . . . '

Amy was about to say what an absurd idea that was, but the words didn't come. Debbie could be right, after all. When she'd pushed the front door wide open to see him standing there, book open, browsing over the words, he'd been reading halfway through the book, not the blurb on the back or the first chapter. It was as if he'd just grabbed it from the shelf in a panic after hearing her shoes clattering over the cobbles. It was very suspicious, now, when she thought about it, without her capricious heart whispering distracting and 'unseemly' sentiments to her.

Amy turned back to the window. The man was still seated on the station bench. As she watched, he straightened up and opened out a newspaper with an unmistakeable flick of his hands, then folded it up and bent over it again, reading. The liar. He'd spun her a tale about needing a book when he already had a newspaper to read. And if he'd lied about wanting a book, then he probably was a burglar after all.

Amy slipped back downstairs, leaving her aunt to sleep while she had a good look around to see if anything was missing. There didn't seem to be, but then the whole of the downstairs was in such a turmoil it would be hard to tell. At least her laptop was still there, though. It looked as if she'd interrupted him before he'd had a chance to pocket anything. But maybe he wasn't a burglar after all.

Her thoughts were scrambled, so she stepped out through the front door into the cobbled private lane between the old bookshop and the deli. Perhaps she should go to the station and have another look at this man, maybe even confront him about the newspaper. Yes, that was a good idea. Go and speak to him on some pretext, see what he had to say about that newspaper, maybe ask for his phone number. If he was a burglar he was unlikely to give it to her. If he was innocent, she'd be able to contact him.

Her aunt's house, originally a Georgian merchant's home, had been divided by her grandfather many years before into a flat upstairs for living in, and a bookshop business downstairs. It was side-on to what was now Runworthy's high street, facing the deli across a cobbled private road which led round the back of the deli and some garages belonging to both of them. Originally the cobbled lane had swung round back onto the high street half a mile further down, but much of it had been sold off and built on nearly a hundred years ago. This left Debbie's house looking as if it was snobbishly cold-shouldering the high street, an impression reinforced by the addition of iron railings and double gates across the cobbled lane.

Amy vaguely remembered her grandfather, Alfred Driscoll, who had set up the bookshop shortly after the Second World War. He'd worked in his beloved bookshop right up to his death in 1998, though by that time Aunty Debbie and Uncle Bernard (rot him) had been doing most of the day-to-day running. Amy had been eight or nine at the time. They hadn't visited her aunt, uncle and grandfather very often, just once or twice a year; but whenever they did, Amy remembered Grand-dad limping through the bookshop to the children's section with her and inviting her to choose a book, something which had always thrilled her because there was so much to treasure. Debbie was her mother's sister and Amy was very, very fond of her. She'd been fond of her uncle Bernard too, until he'd behaved so despicably.

The iron gates across the cobbled lane were propped open as usual when Amy walked out into the high street. The notice 'private property' affixed to the iron railings on either side of the gates should keep most people at bay, surely? The lane looked like private property; it said it was private property. She frowned. It seemed that Aunty Debbie was right about the young man. He'd walked past the sign and into the house, and that was a bit odd, thinking about it.

It was nearly 5.30pm and the shops were beginning to close. Amy still hadn't got used to the small-town behaviour of the local shops. Runworthy seemed to put itself to bed ridiculously early.

The florist was moving her buckets of flowers and pot plants inside. She straightened up as she saw Amy coming up the road. 'How's Debbie?'

Amy stopped, wishing she could just carry on to the station. 'She's over the worst of the first round of chemo, thanks. Very weak, but cheerful as always.' Her voice caught on the sudden lump in her throat.

'I didn't like to ask her, but will she lose her hair, do you know? It's such lovely hair, it seems a shame.'

Amy thought of the long, dark lustrous tresses so like her own. 'Yes, she will. She had it cut short so it won't be such a shock when it does fall out.'

'Has she had an operation then? I'm a bit

confused and I didn't like to ask . . . You know how it is. We were all very shocked.' The florist was chewing her lip, not quite looking into Amy's eyes, but Amy saw the gleam of tears dewing her lashes.

'Not yet. She's having chemo first, four rounds of it, then an op, then radiotherapy.'

'Seems a funny way of doing it. I'd want it cut out immediately, but I suppose they know what they're doing.'

'Everyone's different and they have various treatments for specific types of breast cancer.'

'Did they say what her chances are? They're supposed to be very good nowadays, aren't they? We're all a bit worried.' The florist was babbling the words out in a breathless gush, as if she wanted to ask every question in case she didn't dare ask again. She looked desperate for reassurance, something which Amy couldn't give her.

Amy knew Debbie wouldn't mind her talking about her illness, but then Debbie was like that; she faced up to problems head-on, chin up high, with a valiant smile on her face. Amy blinked. 'She didn't ask, and they didn't say. But as you say, nowadays the outlook is a lot brighter than it used to be.' Amy's voice was too bright — too positive — as if ensuring Debbie's survival through wishful thinking alone.

The florist looked down at the bunches of flowers, selected a couple, and passed them to Amy. 'Give her my love, won't you? Give her all our love, and tell her we're thinking of her. Would it be OK to visit?'

'I would leave it for a couple of days. At the moment she's still very tired and needs to sleep a lot. But every day she's a little stronger.' *Until the next round of chemo,* the thought ran on in Amy's mind. 'This is very sweet of you and I'll get them in water straight away, thanks.'

Bother.

2

Amy headed straight back home at a half-run and dashed through the front door into the hallway, then into what had been the kitchen when the house had been a merchant's house and not a business. It had probably been last updated in the early twentieth century, with an old range, a Belfast sink and old built-in dresser, and a scullery between the kitchen and the dining room, all hardly used since the creation of a modern kitchen in the flat upstairs. Amy shoved the plug in the sink, pulled the tap on so hard it splashed, placed the flowers into the water, dried her hands swiftly, then ran out of the house, remembering to lock the door. She ran up the high street and turned right over the railway bridge. It was only a five-minute walk, really, and a two-minute trot, but as she ran over the bridge a train trundled into the station. She heard the mumbled announcement; then, as she paused on the bridge, she watched it pull away. The platform was empty. She propped herself up on the bridge and caught her breath, both relieved and disappointed.

Never mind, she told herself. *Aunty's*

probably right — he's just a good-looking burglar dressed up in a suit to allay suspicion. Even if he's not, I bet he's married, good-looking bloke like that. And what would you have said to him anyway? Aunty's right; it would have been 'unseemly'. And if he was a burglar, then the last thing you should be doing is panting after him. Just as well, then. But her common-sense self-talking-to didn't stop the feeling of deep disappointment. She muttered silently to herself as she walked home, saying the things she wished she'd said at the time. By this time her heart had resumed its normal rhythm, but pattered like a skittish pony every time she thought of him.

She let herself back into the house and stared round with a potential burglar's eyes. Was the man an opportunist burglar, or had he genuinely thought the bookshop still open? She was standing in a large hallway with a doorway leading to the front room; a door to a downstairs cloakroom; next to that a door shutting off the stairs up to the flat; and lastly, the door to the old unused kitchen. The hallway had bookshelves and a table where Granddad had kept the till. It had looked very different when it was a bookshop, despite her books now covering the shelves. It had looked like an orderly shop, not a cluttered domestic space.

Surely that should have told that man that the bookshop had closed; that and the 'Private Property' sign, and the lack of the 'Murray's Bookshop' sign above the front door? Definitely a burglar, then, thought Amy with a grim nod. Perhaps they should mention it to the local bobby when they saw her next.

Amy went back to the flowers in the sink. They were beautiful and needed arranging in a vase. Her eyes roamed over the old redundant kitchen. This would be hers when she and Debbie had sorted the downstairs out. Debbie's washing machine was down there because it was easier to do the washing downstairs and hang it outside, but all the other modern appliances like cooker and fridge were in the upstairs kitchen. Amy had brought the two-ring tabletop electric hob she'd used at university, a kettle, and her cafetiere, but apart from those modern intrusions the old kitchen looked like a museum exhibit. She'd need a small fridge-freezer, she decided, and a microwave.

She opened the Welsh dresser doors and was startled to see heaps of vintage crockery, but found no vases. Then she looked in the cupboard under the Belfast sink. There were several old-fashioned vases there. She pulled a large one out. It was heavy and made of moulded glass, probably dating from the '50s, probably older than Debbie. *I feel like I've stepped back in time,* she thought as she filled it with water.

She arranged the flowers carefully and gave them an appreciative sniff, checking they weren't overly scented because Debbie was hypersensitive to smells just now, then took the vase upstairs. Debbie was asleep. Amy put the flowers down on a mat on the dressing table. The three mirrors caught the reflections and multiplied the flowers until it seemed like a garden.

Back downstairs Amy put the kettle on, put a generous amount of fragrant coffee in the cafetiere, and while the kettle was boiling, went through the scullery into what had originally been the dining room. Her grandfather had used this as his business study, and then Uncle Bernard and Aunty Debbie had done the same. It still contained a massive desk and cupboards with the old ledgers and the more modern accounts, which her aunt had kept for the statutory six years after she'd closed the bookshop. At the moment Debbie still used it for work as a self-employed book-keeper, but once they had moved Debbie's computer and business accoutrements upstairs, this was going to be Amy's study. French doors led out onto the terrace. Amy sat at the huge desk and stared into the garden. It was going to be the most amazing study.

Another door led from the study into what had originally been the drawing room before the bookshop conversion: Amy's bedroom-to-be. This was furnished with bookshelves and had been part of the bookshop.

Amy gave a little shiver of glee. *I am so lucky to have all this space. Good old Aunty Debbie.* She opened the door into a shower room with ancient fittings dating from when it had been converted from an oversized cupboard in the 1930s. It was green art deco and as much a fossil as the downstairs kitchen. Granddad's parents, her great-grandparents, had had it installed when a proper modern bathroom was all the rage, but when Granddad had converted the house to bookshop and upstairs flat, it had fallen into disuse as anything more than a loo for him while he was at work.

Amy wondered what it had been like for her mother growing up here with Aunty Debbie. Great fun, probably. When her mum had married her dad, they'd set up home a long way from Runworthy, so Amy's family had only visited a couple of times a year while she was growing up, and those visits had been as enchanting as a fairy tale. 'I'd have loved to live here as a kid,' said Amy aloud to herself as she went back into the old kitchen to make her coffee. 'Never mind; I can live here now. I'm so lucky. It's a pity Debbie isn't very well, though. It's put a real downer on it. Still, at least I'm able to help out. That's one good thing.' She pushed the thought aside and took her coffee through the study's French windows onto a very pleasing brick terrace and sat down at a teak table. A path of the same brickwork then went down through the lawn and terraces towards the railway. A low line of hawthorns on the railway embankment marked the end of the garden. The brick paving — old, Victorian, and beginning to disintegrate — threw back the heat of the day. It was a lovely place to sit out of an evening, especially in summer.

That man, the handsome burglar, kept invading her thoughts. The more she thought about it, the sillier her suspicions seemed. He hadn't looked at all guilty when she'd confronted him; no, he'd been indignant. He could easily have found the newspaper at the station — people often just dumped them when they'd finished with them — so needing something to read probably hadn't been a lie after all.

He looked a couple of years older than she, past the gawky-youth stage; a man. Not like the boys at university. She shuddered. So brash, so cock-sure of themselves. It seemed that nowadays boys assumed that everyone regarded sex as a sport, like going for a run or a session of aerobics, whereas she thought it should be something special — a pact, sealing the love between two people. 'You old romantic,' she told herself. 'You read too much slush.' She took a sip of the rich, fragrant coffee. 'But I like reading slush,' she wailed to herself. 'I like reading everything, which is why I'm doing an MA in English Literature.' Another sip of coffee followed the first — mellow, delicious. 'You're a fool; best-looking bloke you've seen for ages and you didn't even get his number. You should have offered him a coffee, never mind a glass of water, because he's hot.' She sniggered to herself over her aunt's teasing. Her smile broadened as she went over the conversation with the man. At the time it had been hideously embarrassing, but in retrospect is was rather funny. *I don't have a lot of luck with men, do I?*

Gareth. Her heart gave a sick lurch over the memory. He was enough to turn the most ardent romantic into a realist. The coffee's savour vanished. She stared over her aunt's beautiful garden, seeing none of it. 'Two months. I should be over him by now.'

* * *

Amy's temporary bedroom, the guest bedroom upstairs, was at the front of the house overlooking the street. After a minute's gazing out of the window, she opened up her laptop to check her emails. Great; an email from her parents, telling her the family had arrived safely in America. Amy's father worked for an American company and had accepted a position in the States for five years shortly before Debbie had been diagnosed. Amy remembered the anguish her mum had felt at seemingly abandoning her sister in her hour of need. Amy had spent ages reassuring her mum that she would be there to help. She could drive Debbie to the hospital when needed. Mum needn't worry. Reading the email, Amy knew that her mum still felt guilty and torn over the whole thing.

Debbie obviously detected the same anguish when she read it. 'Dear old Pat, she does ramble on, over and over the same old things. I know she was pretty cut up over the move, and feels bad about it, but it's just one of those things. I hope it doesn't spoil her enjoyment of the adventure. America's a wonderful place and I always wanted to visit. Perhaps I'll go after my treatment's finished.'

★ ★ ★

A couple of days later Amy arrived back from shopping and picked up the post scattered on the doormat, glancing through it as she wandered into the old study. Her aunt, getting over the first round of chemo and feeling very much better, was tackling the old business paperwork in the filing cabinet. Uncle Bernard had never been very good with his filing and some valuable things had been shoved any-old-how into archived accounts that could now be destroyed. Separating out the precious from the discardable was a slow, tedious business, especially under the circumstances, and the main reason why Amy was still in the guest bedroom upstairs and not in this room.

Debbie looked up. 'I wish I could just dump the lot but I can't,' she moaned. 'I have just found an old life insurance policy that I never knew about. Or if I did, I'd forgotten about it. It was one thing your uncle was very good at. Said we should be insured because if anything happened to one of us, he'd want the other to be all right. This one has lapsed, I expect — I certainly haven't been paying into it — but I wouldn't be surprised if we came across some share certificates or old savings accounts I knew nothing about. He

26

was terribly badly organised, my Bernard.' She showed Amy the policy.

'Blimey, you were worth a fortune if you snuffed it,' exclaimed Amy, blinking over the sum Debbie was insured for.

Debbie laughed. 'He nearly collected it too, when I fell down the cellar stairs.'

'I remember that,' said Amy. 'You had to go to hospital with a broken leg.'

'Oh, I was in such pain, and it thoroughly frightened the life out of me. I hate the stairs and goodness knows what I tripped over; my own two feet, I think.' She shuddered. 'I must confess I just left a lot of the domestic paperwork exactly as it was when he left me; couldn't bear to tackle it at the time. I was more preoccupied by the bookshop business, then the book-keeping business, and it's now become one of those jobs you never get round to unless something happens.'

'Something like me, you mean?' Amy laughed, though she had the horrible suspicion this was a 'straightening of affairs' just in case her aunt didn't survive.

'Exactly. We're dreadful hoarders, the Driscolls. My father used to hang on to all sorts of things 'just in case', and I'm not much better. Good job I have such a large house. Your mum's the same . . . '

'Don't I know it; it was awful trying to sort

27

out everything and pack it up so the house could be let while they're in America. I'm glad you had room in the attic for some of their stuff or they would be paying horrendous storage fees.'

'They'd have had to get rid of it all and start afresh when they came home. Five years would be far too long to pay for storage,' said Debbie. 'It wouldn't make economic sense.'

Amy handed over the post, which looked like a number of get-well cards and a bank statement. Debbie opened the cards first, and smiled and laughed at the contents. She scanned the bank statement briefly, then frowned. 'I've done enough sorting for today. Bring that box upstairs, Amy love, and we can shred later on it whilst watching TV.'

By the time Amy had carried the box up, her aunt was online on her computer, which she had moved out of the study and upstairs into the lounge. She was frowning.

'Cup of tea?' suggested Amy.

'Oh yes please. No, actually, I fancy a coffee. In a few days' time I won't be able to bear even the smell of it, let alone drink it.' Debbie pulled a face. Shortly, when she was sipping some of Amy's excellent coffee, she mused, 'There's a saying, isn't there, about the person who earns two pounds more than he needs is happy, but the man who earns two pounds less, isn't?'

'Mr Micawber, Charles Dickens: 'Annual income twenty pounds, annual expenditure nineteen, nineteen and six, result happiness. Annual income twenty pounds, annual expenditure twenty pounds ought and six, result misery.' It seems true enough, I suppose.' Amy fed some sheets into the shredder. 'I could do with earning a few pounds, but only part-time or I'll never get my MA done.'

'Good idea,' said her aunt. 'I think that would be a very good idea indeed.' Her eyes snapped back to her computer and she scowled at it.

Amy didn't like to ask if there was anything the matter.

3

'All set?' asked Amy as Debbie plugged the seat belt in. It was Thursday, chemo day, and Amy was taking her aunt to hospital.

Debbie nodded. She looked pale and strained. 'Let's go.' Her smile only tweaked her lips, and did nothing to soften the anxiety in her eyes.

Amy eased the car out along the narrow cobbled lane though the iron gates and onto the high street. It was her mother's car, which she was using now the family had gone to the States. She stole a glance at Debbie. *Of course she's going to be OK. Don't let her see you're worried. It'll be a six-month ordeal and then she'll be better.*

Debbie had taken all the medication designed to help her through the treatment. On her lap she clutched a folder containing her hospital card and the sheets she had scrupulously filled in for the nurse. The air of intense focus made Amy feel as if they were about to go into battle.

It's horrible. In a way I'm taking my aunt to be poisoned. But what choice is there? Loads of people go through this. Loads and loads. And they get better. It's no good worrying. Concentrate on your driving.

The journey was spent discussing the future: what Debbie would do once this was all over and done with, how she would redesign the garden, how she would promote her book-keeping business. It was all a little too defiant, but it kept their spirits up.

'That's lucky,' said Amy, grabbing a parking slot close to the oncology department. 'You stay there while I go and pay.'

'Here,' said Debbie, thrusting a bag of pound coins at her. 'I came equipped after last time.' Last time they'd had to scrabble around in the bottom of handbags and the car's glove compartment for enough loose change to pay for the parking. 'Best get a day's worth, Amy love.'

Amy fed the coins into the ticket machine. 'This is going to cost us a fortune when it comes to the radiotherapy,' she said as she displayed the ticket on the dashboard.

'I think I get a special parking permit for that,' said Debbie. She was frowning again, and Amy wasn't sure if it was at the ordeal ahead of her that day, or the thought of paying so much for parking. Less income, more expense; not a good feeling.

A short, fairly brisk walk later they were in the chemotherapy suite, reporting in. They sat in the waiting area and opened the books they'd brought with them. Amy found the words in the novel just didn't make sense, so she gave up, surreptitiously glancing round the waiting room at the other occupants. Some had hair, some didn't; some looked nervous, while others had brittle smiles and laughed a lot. An elderly couple sat hand in hand, saying nothing, just stealing adoring glances from time to time.

'It was so good to hear from Pat,' said Debbie. They'd received another email from Amy's mum that morning, wishing Debbie good luck with the treatment and telling Debbie and Amy that the family were feeling more settled; the house was lovely, made of clapboard on a wide street; and the twins had already made some friends.

A nurse took Debbie off for blood tests and to weigh her and discuss her treatment so far. Amy tried reading the book again, but it was impossible, what with all the coming and goings, and the desultory conversations around her.

Debbie came back all smiles. 'Now we wait for the blood test results,' she said, fishing a magazine out of her bag. 'It was good to hear from your mum, wasn't it? Oh . . . I've said that already, haven't I? I must be losing my marbles.'

Amy laughed dutifully. 'Don't be silly.'

People came and went, the minutes slipped by, and then it was Debbie's turn. Amy came to sit with her while the nurse fixed up the chemotherapy drip. Debbie didn't watch as the nurse put the needle in. Amy saw Debbie smothering a flinch, a bland mask of fortitude fixed on her face.

'I'm not sure I'd want to live in a clapboard house like Mum and Dad,' piped up Amy in an effort to distract Debbie. 'Too much like living in a shed.'

Debbie laughed. 'What about a romantic log cabin?'

'With turfs on the roof?' said Amy.

'I've seen those in Norway,' said the chemo nurse, fiddling around with the drip. 'Really quaint. Some even have trees growing on the roof. I went on holiday there and actually saw someone weeding his roof. There you go . . . running in nicely.' She left to attend to another patient.

The drugs slowly trickled into Debbie's veins.

*　★　★*

The walk back to the car was much further and much slower than when they'd arrived. Wordlessly, Debbie clambered into the passenger seat and picked up the bowl she'd brought along in case of nausea. Amy didn't say anything either, because she'd run out of conversation and anything she did say now sounded false and inane to her ears. She drove home carefully, taking bends slower than usual.

When they got home, Amy dropped her aunt off at the front door, then continued round to the garage to park the car, glancing anxiously in her mirror to make sure Debbie had managed to let herself in. By the time Amy had parked the car and reached the hallway, Debbie had hauled herself up the stairs. 'I'm going to bed,' she muttered.

'Have you got your bell to hand in case you need anything?' Debbie had an old school bell which had quite a penetrating ring to it, and Amy had suggested Debbie had it to hand in case of need. Amy would hear it all over the house.

'Don't worry, everything's under control. I'll leave the bedroom door ajar and call you if I need anything.'

4

Next morning Amy heard the shower going for quite a long time, so long she was beginning to get worried, wondering if Debbie had slipped and hurt herself. She was about to go and knock when she heard the bathroom door bolt flick back. Debbie wandered into the lounge swathed in a fluffy dressing gown. She was bald. 'It started coming out in clumps, so I thought I might as well get it over with. I think it was ready to come out anyway. At least now people will realise why I'm so slow when trundling round the shops and can't cope with opening doors. I feel weirdly lighter. Naked.'

'It actually suits you in a strange way. You have a very elegant neck.'

'I love you too, dear.'

'I mean it. I suppose you could get a wig, except they're expensive.'

'I could have one on the NHS if I wanted, but I don't think I do. It would be awfully hot in this weather and it's only for a few weeks. Besides, I'm not afraid to let people know I'm having treatment, and if it reminds one woman to do their self-examination and they

35

find something, it's worth looking a bit odd.' Debbie ran a hand over her scalp. 'Anyway, what are your plans for the day?'

'I have my tutor group this morning but I don't have to go if you need me.'

'I'll be fine, honestly. I'll stay in bed and rest. I'm sure I can get myself the odd drink or something to nibble. Not that I fancy much just now. You go to your group. Enjoy yourself.'

'I'll be back for lunch,' promised Amy.

After lunch Debbie remained in bed. Amy decided to get on with some studying. She started off with good intentions but she found it hard to concentrate. Unhappy thoughts kept nipping at her heels like bad-tempered terriers. She gave up trying to do some work, and lost herself in a slushy novel. She was curled up on a new sofa in what she laughingly called her library, deep in the book, when she heard stealthy footfalls on the cobbles outside. Her heart clenched. The post had already arrived, so it couldn't be the postie. She tiptoed into the hallway and hovered indecisively, a chill gathering at the back of her neck. Whoever was out there was being very furtive. The letterbox flap rose, so she assumed it was someone delivering junk pamphlets, but nothing was posted through. The flap was released quietly. There was a timorous knock at the door, which she didn't answer. Then another. Why did whoever was at the door not ring the doorbell? She stood behind the door, wishing it had a chain, wishing it had one of those peephole things. She knew she was being silly, overreacting to the cat's-paws on her spine.

The handle of the door went down. Someone was testing it to see if the door was unlocked.

Amy flung the door open. Her heart flipped. On the doorstep was the handsome book-burglar, far more casually dressed today, in jeans and a short-sleeved shirt. Still looked gorgeous, though. He staggered back, shock blatant on his face. She burst out laughing. 'Oh it's you; you gave me such a fright.'

He caught his breath and smiled brightly. 'Hi. Me too . . . you scared the heck out of me, opening the door like that. Sorry, I tried ringing but your doorbell's not working. I brought your book back, thanks. I didn't like to just shove it through the letterbox in case it broke the spine. I got the job and I was just passing.' His smouldering grey eyes gazed steadfastly into hers.

She half stepped outside, pressed the doorbell. Sure enough, no sound issued from it.

He went that fiery red again. 'You thought I was lying?'

'No, of course not. Just testing. I expect the battery's flat. Won't you come in a minute? Have a coffee or something? Congrats on the job by the way. A teacher, wasn't it? Which school?'

He hesitated slightly before entering diffidently. She ushered him into the front-room 'library'. Her heart was galloping. He was far more handsome and far less suspicious than she remembered. Debbie's remarks about him being of dubious character were ludicrous, now he was standing before her. He was probably a little shy, that was all.

'Wow, love the sofa,' he said. 'I don't remember that from last time.'

'It wasn't here last time. It's lush, isn't it? I got it from the charity shop down the road. I don't normally buy second-hand soft furnishings, but that I just had to have. Do you fancy a cup of tea? Or coffee maybe . . . have you time?'

'I didn't mean to intrude, but a coffee would be great, if it's not too much trouble.' He had a super smile — unassuming, slightly shy, but engaging.

'No trouble. Come through to the old kitchen. I'm Amy.'

'Luke.'

Amy busied herself with the coffee things. 'Sugar?'

'No thanks.'

'We'll have to sit outside and drink it. I'll explain in a minute. Can you get the back door please? I'll carry the tray . . . '

Luke opened the door for her. She stepped out into the garden, put the tray down on the table and offered him a seat. She rummaged through her brain for all the intelligent things she planned to say to him if she ever saw him again, but the words seemed to have disappeared, leaving just mush in her brains, so she poured the coffee instead.

'Wow, what a beautiful garden,' he said. 'Love this terrace . . . and the pots.' He took a sip of coffee. 'Oh, good coffee.'

'It's my one vice. I love it.'

'You were going to tell me why we have to drink it out here. Not that I mind; it's a beautiful garden.'

'My aunt is having chemo at the moment. She's just had a round of treatment and the smell revolts her.'

'I'm sorry to hear that.'

An embarrassed silence started to gather, so Amy said, 'So, the teaching job — which school?'

'Sir Gordon Fliney. I went there as a kid.

Hasn't changed much. There are even some of the same teachers, and I swear they don't look a day older than when I left, must be . . . ' Luke examined the sky as he counted the years. 'We moved away from Runworthy the summer after my GCSEs and I was nearly seventeen, so that's seven years ago. Blimey.'

'The bookshop closed down at about the same time, then, because that's when Uncle Bernard did a runner to Canada, the pillock.'

'Mr Murray, you mean?' Luke looked shocked.

'Yes, my uncle, rot him. Murray's Bookshop was struggling, what with online sales and stuff, and he made things worse. He's such a know-all about business, but he's rubbish at it. I mean, like changing the name from 'Driscoll's', for one thing. Granddad Driscoll set up the bookshop after the war and made it into something special, a feature of the town. Well, any fool knows about 'good will' in business, but my uncle wanted to see his own name above the bookshop when Granddad died.

Debbie was dead set against it, but Uncle Bernard did it anyway. Trade dropped off because people thought it was someone new, and they didn't have the same loyalty. He ran off to Canada to start afresh, leaving my aunt in charge of the business. After a long, hard look at the market, Debbie decided to close it down and got a job as a book-keeper — she's qualified. Then she went freelance and she's doing very well.' Amy took a sip of coffee and smiled at Luke, her mind drifting back to the ructions this had caused: miserable phone calls from Debbie to her mum, her mum saying what a rat Bernard was, and how she suspected he'd been up to no good, something which Amy hadn't believed because she had loved her uncle up to the point he had abandoned Debbie.

'That's such a shame. I liked Mr Murray. A charming man; I'm surprised. Your poor aunt. One thing after another.' He looked genuinely sympathetic, his thoughtful eyes clouding over. 'I thought it was Mr Murray's shop and only met your aunt a few times. I never realised it was really her family's bookshop.'

'Oh yes, but Uncle sort of took over, especially as my aunt was suffering from tummy trouble at the time and wasn't very well; it sort of dragged her down. Went on for months. The doctors said it was irritable bowel syndrome but I think she might have been allergic to something. Bernard, perhaps,' she quipped, then laughed briefly before saying, 'Oddly enough her stomach got better once Bernard left, so maybe that's not such a joke after all.'

'Might have been stress-related if things weren't going well with the bookshop. Maybe she felt conflicted over him seemingly taking over like that.' Luke sounded like he was trying to be clever, but Amy forgave him that because he spoke with such sincerity.

''Conflicted? Maybe. Nerves are supposed to make IBS worse, aren't they? Maybe there was a lot more to the break-up than I knew about. All I remember was Mum being on the phone to her for ages, in private, then her grumbling to my dad about what a pillock Bernard had been. He just up and left one day; ran away to Canada. Aunty was miserable for months afterwards, but her IBS got better, so maybe it was because the worst had happened and she could move on. I shouldn't bore you with family stuff like that.' Belatedly Amy thought perhaps she'd been a little too free with personal gossip, babbling on as she had. She felt herself blush. 'Please don't share that with anyone. It is a bit private and I — well, I shouldn't really have mentioned it.'

'I won't. Have you moved in to look after your aunt, then? Are you a nurse?' His eyes smouldered at her over the top of his coffee cup.

Amy found herself telling him about her family moving to the States for five years, and how she was doing an MA with the OU, hoping to become a teacher; how coming to live with Debbie had been fortuitous under the circumstances. 'Anyway, enough about me. Tell me a little about yourself. For instance, you used to live here and moved away aged nearly seventeen. Then what?' Amy leaned towards Luke across the table, her hands cupped round her mug. He was looking at her with an intense expression.

'A-levels, degree in geography, then an MA, then my postgrad certificate in education, and I did my NQT year last academic year. I saw this teaching post come up and I jumped at it, partly because it means I can stay at my parents' and commute. But I'm not so sure about staying with them now. It's not the same, going back home after university. It's not easy sometimes. Especially with my dad, you know. Alpha-male thing.'

'Ooh, I do know. I love my mum and dad, but it's nice to get away. Aunty's house is so big I'm not under her feet, since the upstairs is a self-contained flat. I'll be living downstairs once it's sorted. It's lucky this house is so big because I've accumulated a lot of clutter.'

'Like books.' Luke's lips twisted into a teasing smile.

'Yes. And clothes. And junk. Really

Important Junk. I had to bring it all with me because Mum and Dad let their house out, and there's a lot of their stuff stored in boxes in the attic . . . ' Amy's words ground to a halt as a thought hit her. Had she just now caught him out in a lie about his parents? Perhaps he was a burglar after all, though he really didn't look like one. And, bother it, she'd told him about the family wealth in the attic. 'So your mum and dad are still local then? You said you moved away years ago. I'm confused.' He was drop-dead gorgeous but that didn't stop him being a villain.

'We did move away, but only about 30 miles. Local but not that local. It's commutable by train, or I could drive if I had a car, but what I save in rent gets eaten by the fuel costs or a season ticket, so I've been having a look at flat rental here. That's why I'm here today. But the cheapest places are in the parts of town I'd rather not live in, and the cheapest is all I can afford.' He toyed with his empty coffee cup, frowning into it.

'Um, tricky . . . another coffee?'

'Only if you promise to let me reciprocate sometime. Like a drink out or something.'

'OK, that'll be cool.' Yes, thought Amy, yes. 'So did you find anywhere to live?' she asked as she made another pot of coffee.

'No. I'm going to stay at my parents' and

come in on the train, I think, at least until I'm a bit more settled. I don't have a car. Never needed one until now.'

'Well you know where to come if you miss your train.'

'Thanks. I'd like that. And talking of trains . . . ' Luke looked at his watch. 'I'd better go soon. When I've drunk this coffee. You make a wicked coffee, you know.'

After that, Luke kept checking his watch so the conversation never really took off again. When he walked off Amy was left wondering if something had scared him away. And bother, bother, bother; she'd forgotten to give him her phone number. She jumped up and rushed after him, but he'd vanished already.

She remembered she'd left the front door unlocked and went back to lock it; then, fumbling in her haste, she ran up the road and over the railway bridge. A train was in the station. Her heart lurched. She ran like a gazelle to the station and onto the platform. The elderly stationmaster gave her look of startled recognition as she clattered past. The train was just picking up speed out of the station. 'Luke!' she yelled. 'Luke!' But the train carried on with bland indifference, hissing over the rails; no heads poked out of the windows. She bit her lip and whimpered with frustration. Nothing she could do about it. Perhaps he'd be back, or perhaps she could waylay him at the railway station if he didn't call by again. Maybe she could write to him care of the school.

'You missed it, then,' said the stationmaster. 'You want to give yourself more time. And you must remember to buy a ticket or you'll pay a penalty fare, Amy, and that wouldn't do at all.'

'I wasn't wanting the train, Mr Brown. I was trying to give someone something. Did you see the bloke in jeans with blondish hair?'

'Oh ho!' said the stationmaster with a slow, deliberate wink. 'You saucy minx. Does your aunt know?'

'Oh, give over,' laughed Amy. 'I'm not twelve still, you know.'

5

Amy picked up the post and sifted the junk straight into the recycling bin. The rest was for Debbie until Amy found one addressed to 'Amy Booklover'. She plonked the rest of the post down on the side table where the till used to be, and carefully opened the card addressed to herself, chuckling over the 'Booklover' part. It occurred to her that the postie had done a good job because there was only half a postcode and it was addressed to 'The Old Bookshop' which wasn't the official postal address even if everyone in Runworthy knew it as such. Inside was a pretty card with a photograph of bluebells on the front.

Dear Amy,

I was wondering if you'd like to come out for a meal this weekend. I thought The Shoulder of Mutton, perhaps, since it's within easy walking distance of your house. My parents remember it as doing good food, but if you know differently or would rather go elsewhere, then, you choose.

Luke

He'd put his mobile phone number and email address as a PS. Amy found her heart was pounding so hard it made the card in her hand tremble.

'Was that the post?' Debbie called from the top of the stairs.

'Yes. I'll bring it up.'

'That's OK, I'm coming down. I want to go shopping for a pashmina or two.'

Debbie was ready to go out; she was wearing a long linen skirt and light summer jacket. On her head was a very fetching turban which complemented the clothes. 'I'm not sure I like this much,' she said, fiddling with it. 'I'm not used to it yet, and it's a bit hot to wear. Not as hot as a wig, perhaps.'

'I don't understand why you won't get a wig,' said Amy. 'Surely you'd feel better about going out?'

Debbie picked up the post and went into the library. 'It's only for a short time. My hair will grow back once the chemo's finished. And as I said, I'd rather people could see that I'm being treated for cancer, so they can guess why I'm a bit feeble on occasions and hold doors open for me when I've just had a round and can hardly battle with a door handle. It's nothing to be ashamed of. I'd rather get a couple of headscarves and maybe a baseball cap or two, things which will wash easily. Everything smells so odd, I want to keep washing it. A wig would be a lot of faff, I think.'

'How are you feeling at the mo? Thing is, I've got a tentative date at the weekend, but I won't go if you need me.'

'I'm feeling better daily, so of course you should go. Who is it?'

'It's Luke the book-burglar.' Amy showed Debbie the envelope. 'He doesn't know my surname — I don't know his, for that matter.'

Debbie laughed. 'Shows initiative.'

'What's The Shoulder of Mutton like nowadays?'

'Good as ever. Ask Luke if he has a fifty- to fifty-five-year-old friend.'

Amy grinned. 'I will at that. I bet there are some crusty old academics at the school in need of a good day out.'

'Humph, less of the old and crusty — a virile PE teacher would fit the bill, thank you. Coming shopping with me?'

Amy was about to refuse and get back to her novel, but wondered whether 'feeling better daily' really meant robust enough for a mooch round town, or whether Aunty ought to have a chaperone, just in case she suddenly felt unwell. 'Cool.'

It was a very slow mooch because every twenty yards they would bump into someone

Debbie knew and they would want to know how Debbie was doing.

'It's exhausting being well known,' she said on their return. 'I feel like I should post a daily bulletin on the gate. Bless them all for their concern. It's wonderful to have so many friends.' She kicked off her shoes and padded into the library. 'I'm too worn out to tackle the stairs yet,' she said. 'Phew. Do things a little bit at a time, that's the best way.'

Amy dumped the carrier bags on the settee next to Debbie. 'Tea? Juice?'

'Tomato juice I think, please, love. I find it very soothing for my sore mouth.'

Debbie was rummaging in the carrier bags and pulling out her purchases when Amy brought her the juice. She'd made herself a mug of tea. She opened the charity carrier bag and pulled out her purchases: second-hand books.

'I thought you were going to cull the number of books you have, not add to them,' teased Debbie.

'Yes, well, I always feel sorry for books in the 10p basket. I've saved them from that great recycling plant in the sky. And anyhow, I haven't read these.'

A little while later, Amy phoned Luke's mobile and told him she'd love to go out for a meal, and yes, The Shoulder of Mutton was a great idea. After they'd decided that a meal Saturday night would be lovely, she hung up. She felt all sparkly and shivery.

Debbie was looking at her with an amused expression which faded as Amy watched. 'Be careful, love,' said Debbie. 'Handsome is as Handsome does. Don't lose your heart to Luke just because Gareth made you feel worthless.'

6

The doorbell rang. 'Aaagh, that can't be him already!' shrieked Amy as the towel round her fell to the floor. 'Can you get that please, Aunty? I'm not dressed,' she yelled through the closed door into the living room, where Debbie was curled up with a book. 'Not dressed' was an understatement; she was still damp from the shower, soggy hair wrapped in a towel, no make-up, and what to wear still undecided. She'd gone through her entire wardrobe, discarding this, contemplating that, until everything was higgledy-piggledy on the bed, and the minutes had been eaten up.

'Yes, I'm going,' called Debbie. 'I'll entertain him with some anecdotes of when you were three or four years old, shall I? I remember a certain game of hide-and-seek . . . '

'Just you dare!' muttered Amy. She couldn't get her foot through the leg of her knickers, and when she did and pulled them up over her damp skin, she found they were twisted. 'Oh for goodness sake, what are you like?' she told herself. She heard Debbie open the front door, and the mutter of voices carried up the stairs. Debbie must have left the doors to the lounge and stairs wide open. Suddenly the voices were in the lounge; she could hear them clearly through the door of her adjoining bedroom. 'I'll be out in a minute,' she called. 'I'm nowhere near ready.'

'I'm sorry, I'm horribly early,' she heard Luke say. 'I got to the station in time to catch the earlier train, and did, in case they cancelled the one I was intending to catch. That would be Murphy's Law. I wish I'd dawdled from the station, or had a coffee at the station, though that's only a vending machine. Bit rude of me to be early.'

'Not at all, not at all,' said Debbie. 'You'll have a sherry if you're not driving? It gives me a good excuse to give you the once-over, make sure you're not a potential burglar.'

'Aunty!' yelled Amy, appalled.

'It's OK; your aunt said that with a wink to show she's joking,' called Luke. 'Take your time, there's no hurry.'

'It's OK, Amy; now I've met him, I recognise Luke from when he was a boy and used to pop into the bookshop.'

'I won't be long.'

'Now where did I put those baby photos?' mused Debbie loudly.

Amy heard the plop of the sherry bottle

cork and the clink of glasses. She raked a comb through her hair so roughly it tangled. 'More haste less speed,' she muttered. The hairdryer drowned out the talk in the next room, so that she just heard the murmur of voices. She really hoped Debbie was joking about the baby photos, especially the ones where she was covered in chocolate and not much else.

Amy got dressed and looked in the mirror. She tore the white leggings off her legs. Why had she never noticed how see-through they were before? She pulled on a pair of blue knee-length culottes. They went well with her T-shirt with the ruffled front. Ruffled — how appropriate, she thought, as she pulled her hair back into a low ponytail. She wondered if she'd remembered her deodorant, so gave herself a quick blast up the T-shirt just in case, slapped her sandals on, and rushed out of the bedroom.

'Wow, you look amazing,' said Luke, a sexy grin lighting up his face.

'So do you.' He did; he looked great in some pale brown slacks, a white casual shirt and a brown leather jacket. She had to fight an urge to run her fingers through his hair. Then she realised she hadn't put any make-up on. 'I forgot my slap,' she wailed and turned to flee back into the bedroom.

'You're fine, don't worry about it,' said Luke. He was laughing, his merry eyes dancing. 'Your aunt's poured you a sherry.'

'Sit down,' said Debbie. 'You're like an ill-sitting hen. Enjoy your sherry.'

Amy did as she was bid. The sherry was top quality, and worth sipping slowly, and it helped her relax. It gave her a chance to watch Luke as he told Debbie a little about himself now he was grown up. He was strongly built, but not too chunky, with well-kept hands. She could see a gold watch gleaming under the cuff of his jacket. His shoes were well polished. He looked altogether effortlessly scrumptious.

Debbie glanced at the clock. 'You'd best be off now, if your table's booked for seven thirty. I must say I envy you . . . Do you know any nice, unattached men of about 55, Luke?' She winked.

'Come with us,' said Luke suddenly. 'Why not? After all, it was your home I invaded so rudely. I bet they could make it a table for three.'

Amy winced internally, all her carefully nurtured romantic fantasies falling like autumn leaves. This was just a duty-visit, then, to make up for his rudeness. Luke couldn't fancy her if he wanted her aunt along on the date.

'I couldn't possibly play gooseberry. I was joking about the man,' protested Debbie. But there was a certain yearning about her which said that she was fibbing, that actually she would like dinner out; that actually, the company of two young people was what she really needed.

'Oh come on, Aunty, it'd do you good. You're over the worst of the last round of chemo . . .'

Debbie looked at Luke. 'Were you joking?' she asked. 'You wouldn't really want a crumbly old woman out on your date, would you?'

'You're not crumbly, and you don't look old, and I think it would be fun,' said Luke. He pulled out a mobile phone, dialled and asked if the table for two could be made into a table for three. 'There, sorted.'

Despite her initial mental howl of anguish, Amy decided it would be great fun with Aunty Debbie. It wasn't a serious date, anyway, just a getting-to-know-you type of meal. And why shouldn't Debbie have some fun, as much fun as she could cram in, just in case . . . Amy shivered.

'You'd best take a cardi with you,' said Debbie.

★ ★ ★

56

The town was quietening after a busy Saturday, and the shops had shut. The nights were beginning to draw in but the weather held promise of an Indian summer. They ambled slowly towards the pub, letting Debbie set the pace. As they stepped inside, Debbie was greeted warmly, said she was doing very well thank you, and indicated that Luke had made the booking. They were shown through the crowded public bar to their table.

The only thing that had changed about The Shoulder of Mutton was that the smoke fug had vanished — a vast improvement, Amy thought. The pub dated back to the fifteenth century, but the restaurant was a more modern addition on the back. It was on the same side of the road as Debbie's house, and the beer garden sloped down towards the railway too, though the station and railway line weren't visible. Instead there were views across the open countryside, and in the distance, the sea sparkled. They had a good table by the window and so could admire the view. Soon they were poring over the menu and talking like old friends. Amy thought perhaps this was Debbie's magic; she seemed to get on with everyone. Amy had the horrible feeling if it had been just Luke and herself out for a meal, she'd have disgraced herself by knocking the salt cellar over, or worse, spilling her wine through nervousness, or end up with the clichéd lettuce on the front teeth. As it was, it was just like going out with the family: fun, relaxed, and thoroughly enjoyable. The conversation roamed over Luke's hopes for his upcoming teaching job and Amy's MA (which she was slightly behind with) and then slid round to Debbie's illness.

'You're very brave,' observed Luke.

'Not really,' replied Debbie. 'You just have to take what comes. Grit your teeth and get on with it, trust in the Lord, and hope for a good outcome. But I have to confess I'm not looking forward to the next round of chemo. I know I'm going to feel awful for a few days, but there are other things you don't really expect, like things tasting funny, and my shoulders and the back of my neck feeling stiff and cold. Nobody told me that would happen.'

'Do you reckon it's because you lost your hair?' asked Amy. She flicked her own lustrous ponytail off the back of her neck. It was quite a weight, and warm as a scarf.

'Maybe, but I think it's more than that.'

Luke looked about to say something, but instead put the last of his pudding in his mouth. *Instead of his foot, perhaps,* thought

Amy. 'How's the flat-hunting going?' she said, a tad too brightly.

Luke grinned. 'Found somewhere at last — not ideal but it'll have to do. I was beginning to despair. The previous one I looked at . . . ' He shuddered. 'The best ones are way too expensive. And the others are in rough parts of town.'

'It's quite expensive round here,' agreed Debbie. She fell silent for a good five minutes, with an inward, distracted look, to the extent that Amy wondered if she was getting too tired, but she revived and sparkled for the rest of the evening.

7

Debbie was wearing a fleece hat on her head, complaining of the cold, perhaps regretting her bold stance over the wig. She seemed disinclined to chat and went on her computer immediately after breakfast to do some book-keeping work. Amy didn't feel up to sorting the old study out on her own because she wasn't sure what was valuable and what wasn't, so she decided to have a poke around in the attic. She'd had a quick look when her parents had offloaded the boxes of belongings that they couldn't take to America and yet were too precious to discard. Though they were letting their house furnished, there had been rather a lot of 'extremely valuable junk', as her father had described it.

Amy left her aunt scowling over some spreadsheets on the computer and walked up the narrow stairs to the attic. Both attic rooms were stuffed to the threshold with things. The plastic stacker boxes were her parents', and they effectively blocked in one of the attic rooms entirely. 'Crumbs,' said Amy. The other attic room was almost as cluttered, but it was old junk rather than new, and at least there was enough room for Amy to pick her way carefully from one end to the other. She wasn't sure what she was looking for; just snooping, she supposed. There were old bedsteads and even mattresses, blanket boxes, a wardrobe that looked like a utility wardrobe from just after the War, Lloyd Loom chairs, several occasional tables painted a horrid brown, a linen basket that Amy remembered falling asleep in as a child when playing hide-and-seek, old nursery toys, several rolls of Turkish rugs, a pair of Tiffany lamps carefully stowed in a large display cabinet, vases, jugs, ornaments (some of which looked hideous to Amy), a couple of standard lamps complete with world-weary shades, a tallboy painted art-deco green, some old pictures, a leather bucket chair . . .

'What are you doing up there?' Debbie's voice came up the stairs. Her tone was a little anxious, a little tired.

'Just looking,' called Amy. 'I thought there might be something I can use downstairs. And you said there's a bedstead up here.'

She heard her aunt coming up the stairs. 'The useful stuff is in the one we didn't put Pat's things in. We were pretty sensible about that.'

'It's like an Aladdin's cave,' said Amy. She

could see one of the beds, a single, with dust-cover blankets swathing it. A couple of cardboard suitcases lay on top. Amy picked her way over, shoved one of the cases along, and sat on it. 'That feels really odd. Weirdly firm.'

'It's a horsehair mattress,' said Debbie.

'Ugh,' said Amy. She lifted the dust covers and underneath was a black and white striped mattress about four inches thick. She gave it an experimental poke. 'Can't say I fancy sleeping on that, much. It's a bit hard. And is it altogether hygienic? Horsehair? Yuck.'

'Your mum and dad were happy enough in the double — it used to be in the spare bedroom until I got the divan — and you used to sleep on this one when you were small. Don't you remember?'

'No. I thought I slept in the lounge on camp beds with the twins.' Amy sat still for a few minutes, thinking back. She really couldn't remember the horsehair beds. When Amy had visited on her own when she was older, she'd used the spare room she was currently sleeping in, and only remembered the divan and the camp beds. She gazed round and a vague memory turned over in its sleep: a memory of a nightmare, and of being hideously cold one Christmas. She would hate sleeping up here, she just knew it. 'Nope, really can't remember. I only remember sleeping in the lounge. Those old army camp beds used to be such a fight to put together.' She bounced up and down and the springs complained bitterly. 'Reminds me of 'The Princess and the Pea', though I now think it was the lumpy mattress which gave her a bruise, not the pea, if this one is anything to go by. But the bed itself seems OK, apart from the horrible screechy noise from the springs.'

'There's a double bed in bits over there . . . the one your parents used. I was going to buy a new bed for your room, though, but actually . . . We need to talk, Amy love.' Debbie sat down on a handy 1950s kitchen chair.

'OK,' said Amy blithely as she picked her way over to the double bed. There was a rosewood headboard, tailboard, and metal frame with interlinking metal springs. 'It's lovely. Seems a shame to buy something when this might do. Can't say I'm up for a horsehair mattress, though. Why on earth were you hanging onto them?'

'Just in case, at first,' said Debbie defensively. 'Then it was more trouble than it was worth to deal with them. It's all very well you young things and your throw-away society, but rationing had only finished a couple of years before I was born. But Amy, we really do need to have a little chat, and not up here either.'

Debbie looked worried and Amy wondered what on earth the matter was.

★　★　★

They'd washed their hands and made a pot of tea before Debbie finally got round to telling Amy, and even then, she skirted round the subject and took a while to get to the point. 'Thing is, Amy love, being self-employed is a bit tough; you're reliant on a buoyant market. It was OK when I first started out; there was enough work and people knew me. But some of the businesses I used to do the books for have closed down, or new people have taken over and switched to a competitor. And now, with this cancer treatment, I can't work at full capacity and work has dried up. Maybe people have lost confidence in me. It'll be better when all this is over and done with. Like a fool I didn't take out any critical illness insurance. I meant to ... but it got overlooked.' Debbie looked bleak for just a minute before continuing, 'I had a bit of a shock the other day when I got my bank statement. I've been a bit preoccupied and hadn't noticed that I've got more going out than coming in at the moment. The hope was you'd get a part-time job, and that hasn't happened.'

'I am trying,' said Amy. It was true; all the suitable jobs had gone, snapped up by the summer's crop of school-leavers. Even graduates were struggling against the per-petual conundrum of employers wanting experience, and graduates not being able to get a job because they lacked experience or because they were overqualified. 'I could advertise for some tutoring,' she added dubiously. 'Or even babysitting. I don't know what to suggest . . . '

'I was thinking after what Luke said the other day, about lettings. Would you mind so very much if you stayed in the guest room and we let out the ground floor?' Debbie looked so worried that Amy bit back the instinctive words, *But you promised.*

'But what about my books and stuff? I'll never fit it all in the bedroom.' Amy felt her eyes begin to prick. 'And it would be a real worry having a stranger in the house. I wish you'd thought of this when Luke was still looking for somewhere; we could have let it to him. I wouldn't mind having him in the house.'

Debbie gave her a wry look. 'I bet you wouldn't — so perhaps it's just as well he's already found somewhere. Come downstairs and I'll show you what I've been thinking.'

Amy followed her aunt down into the old kitchen.

Debbie said, 'We need this room because the washing machine is here, and there's no room for one upstairs, but we don't need the scullery, not really.' She walked through the scullery and into the study.

Amy followed, a sinking feeling dragging at her feet. Most of the shelves were now clutter-free, the desk was empty and the place had a naked feel to it, as if by stripping out the rubbish they had stripped away the memories of Granddad, and even the good times before Bernard had let Debbie down.

Debbie looked out of the French windows onto the terrace. 'A lodger could use these as their front door,' she said. 'No reason why not.' She turned and led Amy into the erstwhile drawing room. 'And there's a perfectly adequate shower room through that door, as you know since it was going to be yours, so this could be the lodger's bedroom.' She led the increasingly doleful Amy through into the front room where all her books now graced the shelves. 'We could permanently lock the door between the drawing room and this room so that you have this as your sitting room-cum-study, and the lodger has the old drawing room with its shower room, study and scullery. And we have the old kitchen with its washing machine and you can make coffee in it, even cook in it if you have a fancy to. It makes sense, Amy love. If we lock this door and the kitchen-to-scullery door, it makes a nice self-contained unit. The scullery has a sink and is big enough for a mini-kitchen — table-top hob and grill, microwave, small fridge.'

'But what would a lodger do for a washing machine? There's no room for one in the scullery. It's barely big enough to be a kitchen.'

'Never heard of a laundrette?'

Amy said nothing more. The crushing sense of disappointment had squeezed all the breath from her. It made sense, of course it made sense. She'd lived in a tiny student study-bedroom at university, so the large front room was luxurious enough on its own. It was just that she had so been looking forward to having the indulgence of a study, a bedroom, a library, and her own kitchen. She'd mentally moved in and made it home, and now her aunt was telling her she couldn't have it.

'You could sleep in the spare room, use the downstairs kitchen if you wanted, or the upstairs one if you want, and use the front room as your private study space.' Debbie looked torn, as if she was an honest salesman selling a duff product. 'I know it's not what we planned, what we'd hoped for, but I recently lost a contract when the firm went bust and . . . '

'It's OK Aunty Debbie, I do understand.' Amy swallowed. 'I can't pretend I wasn't looking forward to living in these rooms. That art deco shower room is so romantic, but it's not as if I'm paying rent, so it makes sense to let the rooms and bring in a little extra.'

'The sooner we get the rooms ready and advertised, the better. We'll use the old double bed but I'll have to order a new mattress — more expense.' Her aunt tutted and frowned. 'Let's hope someone wants the rooms, or it's money wasted. We'll furnish it with bits and bobs out of the attic.'

Amy did most of the work bringing the furniture out of the attic, roping in Alison from the deli next door for the really heavy, awkward bits. Although Debbie was recovering from her latest round of chemo, and she still felt a bit feeble, she was well enough to move some of the lighter bits round, provided she took plenty of rest breaks. Soon the Lloyd Loom furniture was in the study and the antique double bedstead was put together in the old drawing room, butted up against the door to the front room, which was now locked. There was a twelve-inch gap behind the headboard because of the book shelving, but that was just too bad. Amy had the bright idea of putting one of the standard lamps in the gap. Then the lodger could read in bed easily, and it saved having to buy a bedside table lamp. Debbie had said that no way was she using the Tiffany lamps for a lodger. They were genuine, and very valuable. Amy secretly wished they could sell the lamps and not bother with a lodger, but it would have been outrageous to suggest such a thing.

They brought a couple of the occasional tables down, too. The linen basket had linen in it but this was a coarse weave, old, and moths had found the blankets. The wardrobe looked a bit plain and dull but was functional. Debbie ordered a mattress to arrive on Saturday, two days hence.

'I'm shattered,' said Amy once it was done. The study clutter they hadn't had time to sort through was piled up in the front room (now Amy's study-cum-library) for the moment, and the new 'flat' was clean and inviting, if somewhat eccentrically furnished. If all this sorting-out had been for her benefit, Amy would have enjoyed every nesting moment; but as it was, she was overcome by a feeling of melancholy.

That night as she lay in bed, she thought about how everything had gone wrong since Gareth had treated her so abominably. She'd not done as well as she'd hoped in her exams (hardly surprising); she'd lost weight, failed to find a part-time job, and was behind with her studies. Thinking about her MA got her thinking about teaching, which led on to thinking about Luke, which turned her heart into a butterfly which bashed its wings to pieces on her ribcage. He hadn't phoned, even though she'd sent a thank-you card to his parents' address, and he hadn't returned her text or phone calls either. Maybe he felt like his duty was done; maybe that was all the meal had been. Amy didn't want to keep phoning him in case she seemed needy, or even desperate. On top of that, now she wasn't to have the whole of the downstairs after all. She sniffled. She should have gone to America with her family after all. She told herself not to be so disgustingly self-pitying, and tried to get to sleep.

8

Term must have just started, judging by the sudden influx of school children on the streets. The doorbell went. Amy saved her work on the computer and went to answer it. Luke was there looking slightly diffident. 'Come in,' she squealed, smiling. 'But if you want a coffee, it'll have to be outside. Aunty Debbie had a round just under a week ago and she's feeling a bit ropey.'

'Sorry to hear that. I've brought her a pressie.' He handed over a heavy package and turned as if to leave.

'Not so fast, mister,' drawled Amy. 'She's not that unwell, it's just that coffee smells revolting to her at the mo. Sit yourself down in the library and I'll see if she's awake. With any luck, you'll be able to give it to her yourself.' Luke came inside and shut the door while Amy ran upstairs.

Her aunt was in the lounge watching TV. 'Who was that?'

'It's Luke, downstairs. Has a pressie for you,' said Amy. 'Do you want to come down?'

'Bring him up, would you please? I'm rather tired . . . '

When Amy had fetched Luke upstairs to the lounge, he went over to Debbie and smiled at her. 'It's not much of a gift, I'm afraid. But I thought you might find this useful. I made it myself on Mum's sewing machine.' He handed over a heavy package.

Debbie took it with a bemused expression. 'I can't guess what this is,' she said, groping at it. 'Not a clue. How exciting.' She tore the paper off, revealing something akin to a draft excluder, like a beanbag but longer and thinner. She looked utterly perplexed.

'You heat it in the microwave,' said Luke. 'A friend from university's mum had chemo. She had the same problem with a cold, stiff neck and shoulders. She made herself a long, thin wheat-bag like those wheat-bags you get for the microwave. She'd warm it up and drape it over her shoulders. Helped a lot, she said. So I thought I'd make you one to see if it made you more comfortable, only it's pearl barley, not wheat, and it has some lavender in it from Mum and Dad's garden — luckily Mum picks it and dries it to make lavender bags.' As he spoke his blush grew and grew.

'That is so sweet and thoughtful of you, thanks. Can you show Amy how to heat it up, please?'

Amy took him through to the kitchen,

which was above the original kitchen downstairs. He looked round at the modern cupboards. 'Wow. I had romantic thoughts of you cooking over that range downstairs.'

'Not likely; far too much hassle, and far too hot in the summer. What do you do with this then?'

'I think you curl it round half a mug of water on the glass plate, and set it going in the microwave for a minute. The water stops it drying out too much. You mustn't put it on for too long or it'll burn.'

They experimented together, feeling it after a minute and deciding another thirty seconds should do it. Amy's heart squeezed when their hands brushed accidentally, and she found herself smiling into Luke's eyes.

When it was warm enough they took it back through to Debbie and draped it over her shoulders. 'Ooooh, that's lovely,' she sighed. 'That's very comforting actually. Thank you. How's your friend's mum now? Is she OK?'

'She's . . . ' Luke's face turned to stone. 'She's fine now.'

'Oh good, glad to hear it. Thanks for this, Luke. It was more than kind of you; it's so thoughtful and considerate.' Debbie settled back into the settee with a sigh. She looked like porcelain again, wan and tired.

'We'll have a coffee outside, I think,' said Amy, with a look at Luke. 'Have you got time before your train?'

Luke looked at his watch. 'Yeah. That'd be cool.'

★　★　★

'Your mum's friend isn't fine, is she?' asked Amy quietly as they took their coffee outside. She looked up at the open bedroom window, grimaced, swore mildly, then led Luke further down the garden path to a set of steps. 'I hope Aunty didn't hear . . . I forgot how the sound carries up to the window.'

The steps were old and lined with clouds of pink and white fleabane, soft and romantic. They stepped down into the rose garden. Most of them were old roses which flowered but once and had finished, though some bore interesting hips. Lining the path was lavender which Amy had trimmed hard back. She pulled an overlooked stalk from a bush and twizzled it in between her fingers. A slightly camphorous lavender smell drifted up from it. 'I saw you hesitate when Aunty asked . . . you lied, didn't you?'

Luke reddened. 'That obvious, huh? I'm not a very good liar, I'm afraid. I nearly opened my big mouth and put my foot in it the other day when we were eating. But your aunty is going to be all right, isn't she? Isn't she? She seems so strong, so spirited . . . '

'She never looks on the dark side,' agreed Amy, throwing the mangled bit of lavender away. 'So I think so, but it's hard to tell, especially at the moment. She's making out it's just a nasty six months' treatment to get over and done with, and then everything will be fine and carry on before. But sometimes she lets her guard slip and I think she's scared. We all are.'

Luke took her hand and her insides melted. 'Lots of people survive cancer nowadays. And she's got you here . . . '

Amy didn't want to talk about it anymore, so she said, 'How was your first day?'

'I'm exhausted. I've actually been there a couple of days. Yesterday was getting ready for the kids. I have loads of lessons to prepare for the national curriculum . . . and loads of paperwork to keep up to date to show that I'm doing the Government Approved Job of it all.'

Amy laughed. 'You sound cynical and you've hardly started.'

'No. I'm just a bit bogged down and overwhelmed, that's all. I'll get used to it. If you're serious about being a teacher, you could do some voluntary work experience there. Apparently there's a literary festival at the beginning of October. I'm sure you could help with that . . . '

'Sounds good, but get your feet under the desk before you start asking favours for me, perhaps.'

'You'd be doing them a favour, I think. They're a bit short-staffed. The last geography teacher couldn't even spell 'floe' as in 'ice floe', apparently.'

'Oops.'

The evening wore on, the coffee was drunk, and the cups grew cold. Luke's face looked burdened with thoughts. Eventually he cleared his throat. 'Amy, I think you're rather special, and I'd like to start going out with you. Once I've moved into the flat it'll be a lot easier. I get the keys at the weekend.'

Amy found herself grinning idiotically but couldn't think of anything romantic to say, so just said, 'Cool.' She raised her face towards him in the growing dusk. He took her in his embrace and touched his lips to hers, gently questing, then broke off just as she needed air.

What a fantastic kisser. Much better that Gareth, who'd seemed to want to lick her tonsils. She winced at the memory.

'Cold?' asked Luke.

'Not now.' She walked with him to the station and kissed him goodbye as the train drew up. He got on the train and she waved him off, and mentally hugged herself gleefully as she walked home.

9

Amy kicked off her rubber garden clogs, removed the gardening gloves, stepped into the downstairs kitchen, and got a fright. 'Who on earth are you and what are you doing in here?' she asked, a feeling of déjà vu washing over her. A very attractive woman had a vase in her hand, which she nearly dropped into the Belfast sink as Amy spoke.

'Goodness, you made me jump there. I'm Gill, the Macmillan nurse. You must be Amy. I've heard lots about you.'

'Sorry, you startled me. I wondered who you were. I didn't know you were here. Aunty Debbie hasn't said anything about a Macmillan nurse coming today.'

'I've been coming every Friday morning for a while now. I'm surprised Debbie didn't mention it.'

'Oh, that's right, I remember now. She did mention it a while ago, but I didn't realise you were coming regularly. I thought it was a one-off. I'm usually out Friday mornings at an OU tutor group, that'll be why I haven't met you before, but there isn't one today. Do you mind if I get to the sink, please? I need to wash my hands.'

Gill moved away with the vase unfilled as Amy scrubbed her hands. Amy had completely forgotten about the Macmillan nurse until now. Debbie didn't really discuss her treatment. Any conversations they had were in response to enquiries from well-wishers or remarks about the appointment times. Other than that, they mostly avoided the subject, instead voicing ambitions for the future. Maybe Debbie didn't want to be constantly reminded about things. Amy dried her hands on the towel and Gill went to fill the vase. She turned the tap on too hard and it splashed over her. She squealed, they both laughed and the reserve between them was broken.

'Someone sent some flowers,' said Gill. 'Debbie said she couldn't face arranging them when they arrived and dumped them in a bucket just before I came.' Gill indicated a bucket in the shady part of the kitchen. A large bunch of flowers was sitting there waiting for attention. 'I said I'd sort them out for her.'

'I prefer the ones which come with a reservoir of water. Sometimes it's just too much effort to deal with things there and then, and it seems criminal to neglect them.' Amy filled the kettle. 'Coffee? If the answer's yes, can you drink it down here, please? It's too soon after the last round. Just a week.'

'Last round in two weeks' time.' Gill unwrapped the flowers and started cutting the ends of the stems off and making an arrangement.

'Thank goodness.' Amy poured water on the coffee grounds and they frothed up, the aroma hitting her. She stirred, pushed the plunger down and poured out the coffee. 'Look, shall I sort the flowers while you enjoy your coffee? I expect you have a busy schedule.'

Gill took a sip. 'Oh, that's gorgeous. So nice to have real coffee.' They chatted for a while about cancer treatment in general. 'Are you OK with all of this?' asked Gill. 'Friends and relatives often get overlooked because all the focus is on the patient.'

'I'm fine, mostly,' said Amy. 'But sometimes it gets to me, especially when I see my aunt being brave during the actual chemo treatment. But I can't show my feelings or it might upset people. People laugh and joke during the session, but there's an undercurrent of tension.'

'If you want or need to offload, here's my card,' said Gill. 'There are lots of websites with help too. Anything, no matter how small . . . '

'Thanks.'

They both went up to see Debbie. Gill carried the flowers up and placed them on the coffee table in the lounge. 'As you can see, I've met Amy at last. She's given me the most delicious coffee.'

'We should do one of those Macmillan Coffee morning things in aid of Macmillan nurses,' said Debbie. 'As a way of saying thanks.'

'You mean the World's Largest Coffee Morning? Are you up for it, do you think? It's the last Friday in September.'

Debbie pondered for a few moments. 'I should be over the last round of chemo by then. Two weeks; I'm usually good by the end of the second week. It would be a nice way to celebrate one-third of the journey and the end of chemo. People say it's the worst bit. How about you, Amy? Interested? Oh, but what about your tutor group?'

'We could have it here that week, perhaps. We could put some tables outside on the cobbled road, or the back terrace, if the weather's nice. Or have them in the library if it's not. I think I saw some old chairs in the attic.'

Gill stood. 'Sounds great, and much appreciated. Have a look online; it's all on the website. Should be fun. I'd best get on and leave you to your planning.'

Over the weekend when Amy phoned Luke, he didn't answer and his phone went to voicemail, nor did he reply to her texts. The first few times it happened she didn't worry that much because she imagined he must be busy getting ready to move into his new flat in Runworthy, though now that they were officially an item surely he could spare a few minutes to talk? Maybe he was really bad at using his phone, but that would be weird. She wished she'd made a Facebook friend of him, but she hadn't and as she didn't know his surname she couldn't exactly find him and send a request.

By Sunday evening she was really worried because it was beginning to feel like Gareth all over again. She badly needed to talk about things, and not with her aunt, either.

★ ★ ★

On Monday morning at breakfast Amy said, 'Now the flat's ready for the potential lodger, do you mind if I go back up to Leicester for a couple of days? Millie's invited me up. Sort of an impulse.'

'Of course I don't mind, Amy love. Who's Millie?'

'One of my friends from university. She

stayed on to do a PhD there, and she's suggested I pop up before term starts and the place gets full of students.' That wasn't strictly true. Amy had texted Millie and asked if she could come up. She needed to talk with her best friend, face to face, and if Luke happened to call by in person while she was away, it was just too bad. In fact, if he felt he could treat her like dirt, ignoring her phone calls, he could shove off. She drafted a text to that effect but deleted it when she remembered his intense eyes and wonderful kiss. Maybe there was a good reason why he hadn't returned her texts and calls. Millie would know what to do. Amy knew her own judgement wasn't up to much just now.

Amy didn't feel guilty leaving Debbie on her own because it was mid-cycle with the chemotherapy and Debbie was feeling much more herself. If anything, it might be that Debbie needed a bit of time and space to herself. On more than one occasion she'd commented how all the well-wishing was getting exhausting.

Her aunt suddenly put down the piece of toast she was munching on. 'Gareth won't be there, will he?'

Amy's stomach lurched. She shook her head. 'Not likely; he went home to his daddy in Preston so he could work in the family

83

business.' She surprised herself with the depth of bitterness in her tone. *I'm turning into a miserable shrew. Perhaps I should change my name to Katherina.*

★ ★ ★

After a leisurely and careful couple of hours' driving, Amy found herself getting lost in the city she'd spent three years in as an undergraduate (on foot, not in a car). Normally her mum or dad had driven her there, and though she'd had her driving licence for a while, she was fairly inexperienced. She eventually managed to find her way to Millie's, a terraced house quite close to the university. It was a cheap part of the city, and Millie's parents had bought the property at the end of Millie's first year so she could live in it and rent out rooms to other students, Amy included. They were very reasonably priced Victorian back-to-back properties, and here and there on the side streets, the tarmac had lifted to show the old cobbles underneath. Amy thought it very romantic, despite a dubious reputation that the area was trying to shrug off. She'd loved her time in Leicester, with its interesting shops and multicultural population.

She parked carefully on the street. Millie

rushed out of the front door to give her a hug, leaving her bowled over and breathless. 'I'm glad you got here so early. I need to go into the university to see someone and I was worried you'd be late. I tried ringing your mobile.'

'I don't have hands-free yet, so I couldn't answer,' said Amy. 'You look amazing.' She gazed at her friend happily. 'And I want to go and say hi to my personal tutor. I found a book of hers in with my clutter and I want to return it. We can walk in to the campus together.'

'Cup of tea first.'

Over a mug of tea they exchanged gossip until Amy's jaw ached. Amy told Millie about her first meeting with Luke. Millie howled with laughter, then said, 'He sounds a bit dodgy to me.' When Amy told her about their subsequent encounter, and how he'd asked her out, Millie sobered up. 'I'm not sure that's a good idea. You've hardly met each other, and that in rather suspicious circumstances; I bet he's trying to inveigle his way into the house via your heart. It's a very posh house, after all. Worth a good snoop round. And even if he wasn't, I don't think it's sensible for you to start going out with him on the rebound from Gareth. There's plenty of time and plenty of men.'

'Funny you should say that.' Amy told Millie about how, after asking her out, Luke had ignored all her texts and phone messages, and hadn't even had the courtesy to mention them when they'd next met up.

'That's bloody outrageous,' said Millie. 'Sounds like a real git. Dump him; he's obviously not really interested, or already has a girlfriend and doesn't dare answer his phone while he's with her.'

'Good point.' It sounded like it could be true. Luke was so good-looking, he must have girls after him. That could explain the offhandedness after taking Debbie and herself out, as well. Blowing hot and cold, or playing the field like Gareth.

'How about your tutor group for the OU? Any fit men there?'

Amy snorted with forced laughter and shook her head. 'Not really. There's one man, good-looking, but he's awfully earnest and awfully, awfully self-satisfied.'

They walked to the university campus, agreeing to meet outside the library café. As they wandered through the campus, much quieter during the summer vacation when fewer students were around, Amy felt a mixture of familiarity and strangeness, as if her recollections of the university had fossilised in her mind at the moment of leaving. Nothing had changed, really, except herself. She felt a small pang of nostalgic mourning. She'd had a wonderful time there, mostly, the only major disaster being when she'd discovered Gareth's perfidy.

Her erstwhile personal tutor was in and was pleased to see her, asking what she was doing and how she was getting on. They chatted for a few minutes, Amy returned the book with a guilty smile, and then they'd run out of words. The silence gelled; her tutor glanced down at the work she'd been doing before Amy interrupted her.

'I ought to go,' said Amy. 'I'm meeting Millie soon.'

Her tutor gave a little start as if a thought had hit her. 'Hang on; I've got something you might like to read, right up your street.' She handed Amy a book by an author she was unfamiliar with. 'I've finished with it so you can keep it. I'm sure you'll like him.'

Amy beamed. 'Thanks.'

Amy walked to the plaza and sat down to wait for Millie. Soon her nose was stuck in the book and she was oblivious to the real world. Two warm hands covered her eyes. Millie. She froze for a couple of seconds, smiling.

'Guess who?'

Gareth.

She ripped his hands from her eyes and turned, blazing. 'How dare you touch me like that? What are you doing here? I thought you'd gone home to be Daddy's Little Pet in the family business.' Her heartbeat thudded sickly against her skull.

'Ooooowh, get you. Changed my mind; doing an MSc now.' With a feline movement he was suddenly in front of her, his hands gripping the aluminium chair arms, trapping her, looming over her, grinning. 'Just as beautiful as ever, aren't you? And just as hard to get.'

'Get away from me.' Amy shrunk back into the chair, the metal back pressing cold against her spine. She was trembling, partly with fear, but mostly with rage.

'What about a kiss for old times' sake?' He had a lovely seductive grin and was good-looking, expensively dressed — and utterly repulsive. She felt no emotional pull, nothing. She was finally over him.

'You have to be joking. After the way you treated me, you can just shove off.' She looked round. The precinct was deserted, the people in the café busy and unconcerned.

'I've chucked Shannon. We could get back together.'

'If you don't back off this minute I will kick you where it hurts.' She could do so easily, the way he was standing over her, but she wasn't used to aggression, and he knew it.

'Yeah, right you will, babe,' he sneered in a disbelieving tone, but pushed himself out of range just in case. He seated himself next to her and leaned in so close she could headbutt him, if she were that sort of person. But he was safe enough. 'You and me, babe: it was great, I see that now. I really miss you and I'm sorry I treated you so badly. You're not like the other girls and I want you back.' He was looking at her as if he expected her to give in, to forgive him, just as she'd always done, lips slightly parted in a self-satisfied smile. 'Go on . . . you know you want to.'

How slimy was that? How juvenile. He was seriously starting to creep her out. Amy fished her mobile out. 'You chucked Shannon, did you? Let's phone her and find out then, shall we?'

'You can't. Don't . . . ' Gareth's smirk fled.

Amy was bluffing. She didn't have the other girl's number; hadn't a clue who this Shannon was. 'Oh, so you haven't chucked her, then, you liar. But that's irrelevant, really. I wouldn't go out with you again if you were the last man on earth. The reason I chucked you wasn't just because you were two-timing me — or was that three-timing me? It was because you were bragging about us to your mates. How disgusting is that?'

'Aw, everyone does that. It's because I was proud of you. I wanted people to know how great you are.'

'So great you were shagging two different girls on the side, eh?'

'That was just casual sex; everyone does that nowadays. We should get back together. I've got my own house now, and a BMW. You don't know what you're missing.'

'Oh I do, Gareth, believe me.' Amy stood and pushed past him. 'I miss you like a dose of plague.'

He stood. 'You can't mean it. I know you still love me really. I love you, babe. I just didn't realise it until you'd gone. Forgive me; Shannon means nothing to me.'

'I've moved on, Gareth, so just drop it.'

'I'll come and visit you, babe — make sure you know how much I really love you.'

'That's not what I meant. I meant I've mentally moved on; you mean nothing to me now. Anyhow, you don't know where I live.'

'Yes I do, babe.'

'I've moved.' *Go, just leave him to it,* she urged herself. She started walking away, but he followed.

'I can still find you. Don't go. I'll make it up to you, I promise.' His voice had risen half an octave.

'I have a new boyfriend, one who really cares for me.' As she said it, she knew this wasn't true. Luke was just as bad as Gareth.

'Yeah right, babe.' He made a grab at her arm, but she slid away, almost running, and stomped into the library, catching a librarian's attention. 'That man is being an oppressive nuisance,' she said, pointing. Gareth saw, and with a last leer, sauntered off.

'I'll report it to security.'

'Amy!' Amy jumped and spun round. It was Millie. 'Amy . . . was that Gareth? You know, he was pretty cut up when you chucked him . . . '

'Served him right,' said Amy, and she told her what he'd done.

'The scumbag,' said Millie. 'You didn't say at the time. I just thought you'd chucked him. He was really upset.'

'*He* was upset? I was devastated. I mean, how humiliating is that? He never really loved me like I loved him. Or thought I loved him. He was just after a . . . '

'Has he gone?' Millie peered through the glass.

'Think so,' said Amy. 'Let's go into town. I want to look round the shops.'

All the way round town, and all the way back to Millie's, Amy found herself looking over her shoulder, wondering if Gareth was following them. She told herself not to be so paranoid. Gareth had just been opportunistic in harassing her when he saw her sitting outside the library, a spur-of-the-moment thing. It was hardly likely he was going to stalk her, not when he had another foolish girl, Shannon, dangling from his car keys.

★ ★ ★

'I really think I'm free of him, at last,' Amy said as they sunk into Millie's sofa, supper eaten, wine bottle half empty. 'I was scared today, but it's like I've exorcised him from my life. He's lost his power to hurt me. I can see now what a spoiled self-indulgent brat he really is. I was upset when I found out about the other girls and chucked him on principle — if he'd asked for forgiveness then, I would have forgiven him and let him back into my life. I was devastated when he just laughed and said, 'All right babe, plenty more fish in the sea,' but as time went on I could see what a nasty slimeball he really is. That little episode today just showed me how right I was. He's an utter, shallow, spoiled brat who has no idea how to treat a woman, and I really don't understand what I saw in him. I feel like I can move on now, put it down to experience and vow not to make the same mistake again.' But she was making exactly the same mistake again, wasn't she? She'd opened her heart up to Luke and he was turning out to be just the same.

Millie's voice cut into her reverie. 'Poor old Amy; you were in a right old mess at the time, never could get the full story from you. Just before exams too. Boyfriends — they're not worth the trouble. You'd best chuck this Luke right now, this minute, since he can't be bothered to reply to your texts.'

'You're right. I'll do it right now. I'm fed up with being treated like an easy lay.' She typed in a snide message, then back-tracked into typing something less offensive, and even then she hesitated.

'Just send it,' said Millie, and she pressed 'send' for her.

10

Amy got home late Wednesday evening. The iron gates across the cobbled private lane were closed, which surprised her. Amy straddled the car across the pavement, got out and opened the gates, then once she'd driven through, closed them again before parking the car in Debbie's garage round the back behind the deli. She was bone-weary and yearning for a cup of tea. The downstairs was in darkness as she unlocked the front door and snapped the hall lights on. 'Hi, I'm home.'

'That you, Amy, love?'

Amy clattered up the stairs and dumped her bag on her bed, then went into the upstairs kitchen to find her aunt filling the kettle.

'Good time?'

'Great, thanks.' Amy flopped into one of the kitchen chairs. 'I'm shattered.'

'I've got some good news. I've let the rooms already. I put a sign in the window Monday afternoon and within two hours I'd had a couple of queries, and one chap said he'd take it straight away. Mr Armitage.'

Debbie seemed very smug, almost as if she was teasing Amy over letting the rooms out. 'Seemed vaguely familiar, but I can't place him.' Debbie winked at her. 'He spent yesterday evening moving his things in. This evening he did a couple of odd jobs round the place, like fixing the dripping bathroom tap, as well as moving the rest of his stuff in and unpacking. He's so shattered I think he's gone to bed early, poor old thing.' Debbie chuckled and poured boiling water into the teapot. She found the biscuit tin and put it on the table next to Amy. She looked a little chagrined at Amy's lack of response.

Amy was a bit put-out about Debbie teasing her like that. It was rather cruel, considering how those rooms had been promised to her, and then let from under her feet. Debbie wasn't normally so thoughtless with her teasing, but the joke, whatever it was, fell rather flat, so Amy decided to ignore it. 'I'm shattered too, so I think I'll just have a sandwich and go to bed.' A tiny, selfish corner of her heart had hoped that the rooms wouldn't be let — that every potential lodger would turn their nose up at the old bedstead, the tatty tub chair and the cramped scullery kitchen — but it seemed not. Just as well, perhaps, if her aunt needed the money. And if Mr Armitage was helpful

95

around the house, that was all to the good. As Debbie vaguely knew him, Amy imagined him to be about fifty, a bachelor with crooked teeth and a leery look, and round-rimmed glasses perched on his nose. He would wear nothing but brown corduroy trousers and a moss-green jumper with elbow pads. She laughed at herself and wondered what had brought that vision to mind. Then she remembered the janitor at junior school, Mr Armstrong. She giggled and started to relax.

Debbie was busy in the fridge. 'Cheese or ham? Or even cheese and ham?'

'Oh Aunty, there's no need; I'll do it.'

'Oh shush and let me mollycoddle you. Let me mother you while Pat's in America.' Debbie never had children, which Amy thought was a shame. She would have made a wonderful mother. On the other hand, Bernard would then have broken any offspring's hearts, as well as Debbie's.

'Ham please, and then I think bath, bed and read. Oh, by the way, why were the gates across?'

'PC Bishop suggested it would be a good security measure. It'll stop casual snoopers at night, and we had an unfortunate incident with a steamed-up car parked in the lane late last night and some disgusting litter this morning. Honestly, you'd think people would see that it's private, wouldn't you? I wish we had infra-red CCTV, then we could put it on You Tube. Alison and I have decided to keep the gates open during the day, and closed at night. I'll go and lock them now you're back.'

★   ★   ★

Amy's early night meant she woke very early. The light was streaming into her bedroom and it seemed too good a day to waste. She had a sudden fancy for coffee on the terrace, so she tiptoed downstairs and put the kettle on in the old kitchen. It seemed odd with the scullery door closed and locked. The view from the kitchen window wasn't great: the old wash-house building, which still had the old copper and outside loo and was a dumping ground for all sorts of junk. Amy expected that a good view from the kitchen hadn't been a priority when people had servants, but it did kind of spoil things now, though the wash-house itself added to the seclusion of the terrace, the walls trapping the heat of the sun, making it a warm spot even in winter. Maybe she should put hanging baskets up. Winter pansies, perhaps.

It was quiet and the kettle boiling seemed unnaturally loud. When the coffee was made she slipped out of the back door and walked round the back between the house and the wash-house, towards the terrace. Someone wearing a dressing gown and pyjamas was sitting at the teak outdoor table, facing her direction, with a mug of something on the table, elbows propped on the table, a book held up in his hands. On hearing her gasp, he lowered the book.

It was Luke.

Amy took the scene in: Luke sitting at the table, the French windows open, diaphanous white curtains embroidered with gold thread leaves gently being pulled outside by a vagrant breeze. 'Mr Armitage?' she asked, the vision of the fifty-year-old janitor withering in an instant.

Luke smiled. 'The very same.' Then his face fell. 'You chucked me! How unjust is that? I mislaid my phone and that's why I didn't get your texts and my phone was on voice message.'

'Oh.' Amy sat down so abruptly her coffee spilled. She believed him utterly. 'Sorry. I never thought . . . '

'You just assumed . . . '

Then the doubts started to creep in. 'But it's now Thursday. When did you lose it? When did you find it? You could have phoned me. You men are just the same.'

'So you said in your second Dear John text. That was a very nasty text, Amy. You've shown your true colours.'

'Eh? I sent you several texts but only one dear John text. I wasn't even sure about sending that, but Millie told me to. In fact it was she who pressed 'send'. And I thought you had a different flat lined up . . . so why take this one, especially as . . . It's not that I don't believe you, it's . . . just I'm a bit confused.'

His eyes blazed at her. 'It's clear that you don't believe me, and I find that very hard to take. I lost my phone the day we went to the restaurant. I thought I'd left it there but when I went back it hadn't been handed in, so I thought maybe someone had just found it and pinched it. I tried ringing it in case I'd left it at home somewhere, but like you, I found it just went to voice mail. I did wonder if I'd left it at school, but no. And it was really frustrating because the flat rental went pear-shaped . . . the landlord wanted more rent and a hefty deposit, which the other neighbours warned me he contrived to keep every time a tenant left, and never attended to repairs and things, so I backed out and told the agency what he was like, and luckily got my deposit back. But it left me with a problem . . . until I saw your aunt's sign in the window when I popped round to see you and explain about the phone. I thought you'd be delighted, but obviously not.'

'Oh, I am. I mean . . . ' Amy took a sip of coffee for the sake of something to do. It was cooling and had lost its fragrance. 'So where was the phone?' Her heart had slowed to a dismayed thumping in her skull.

'I found it yesterday evening in your aunt's flat, of all places. Debbie found it down the side of the settee the other day, thought it was yours, put it on the side and forgot about it. It was on silent. I saw it when she gave me a cup of tea after I fixed the dripping tap.'

'I'm so sorry I misjudged you. If I'd guessed then I would never have chucked you.' A lump of flint had formed in her throat. She tried to squeeze some words out, but they were very hard to say, mainly because she was suddenly very afraid. 'Can we . . . ? If I'd known I'd never have sent that text. I thought you were behaving just like Gareth did. He never replied to texts or phone calls. Can we still go out together, please?'

Luke looked at her with his compelling eyes as if considering the request, then said, 'I don't think that's sensible, not after those horrible texts. You're far too immature to be of interest to me; I see that now. On the outside you are a beautiful woman, but it seems on the inside you still have a lot of growing up to do.'

'It wasn't a horrible text. I just said that if you couldn't be bothered to answer my calls I thought we should cool it; what's so horrible about that?'

'That I could understand, and I was intending to explain when you got home, but after the next text — well, that was utterly bitchy and immature. Effing slimeball, indeed!'

'I didn't say that.' *Millie. It had to be Millie, 'helping'.*

With a lithe movement Luke stood and fetched his phone, found the text and showed it to Amy. He was right; it was really nasty and immature. Amy noted in passing that he had the same model phone as hers; no wonder Debbie had assumed it was hers when she found it. 'I didn't write that. Millie must have done it. She was trying to protect me. I had a bad time with Gareth and she was trying to protect me from breaking my heart over another guy who never replies to texts. I'll admit your name was mud on Monday night but I never sent that.'

'Oh. OK. Why didn't you phone my parents' house on the landline?'

'I don't know their number, and I don't

know your surname. And you could have phoned the house, too. Or used your parents' phone to give me a ring on my mobile. Or dropped by or something. And, come to think of it, you never mentioned it the other day when you did drop by. You surely must have guessed I'd be texting you and you'd already lost the phone by then if you thought you'd lost it in the restaurant. You could have said about losing it then.'

Luke chewed over this for a minute before saying, 'That's true. I'm sorry, Amy; it's been a hell of a few days. I haven't got Debbie's phone number and it's ex-directory . . . at least, I couldn't find it. And the only record of your mobile number was in my phone's memory, and your surname's not Murray nor Driscoll . . . I still don't know what it is, for that matter. You never said you'd been phoning me the other day, and it never occurred to me to mention it . . . I was too busy chatting. And then I was run ragged over the flat-letting.'

'So we're still an item?'

Luke pondered, a faraway look in his eyes. 'Let's just be friends for a bit and get to know each other a little better before we start going out as a couple. I think maybe I rushed into things.'

He didn't believe her, then, and thought

102

that horrible text was hers. Oh, she could kill Millie for that. She looked away, blinked twice, and fled.

* * *

When Amy got upstairs, emotions sloshing round her head like dirty bath water, Debbie was in the upstairs kitchen, also in her dressing gown, up uncommonly early. It was barely half past six. Debbie looked tired and crumpled, as if she'd spent half the night awake.

'You could have told me it was Luke instead of playing games with me last night,' Amy blurted out.

'I did. I told you it was Mr Armitage but you didn't seem that interested, so I dropped it. You seemed very tired and something had upset you, so I left you to it, thinking you'd tell me in the morning.'

'I didn't know his surname's Armitage. I wish you'd just said 'Luke'. Everything's gone horribly wrong.'

'Oh, sorry Amy love, I didn't realise. Do I take it you and Luke have split up already?'

'Yes, but it's all so embarrassing, and I don't know what to do.' Amy explained what had happened. 'I could kill Millie.'

'Hadn't you best ask her if she sent it

before jumping to conclusions?'

'Who else could have done it? My phone was on the side in her house and she could have done it when I went to the loo or something. Maybe I could ask her to confess to Luke.'

Debbie pressed her lips together and sighed. 'I don't think that's wise, Amy love. What's to stop him thinking you asked Millie to confess when it was you all along? It will just add to you seeming immature to him. Just be friends, as he suggests, and get to know each other better. In some respects I think that's better than having a boyfriend within easy reach. Less temptation.'

'For goodness sake, I'm old enough for sex if I want. Everything keeps going wrong for me. First it was going to be awkward for me to go the States with Mum and Dad, then you had to rent out the rooms instead of me having them. Now I won't be able to sit comfortably in my favourite spot in the garden because I'll be too embarrassed . . . he'll think I'm stalking him.'

'Oh dear.' Debbie's face softened in sympathy. 'So now isn't a good time to mention another problem, but I must. I'm not sleeping at all well at the moment. The trains aren't too bad normally, even with the windows open. I'm acclimatised to them, but lately I'm waking up every time one goes past in the night. You using the bathroom is also waking me up and I'm at the end of my tether, just when I need my rest most. I was going to ask if you'd mind swapping bedrooms so that you have the one at the back. There's the airing cupboard and built-in cupboard between the front room and the bathroom, and you can't hear the floorboards squeaking so much either. I know it's smaller, but you'd get the nicer view . . . '

'Oh now, that I don't mind, if that's what you want. In fact, I think it makes sense. Do you mean swap everything over or what?'

'I'd want to move the furniture round, if that's all right.'

11

Of course, it was the sort of task that becomes bigger once you start it. They moved all the furniture into the lounge and landing, then decided that the bedrooms needed a jolly good vacuum . . . and how about renting a carpet-cleaner and doing a thorough job of it? Seemed like a plan, especially as Debbie was hypersensitive to smells at the moment, so a nice clean carpet would be lovely.

Halfway through the day, letting the carpet dry out a bit before moving the other furniture in, they sat in the upstairs kitchen over some lunch. 'It's taking longer than I expected,' confessed Debbie, 'But not before time. When your Uncle left he tore the heart right out of me, and though I carried on from day to day, sorting the business out and closing it down, it was as if I was on autopilot, not daring to think, not daring to feel anything. Then when I went self-employed with the book-keeping, I was so busy it was all I could do to keep up with the housework; when someone gives you a job, you do that in preference to housework because housework will keep but the job won't. Though this cancer has been one heck of a shock, it's made me slow down and take stock of my life, decide what's a priority. And getting things sorted has become important because . . . because you needed the room. I'm sorry things haven't worked out exactly as planned.'

'Awwwww,' said Amy. She laid her hand on her aunt's arm. She knew what Debbie really meant about getting things sorted out; she didn't want to leave a mess if the outcome of her treatment wasn't good, but nobody actually liked to consider that possibility. 'I do appreciate you giving me a home while Mum and Dad are in the States, and I know it's not your fault you've had to let the rooms instead of letting me have them, but it'll all work out OK.' She took a bite of sandwich. 'I do feel all stirred up and disorientated, though. Did I tell you I bumped into that rat Gareth up in Leicester?' Amy found herself telling Debbie about the encounter. 'He scared me a bit, like there's an underlying core of self-centred violence that I'd never noticed before.'

Debbie shuddered. 'Men. No wonder you're all stirred up. Poor Luke caught some collateral damage when you and Millie sent those texts, I think.'

They were still busy when they heard the French windows open and close. Luke must be home. Amy tried not to think about it as she set out her belongings and ornaments in the back bedroom. It was a lovely room, catching the evening sun. She set a small table for her laptop near the window so she could look at the view when sitting at it, studying. Even the station was picturesque. She looked down and could see Luke sitting at the outdoor table on the terrace, with a pile of paper under a stone. He appeared to be doing some marking. Amy heard the phone ring, and an excited, 'Ooh lovely,' from Debbie.

Debbie came into the bedroom. 'Alison next door has just phoned to say she has some gateau that needs eating up. She can't sell it tomorrow, and it's too much for her, and her parents are away just now. I said we'll meet her on the terrace with plates and coffee.'

The thought of gateau after their exhausting day was very appealing. Amy made the coffee downstairs while her aunt sorted out a tray of plates, forks, a jug of milk and a bowl of sugar. When she walked outside, Amy saw that Alison and the gateau had already arrived and she was sitting down, deep in conversation with Luke. She felt a stab of envy because Alison was good-looking and had a svelte figure despite temptation, though surely she was a little too old for him? Alison's parents owned the deli, and Alison had done a degree in business studies before taking over most of the running of the deli.

'It was hard at first,' Amy heard her say, 'But I just don't get tempted any more. I didn't like to just throw it away and there's masses here. Hi Amy, have a slice.' Alison beamed at her and cut off a huge portion of gateau while Debbie poured the coffee.

Amy gave Luke a tentative smile. He smiled back warmly and she felt a frisson of excitement run through her, closely followed by a feeling of sadness.

'Oh well, bang goes my diet for another day,' said Debbie, without much dismay in her voice. 'Such a treat.'

There was a sound of footsteps on the cobbles. 'We really must keep that gate locked at night,' said Alison, just as Gill the Macmillan nurse appeared.

'I thought I heard voices. I tried ringing the doorbell but . . . '

'We're all out here scoffing cake,' said Debbie, introducing Gill to everyone. 'It's a lovely evening.' Her tone was regretful, as if she didn't want to leave the gathering for a private word with the nurse.

'Why don't you have a slice?' said Alison, smiling up at Gill.

Amy was looking at Luke's facial expression. He seemed stunned by Gill's appearance, and no wonder, because she had a great figure and a lovely air about her. It wasn't fair, having two beautiful women to compete with. Amy had a sudden urge to rush back indoors and attend to her make-up.

Gill stole a look at her watch. 'That would be lovely. You're my last call anyway.' She seated herself next to Luke with a guilty little smile and boggled at the hunk of gateau Alison cut for her.

The cake was delicious, and Alison complimented Amy on her coffee. 'You seem to have a real knack for making it.'

'We're going to hold a Macmillan Coffee Morning,' said Amy.

'Cool. I'll bake a cake,' said Luke. 'But it'll have to be a microwave cake and I haven't done one of those before.'

'You can use our oven,' said Debbie.

'I think we still have a functioning urn you could borrow in case you get a lot of people all at once . . . a kettleful won't go far, believe me,' said Alison.

'I'd best get on and leave you to your planning. I'll pop by at a more convenient time to see you, Debbie.'

'Oh, thanks,' said Debbie, looking contrite. 'We've diverted you from your duties.'

'Not at all, it's been a treat to sit down to delicious coffee and cake.'

* * *

Late the next afternoon Luke was on the front doorstep looking very teacherish with a sports jacket and tie, and his briefcase in his hand. 'Hi, I've got some news.'

Amy ushered him through to the library where Debbie was sitting quietly, reading, because the back of the house and upstairs were far too warm in the evening sun. The weather was sultry, in need of a good thunderstorm.

Luke sat down, flashing a grin at Debbie. He pulled a form from his briefcase. 'I've been talking to the head teacher, Donna Phelps, and she'd love to talk to you about voluntary work, gaining some work experience and so forth. Is Wednesday OK? I've brought one of those horrendous CRB forms for you to fill in, so you have it ready if Mrs Phelps takes you on ... the sooner it's submitted the better because they can take ages to come through. The school will pay the fee as it's for their benefit.'

Amy took the form. 'Thanks, that's excellent. That's so exciting. I've filled these in before.'

111

★ ★ ★

Aunty Debbie drove Amy to the school for her interview so she would arrive unflustered and cool, though Amy walked home with a bounce in her step. She hadn't seen Luke at the school but couldn't wait to tell him she would be helping out one day a week: Mondays, starting the following week. She wouldn't be on her own with the children at first, so her previous CRB check was deemed sufficient until the new one came through. Donna Phelps, the head teacher, seemed like one of the nicest, most sensible and approachable people Amy had ever met.

When Amy got home Debbie said, 'There was a delivery of flowers for you, beautiful red roses. I put them in a vase on the table in the library for you; it's cooler in there.

'Flowers?' Who on earth would be sending her flowers? It wasn't her birthday or anything. She went downstairs. They were lovely roses, red as wine, but lacked scent, something Amy thought a shame, as if they were all show and no substance. Shoving that ungracious thought aside, she opened the card. 'To Amy, just to say sorry. x'. It must be Luke with a rather extravagant gesture. A bit confusing, really. Was this a romantic gesture to say he'd forgiven her and believed her now? Why couldn't he have just given her a token bunch of flowers if he wanted to say sorry? This was way over the top, so way OTT it left her embarrassed.

★ ★ ★

When Luke got back that afternoon, she waylaid him on the way round to his flat and said, 'Thanks.'

He grinned. 'My pleasure.' He was reserved; a little distant, even. She stood there waiting for him to follow it up with the suggestion that they start going out together after all, but the suggestion never came.

The awkward silence lengthened but she refused to be the one to suggest they go out. If he wanted to lay it cool, she'd play it cool. 'Can you help me have a look in the cellar for tables and chairs and things for the coffee morning, please? Debbie's convinced there are some boxes of crockery but she won't go down the steps after her accident.'

'Cool. Where's the cellar?'

She led him into the old kitchen. 'It's locked, and that's the key hanging on the doorframe. Be careful because it's rather dangerous, which is why the door is kept locked. We were never allowed in there as children.'

Luke unlocked the door and pushed it in. 'Whoa! I see what you mean. That's quite scary.' The stairwell gaped in front of him. He fumbled for the light switch. It was old — Bakelite — and it didn't work. 'That's dangerous, too. Perhaps I can change the lightbulb, or at least check it out.'

Amy passed him her house keys which had a torch on the keyring, but it was barely adequate, a wan glimmer against the darkness. 'Careful,' she said as she followed Luke down into the abyss. 'I don't think anyone's been down since Uncle Bernard left; Aunty hated it after her accident.'

Luke laughed. 'Maybe he never ran off. Maybe he fell down the steps never to be seen again. Maybe she did him in and buried him in the cellar. Mwuahahahaha.'

Amy laughed and shuddered. 'Don't be awful.'

They reached the bottom of the steps, much to Amy's relief. They were steep and narrow, though the banister hemming them in made them safe enough if you took your time. If the handrail broke with your weight on it, it could prove very nasty, though, as poor Debbie had found out. She shook it carefully just in case, finding it solid and trustworthy.

Luke flicked the wan torchlight over the

walls, ceiling, and various items of unidentifiable junk. Amy caught a glimpse of a body on the floor, gave a strangled squeak and grabbed at Luke, fear raking her hair with chilling fingers. Luke froze, then played the torch beam over the body. It was half-hidden under a sheet, one hand peeping out from under it, and a waxen, bald head poking out at a strange angle. Neck broken, most likely.

'What the — ?' Luke bent over, then laughed. 'That gave me such a fright. It's a mannequin. You know, for dress shops. Look.' He whipped the sheet off with a cloud of dust. He was right. The plastic nude stared back at them with blank-eyed indifference. 'Did your uncle ever keep a clothes shop?'

'Not that I know of. That really scared me.'

Luke moved as if to give her a comforting hug, but must have thought better of it. He flicked the beam to the faulty light fitting. It looked old, a two-ply cloth-coated cable descending to a brass bayonet lightbulb fitting. 'I'm going to buy a decent torch. Come on, Amy, this is a bit too dangerous stumbling around in the dark, I think. We don't want to break our necks falling over something.'

A little later he was back with a decent torch, a stand-alone halogen lamp and extension cable. 'I don't actually trust that light fitting,' he explained. 'We'll run this down into the cellar, and plug it into a kitchen socket every time we need a light down there.'

'I told Debbie about the mannequin and she laughed, saying Granddad was a bit of an acquirer and hoarder of things that 'might come in handy some time'. But there should be some antiques down here, she thinks, and some old bits of silverware from the kitchen and stuff. She remembered putting them down here in a seaman's chest when she was younger, sprightlier and before she had the fright.'

'Fright?'

'She fell down the stairs and broke her leg . . . the handrail broke. Swore she'd never come down here again.'

'Crumbs; that's what you meant by her accident. Now you tell me. Better check the handrail out then.' Luke played out the cable and set up the light. When he turned it on the cellar became just an ordinary, if very cluttered, room. He examined the handrail. 'Looks safe enough.' It was a simple handrail supported by wide upright struts every couple of steps. No wonder they hadn't been allowed to play in the cellar as children; a child could easily have fallen between the struts. A bar along the middle of the struts helped strengthen them. The steps were solid brick and concrete built against the wall, and the struts were quite crudely screwed onto the outside edge of the steps, as if the whole handrail were an afterthought.

'Those struts look newer than the handrail.' Luke frowned. Discarded at the bottom of the steps was a heap of what looked like the old struts, bits of wood about an inch square and two-foot-six long. He picked one up. It was shorter than it needed to be by about six inches, broken at the end. All the old struts were broken and nearby were some other bits of wood, about six inches long. They looked like the broken-off ends. They'd all broken at about the same place, across the screw holes, which had acted like perforations. Luke held up a six-inch piece against a longer bit and shook his head. 'Three screws in that narrow bit of wood. Weakens it. Some fool tried to make the rail stronger, and ended up actually making it weaker. Your aunt was lucky not to kill herself, I think.'

'It seems to have been mended sensibly, though. Is it safe?'

Luke shook the rail. 'Seems solid. It's been mended with thicker struts, for a start, and well-spaced screws into the brickwork.' He pulled in a breath as if to say more, but shook his head instead. He was frowning, eyeing the struts up. 'Something doesn't seem right,' he said, but Amy wasn't really paying attention, not when she had a new Aladdin's cave to explore.

They had a good poke around the cellar. There was a drop-leaf dining table with fold-out chairs, a strange-looking cupboard without a top on it, a marble slab, some copperware green with verdigris, and through a door into another part of the cellar, a large heap of coal.

'That must have been here for ages,' said Amy. 'The range hasn't been used for years, as far as I know.'

'There's a book down here,' said Luke. 'One of yours?' He held up a large book about antiques.

'No. I expect it's Debbie's.'

There were a couple of occasional tables as Debbie had thought, and some random chairs, as well as a tea chest full of sets of china tea services or coffee cups with one or two items missing. Perfect for a coffee morning, once they were cleaned up. There was even an old tea trolley.

They moved the important pieces to the bottom of the cellar steps. Luke bent, picked up a screw, and spent a minute looking at it carefully before putting it into an old jam jar which stood on a three-legged bamboo table.

'Ugh, I'm all covered in cobwebs. Let's call it a day,' he said.

'We can bring up the crockery a little at a time, and get it washed ready. And leave the furniture down here until nearer the time,' said Amy. 'It depends on the weather forecast.'

★ ★ ★

When Amy told Debbie about the coal, Debbie said she used the range when it was very cold, but burned wood in it. That coal would come in handy, if Luke would be kind enough to bring it up when needed. 'I want that old chest of silverware,' Debbie added. 'See if you can find it because I'd quite like to sell it. I wish I'd sold it thirty years ago because the price of silver went through the roof, though it's dropped again now, but it seemed all wrong selling the family silver. But now it seems wrong to hoard it in a box out of sight. There are also one or two bits of old majolica, if I recall correctly. Those could go because I always hated that stuff. And some willow-pattern stuff. But we'll try selling the silver first, I think.'

Amy carefully went back down into the cellar, mentally thanking Luke for his foresight over the cable extension and lamp, and had a good poke around. 'I can't find any silverware,' she told her aunt later. 'But I did find an old sea chest . . . was that where you put it?'

'Yes.' Her aunt sank back into the pillows. 'Or at least, I thought I had. But it was years and years ago. How mysterious. Maybe I misremember.' She sighed. 'I'm tired, need to sleep, and I can't be bothered to fret about it now.'

Amy said nothing, but wondered if the silverware had been stolen. And if it had been stolen, when had it been taken? Luke had been caught snooping around the house, though with an innocent explanation, and now some valuable items were missing from the cellar. Perhaps he'd gone back down into the cellar and stolen them. But how could he? He didn't have a key to the main house. Besides, if he were a criminal, surely he would have said yes to going out with her, just to look out for nickable stuff if nothing else. *Don't be so daft,* she told herself. *Debbie has just forgotten where she put it, that's all.*

12

On Monday Amy and Luke walked to school together. This might have been a mistake because Chloe, one of the girls in the class she was helping out with, asked, 'Are you Mr Armitage's girlfriend, Miss?' Her sidekick Samantha sniggered.

'That's an impertinent question,' said Amy.

'What's impertinent, please, Miss?' drawled Chloe through her nose.

'Irrelevant to the point of rudeness and insolence,' said Amy. 'I suggest you either look it up in the dictionary or we can continue this discussion in detention after school.' Chloe shot her a poisonous look, but Sam sniggered, this time at Chloe, whose scowl deepened.

★　★　★

'Enjoy yourself?' asked Luke as they walked home with a two-foot exclusion zone between them.

'It was fun, though some of those kids just don't seem interested in anything apart from what happened on the soaps and what the latest lippy colour is,' replied Amy. She told him about Chloe and Sam. 'They must have seen us walking in together and put two and two together and made five. Honestly, it's not as if we were holding hands or anything remotely suggestive.'

'Oh, those two,' said Luke. 'They came to my attention very early on. I have them in my geography class, and they're really cheeky. Wearing.'

'I'd like a snoop in the charity shops on the way back,' said Amy. 'I could do with a few more mugs for this coffee morning, and maybe a teapot or two. Did you know Debbie has asked at least 30 people . . . and she keeps saying 'bring a friend', so I have no idea how many are coming.'

'Let's hope it's a fine day and they can spill out into the garden or onto the cobbled area,' said Luke. 'Why not ask them to bring a chair with them?'

'I can't do that,' said Amy. She laughed. 'Can you imagine thirty people carrying chairs up the high street?'

She mentioned the seating problem to the people in the charity shop where she'd bought the sofa. They said they had a number of chairs and a couple of tables which had been in the shop for a few weeks and spurned by the customers. Amy could have them for a sensible donation. They also had some coffee pots, which Amy nearly declined since she preferred serving coffee in a cafetiere. 'Don't be daft,' said Luke. 'You can make it in the cafetiere and transfer it. You might find yourself really busy.'

Amy couldn't resist a few more books. Luke just laughed at her.

'Good job Aunty Debbie has a cellar,' said Amy as they walked home with a couple of the chairs; a matter of a couple of hundred yards. 'At least we have somewhere to store these before the big day.'

★ ★ ★

The next day Luke came home from school grumbling that someone had spread a rumour that they were getting married. Amy was furious.

13

Amy was thumbing through a cookery book when Luke joined her at the outdoor table. 'I'm wondering what to bake for this coffee morning,' she said, glancing up at Luke.

He plonked a mug of tea down, then a pile of marking. 'I could bake something too if I could use your oven — I don't trust the microwave. I'm not bad at fruit cake.'

'Great idea, thanks.' Amy slowly turned the pages, looking for something simple but yummy-looking. 'Debbie would like us to go up to the attic and help bring down some bits and bobs from up there. When you have time, and only if it's convenient.'

'Course I will,' said Luke.

'She wants us to keep an eye open for the silverware and majolica which she thought was in the cellar. I've looked all over but there's nothing like that down there, so it must be up in the attic. Seems a more likely place for it anyway.'

'Did you bring that book up from the cellar? The antiques one. She can see if it's got what she's after in it so we know what we're looking for. I've no idea what majolica is.'

'It's this hideous china stuff,' said Amy. 'I wouldn't give it houseroom, but it's valuable. But no; I forgot about the book. It's ten years out of date anyway.'

★   ★   ★

The evening before the coffee morning, the downstairs kitchen table was laden with cakes, home-baked tarts and biscuits; some tea trays had been pressed into service and about fifty mugs had been found. Teapots and proper china teacups were laid out, and several jugs of assorted sizes had been put ready.

'If nobody comes we'll be eating cake for weeks,' said Debbie.

'How many have you invited?' said Luke, reaching for a jam tart.

Debbie slapped his hand away. 'FHB. About thirty, but not everybody's replied.'

'FHB?' asked Amy.

'Family Hold Back. Mum — Gran used to say it if we had guests and were a bit short of something. War-time habit, I think.'

There was a knock at the front door. 'I'll get it,' said Amy.

It was Gill the Macmillan nurse. 'I thought I'd pop by this evening rather than tomorrow, as you're having the coffee morning,' she said.

'We're all in the downstairs kitchen ogling the cakes,' said Amy, showing her through. She was in the perfect position to see Luke's eyes fly open with appreciation of Gill's beauty. Amy's heart flipped and hurt itself on her rib cage. Gill seemed oblivious to Luke's admiring looks. Amy's hands clenched and unclenched and she swallowed a couple of times.

'Wow,' said Gill, looking at the spread. 'Maybe I should come round tomorrow after all.'

'Why not?' said Luke.

'I don't think so, it's Debbie's coffee morning.'

'If you've come to see, me shall we go upstairs?' said Debbie.

* * *

'I thought you said thirty guests. We're running out of coffee and I'm getting low on cake,' said Amy to Debbie as she entered the kitchen the next day. The coffee morning was in full swing. Very full swing.

'Thirty friends plus friends of friends, it seems,' said Debbie. 'I've brought some of the money through to hide away.'

'I'm rushed off my feet. Can you pop next door and get more coffee from Alison, please?

126

Thank goodness we got the extra cups and plates and things.'

One or two of the coffee-morning guests had brought home-baked cakes to contribute, which was just as well because otherwise Amy didn't know how they'd have managed. Lunchtime came and went and the coffee morning segued into afternoon tea. Eventually the frenzy died down, Debbie locked the gates early, and Amy took her coffee and the last remaining slice of cake into the library. She was rather startled to see one or two guests with noses deep in some of her books.

'Coffee, cake and a good book,' said one lady. 'What could be better?'

'Isn't it a fact that English women prefer chocolate to sex?' said the most elderly-looking lady. She dabbed a serviette to her lips. 'I really enjoyed that. Debbie must be very proud of you — Amy, isn't it?'

'A great success all round,' declared another. She pulled a little moue with her lips. 'I suppose we'd better make tracks. Shame I'm only halfway through the book. I've got to the point where the hero and the heroine have fallen out with each other. I don't like to leave him dangling.'

'Doesn't do to leave any man dangling,' said the lady who had made the remark about chocolate. She gave a slow, knowing wink.

Amy was struggling for something to say. In the end she said, 'Cool. You could take that book if you like. I'm trying to cull them, but I keep buying more.'

'Oh, thank you. I must make a contribution for it though,' said the lady, dropping a couple of pounds into the kitty as she left. Debbie had to go and unlock the gate again to let them out.

* * *

When Luke got back from school he was most miffed to find that all the cake had gone, until Debbie told him she had put some by for him. He was very impressed when they told him how much money they'd raised.

'I think we had well over a hundred people throughout the morning,' said Debbie. 'Must have done, but I lost track after about ninety. I didn't know everyone. I expect some of them were friends of yours, Amy.'

Luke glanced at their faces. 'You look utterly worn out, the pair of you. Let's have a sit down. I'll make you a cup of tea, then I'll help Amy put the chairs and stuff in the cellar in case it gets damp tonight.'

Debbie laid a grateful hand on Luke's arm. 'You're very thoughtful.'

'This is hideously scary,' said Amy. Luke was walking down the steps backwards and they were carrying a table between them. 'I'm terrified one of us is going to slip.'

'Like Debbie,' agreed Luke. 'There, I'm down. I might just ask you to pass the chairs over the banister. Safer. How did Debbie's accident happen?'

'I don't know. I wasn't here. I just remember a phone call from Uncle Bernard to say there had been an accident, the banister had given way and Debbie was in hospital with a broken leg. Dad said he'd come over and help Bernard mend the banister, but Bernard said it was all right; he'd got someone in to fix it already.'

Luke shook his head and frowned at the steps. He shook the banister. 'This doesn't look like a professional job, though. I wonder who was idiot enough to drill the extra holes in the original struts.'

'Bernard, I expect. From what I remember of him — mostly from what Dad used to say to Mum — Bernard thinks he's bright and clever, but actually I think he's rather stupid and not very forward-thinking. I adored him as a kid, but see things differently now. I think that's why Dad wanted to come and fix the banisters. He was afraid Bernard would botch the job. He was pleased to hear Bernard was getting someone in.' Amy shoved the table a little closer to one of the walls. 'Oh, by the way, thanks for the card. But really, you shouldn't have.'

'Card? What card?'

'Came in the post this morning.'

'I didn't send you a card.' Luke crushed some perspiration from his brow.

An ice cube slid down Amy's back. The cellar walls crushed down on her lungs. 'Let's get out of here, it's beginning to creep me out. I'll go and fetch the card. Meet you on the terrace.'

Back in the downstairs kitchen, Amy picked up the card and retrieved the envelope from the recycling bin. It was printed with her name, address, post code, and posted in Derby, sent via an internet card site. The card, with some daft cartoon fluffy animal on the front, said, 'Hope you liked the roses.' Amy had assumed it was another profligate gesture from Luke, one which she actually found rather unnerving.

'What roses?' asked Luke. 'Why on earth would I be sending you a card?' He turned the card over and over but it was utterly anonymous.

'I thought you sent me roses. When they

arrived I said, 'thanks,' and you said, 'That's OK,' or something. Then the card arrived and they're obviously connected.'

Luke frowned. 'When? I don't remember.'

'It was the day of my interview with Donna Phelps. They were waiting for me when I got back. The card on the roses just said 'sorry.' I assumed they were a rather extravagant gesture from you, I thought it was a bit much, really, but didn't like to seem churlish, so I thanked you. I thought maybe they were a prelude to you asking me out, but you didn't and you seemed so offhand that I didn't pursue it. You seemed to know all about them, and now you deny sending them.' Amy had a slightly hysterical undertone to her voice.

Luke sat still, frowning for a minute before saying, 'I don't remember you mentioning any flowers. If you said thanks, I expect I assumed you were thanking me for the heads-up about the voluntary work. I didn't send you roses and I didn't send you this card.'

Amy said nothing more, but she could guess who they were from, now. Gareth. Unless Luke was lying and playing silly games with her, which seemed unlikely. But how did Gareth know her address?

★ ★ ★

On Monday Amy was helping out at the school again. They were preparing for the literary festival on Thursday. Donna Phelps asked her if she was free over the half term holiday. They needed another female helper on a geography/geology field trip to Pembrokeshire because three out of the four geography teachers were male, and the female one wouldn't be going. Amy said yes without hesitation. She was still at the anything-to-oblige stage and it never occurred to her to give it some serious thought. If she had, she might have realised it wouldn't be easy being on duty twenty-four hours a day in the company of rumbustious teenagers and a rather attractive man who was, regrettably, not her boyfriend, despite the beastly school rumours.

* ★ ★

The next day she was sorting her clean clothes into their various drawers, when she heard the mumble of voices from the garden. It was utterly audible, as if those speaking were in the room with her; some discussion about the merits of a couple of fruit stalls at the Tuesday market. The voices were so loud she felt she could reach out and touch whoever it was. She frowned and looked out of the window. Two women and a child in a pushchair were sitting at the outdoor table on the brick terrace, as bold as if they owned the place.

Amy remembered the previous occasions she'd accosted a 'trespasser' in her aunt's house. She'd come across as rude and aggressive. This time it would be better, she told herself as she strode down the stairs and into the back garden. The two women looked up with smiles as she approached. 'Can I help you?' Amy asked politely as she reached them.

'Two coffees please,' said one. 'And do you do soft drinks?'

'You're not as busy as Friday, very quiet today,' said the other. 'I'm so glad you've opened, because Lucy's bus only comes every two hours, and there's nowhere else that serves coffee except The Shoulder of Mutton and the burger bar.'

'My feet are killing me,' confided the first woman. Amy noticed that she was sitting as if she had a lump in her midriff. She vaguely recognised the second woman from Friday, someone she'd assumed was one of Debbie's friends.

'Oh dear,' said Amy, thoughts tumbling into a new pattern. 'This is a bit awkward; this isn't a café, we were just having a

133

Macmillan Coffee Morning; but if you like, I'll put the kettle on, as you're here and need a sit-down. You're welcome to a drink. I'd be pleased of the company, to be honest.'

Both women's faces fell, then reddened. 'Oh my goodness,' said the second. 'I saw you were open on Friday and thought, thank goodness, a new coffee shop. I just walked in off the street and had coffee and gateau. I never realised . . . '

Amy laughed. 'You were more than welcome.' She told them how much they'd raised for Macmillan. 'Honestly, please stay and have a cup of coffee. I hardly know anyone in Runworthy.'

A little later she'd brought out some coffee and mugs, and rustled up some apple juice for the toddler. The women, Lucy and Emily, had grown up together at school and now met up on Tuesdays, market day, nearly every week. 'I live out in the sticks,' said Lucy. 'Terrible bus service. But it's nice to get out the house with Josh.'

'I live in Runworthy, and my kids are at nursery and playgroup,' said Emily.

Amy told them about herself and her ambitions.

'Forget being a teacher; you should open a coffee shop,' said Lucy as they stood up to go. 'You make a wicked coffee. It would be great in the summer, sitting at tables on the cobbled lane, watching the world go by, like on the continent.'

Later, when Amy was phoning Millie, she told her what had happened. When Millie stopped laughing she said, 'Perhaps you should open a coffee shop if that's what the town needs. Do your MA around it. Earn some money.'

'Might not be viable,' said Amy, lying back and studying her bedroom ceiling, phone clamped to her ear. 'I think that if there's a gap in the market which nobody has filled, there's often a reason.'

14

A week before the half-term trip, Luke, Debbie and Amy were sitting outside drinking coffee. There was a distinct autumnal nip in the air. 'Do you think you could get some coal up from the cellar for me please, Luke dear,' Debbie said. 'I'm too scared to go down and as it's turning chilly I might see if the range is working OK.'

'Amy said you had an accident,' said Luke.

'Yes,' Debbie laughed. 'I tripped over my own feet, grabbed hold of the banister and it came away from the steps, one strut at a time, crack, crack, crack, crack, like dominos . . . luckily it was enough to slow my fall, but I still ended up with a broken leg. The banister's fine now, so it's safe for you to go down. I wouldn't ask you if it weren't safe. Bernard mended it shortly after I came home from hospital, but I still can't bring myself to go down there.'

'Oh,' said Amy. 'I thought Uncle Bernard got a carpenter in to mend it.'

Debbie shook her head. 'When did Bernard ever take the sensible option if he thought he could save a penny or two? No, he did it himself. Took him days, but he wouldn't hear of having help.'

'But Dad offered . . . why didn't he accept help? Mum wanted to come down to look after you, but Uncle Bernard wouldn't hear of it.'

'I expect he was a bit embarrassed,' said Debbie. 'I think it was his 'improvements' which caused the thing to collapse in the first place.'

Amy laughed, but Luke just looked pensive. 'That must have been awful breaking your leg like that in that horrible cellar. Did Bernard hear you or something?'

'He was out all weekend visiting his cousin in Stockport, but luckily Alison's Mum heard me calling. I must admit it was very frightening, I was in such pain and couldn't move. Good job the back door was open or I could have been there for hours. I could have died by the time Bernard came home. I really can't stand the cellar now.'

'I'll fetch the coal up now, before I forget,' said Luke.

While Luke was fetching the coal, there was an angry snarl of car engine being revved very hard. It sounded as if it was coming from the cobbled lane. Debbie and Amy exchanged a look, stood up together and rushed round.

A soft-top BMW was in the middle of the

cobbled lane, and Gareth was pounding on the front door. 'Amy! It's me; open the door.' He turned and stared at her. 'There you are,' he said, walking briskly towards her. 'I've decided I can't live without you. I've definitely chucked Shannon this time, for good. Honest. Here.' He thrust a bunch of red roses at her. They were wilting already, heads bowed.

Amy backed away. 'I've told you to leave me alone. It's over, Gareth. Over.'

'You don't mean it. You were just playing hard to get. You know you love me really; you were really cut up about chucking me, I know. I've learned my lesson and I promise I won't two-time you again. I'll play it your way, be all romantic and stuff. That's what the roses are about.' He advanced on her, panting slightly, a soppy puppy look in his eyes.

'Go away!' she shrieked. The world was beginning to spin. 'I told you to leave me alone.'

'But it's you I love, only you. You haven't got a boyfriend; I looked at your Facebook status.'

'How? You're unfriended.'

'A mutual friend let me look on her computer. Come on, babe; get in the car, I'll take you out to dinner.'

'No. Just go. And don't you dare sent me any more anonymous cards or flowers. It's not romantic; it's stalking. You're obsessive — you're nuts. You just don't get it, do you, Gareth? You just don't understand.'

He wasn't going to go. He was going to stand there, making a scene. She tried to retreat through the front door but it was locked. Debbie had vanished. Amy turned and ran towards the back door, heart thundering, but Gareth's hand grabbing her shoulder brought her up short. 'Don't! Please listen,' he begged.

Luke leaped out of the back door, closely followed by Debbie. Luke took one look at Amy's face and rushed over as she turned and brushed Gareth's arm away.

'Gareth, you heard Amy; please go.' Luke stood next to Amy, poised for anything.

'What's it to you?' Gareth's body language was cocky, sneering, but his face was pale with livid blotches on his cheekbones, his eyes imploring.

Luke put a protective arm round Amy's shoulder. 'Gareth, I've heard all about you, and what I've heard I don't like. You're not wanted here, not welcome. If you don't leave Amy alone, we'll apply for a non-molestation order or something. Go away.'

'Amyeeeee.' Gareth begged her with his

eyes, the petulant expression ruining his good looks.

'Just go; I don't know what I ever saw in you.'

'Is he your boyfriend?' Gareth's tone was rich with disbelief. 'It's not on your Facebook status.'

Amy paused, then said, 'Yes, yes he is, now go before we call the police.' Luke's embrace felt comfortable; it felt right, reassuring. Luke bent to her, his soft lips on hers as he gave her a possessive and hungry kiss that left her dizzy.

Luke broke the kiss and looked up at Gareth. 'I suggest you just go. Now.'

Gareth's face fell into planes of utter desolation, and a few tears started down his face. He looked like a four-year-old whose toy has broken. He backed off and slid into his car.

'Take care as you reverse out,' said Amy, because a crowd of curious people had gathered. 'Honestly Gareth, I don't know what you think you're doing.'

Gareth reversed out slowly, and the last she saw of him was his woebegone expression as he set off up the high street.

'Come inside, Amy. You look as white as a sheet. You too, please, Luke,' said Debbie. 'I'm going to lock the gates early.'

Amy and Luke went into the library and sat down on the green sofa. Amy felt strangely numb, yet she could sense Luke's body heat as he sat so very close to her, yet without touching.

He was studying the floor, sitting tightly, hands clenching and unclenching. 'I'm sorry about acting like your boyfriend after telling you I'd rather we were just friends, but Debbie told me it was an emergency.'

'I'm sorry I told him you are my boyfriend when you've said you don't want to be, but I couldn't think what else to do to put him off.'

'It was an awful liberty to kiss you like that, but I didn't think he believed me until then.'

'I'm not sorry about the kiss; it was a lovely kiss.'

Luke said nothing to that; didn't suggest they get back together, that cooling it had been a mistake. The numbing chill had reached Amy's throat, tightening her voice as she said, 'He was always persistent, as if he can't understand the word 'no', but I never expected this. He's a spoiled brat; Daddy's rolling in wealth, as you can guess from his car. I expect he always got his way as a kid. What a fool I was, taken in by all that glamour. And if that was Millie who let on about my Facebook status, I'll kill her. Though I doubt it was.'

Luke shook his head. 'I feel like I've started watching a very complicated film halfway through. I know I said I'd heard all about him, but that was a fib. Debbie just said your ex was here, she didn't trust him and could I come quick. Do you mind telling me what's going on?'

Just as he asked this, Debbie came in with some mugs of tea. 'You'd better tell him, Amy love. I'm beginning to wonder about that man's sanity.'

Amy nursed the white-hot mug of tea, chewing her lip. She lifted the mug to her lips and drank a scalding sip, then another. Debbie had put sugar in it, which normally tasted disgusting, but now she welcomed it. She told Luke about the confrontation with Gareth over his two-timing her and sharing bedroom secrets with his mates. As she spoke, it sounded so silly — banal, even. Luke's knuckles grew white as he hugged his knees. He frowned. 'If I'd known, I'd have thumped him just now.'

'And what good would that have done? It would have caused a lot of problems for you and not really taught him anything. I think he's a fantasist who doesn't understand people very well. All glamour and no substance.'

Luke nodded reluctantly. 'You're right.

Forgive me, but I think you're well rid of him. Provided you are rid of him.'

'You certainly are well rid of him, the toe-rag,' said Debbie.

'It's weird. I thought he loved me at first, but when I heard about the other girls I chucked him even though it broke my heart. I knew I'd made the right decision, though I felt really muddled about it, like the sensible part of me knew I was right but part of me still loved him. I didn't know what to think, what to feel, even.' Amy felt the tears pricking, so swigged some tea. She was shaking less, now. 'But today the look on his face when he saw your arm around me and I told him you're my boyfriend; well, I think he's genuinely in love with me. Maybe he always loved me and truly didn't understand why I was so upset and chucked him.' She let out a shuddering sigh. 'Thanks, Luke; I feel safer now.'

'He's a fool to treat you like that, and it explains a lot. No wonder you were so upset when I didn't return your texts.'

Amy pulled her phone out. 'I'm going to phone Millie and ask her if she gave him my address.' She dialled. 'Hi Millie, did you tell Gareth where I live or show him my Facebook status?'

The denial was instant. Then Millie

gasped. 'But he did come round in a bit of an emotional state a couple of days after your visit. Crying he was, so I left him in the living room alone while I made a cup of tea. But he wouldn't have peeked at my laptop would he? I was only gone for a couple of minutes.'

'Is your computer password protected?'

'Um, no.'

'Honestly Millie, one of the favourite games in the first year accommodation is to sneakily use someone's computer to change their Facebook status and things. You ought to have it passworded. He's just been round here and made a scene.'

Millie swore horribly. 'Oh I'm so sorry, Amy. I never thought . . . '

'And another thing, did you send an extra text to Luke after the one I sent?'

'That slimeball? Too right. He's another Gareth in the making. Your email wasn't nearly firm enough.'

'Another Gareth, who you felt so sorry for when he turned up on your doorstep all miserable, you made him tea and gave him an opportunity to sneak a look on your computer? Honestly, Millie, that was a bit much.'

'Yes, well, sorry, all right?'

When she'd hung up Amy sat there staring into space for a few moments. The world around her felt as if it were made of sponge. 'She's my best friend, but she's always interfering with the best of intentions. Drives me nuts at times. I don't understand how Gareth got my address from my FB page because it just says 'Runworthy'.'

'There's a photo of this house, though, Amy. It wouldn't be hard to find on Streetview. Best take down the photo, I think,' said Luke. 'FB isn't as safe as people think. I'll leave you in peace now, if that's OK. I think it's for the best.' Luke stood, bent over her and after a moment's hesitation, kissed her cheek lightly as a brother might, but she felt his lips on her cheek as if they were branding irons.

★　★　★

Amy joined Luke at the outside table the next afternoon. 'You look very pensive,' she said.

He turned his eyes to her. They were troubled. 'I know it's none of my business, but when did Debbie have that accident? Do you remember?'

Amy considered, trying to remember how old she was. 'It was a couple of years after Granddad died, so it was eleven or twelve years ago, I think.'

Luke brooded for a minute. 'Was that

antiques book we found in the cellar your aunt's?'

'She said no when I asked, so I said it must have been uncle Bernard's, but she laughed and said he didn't know the first thing about antiques, and wasn't interested, so it must have been Granddad's.'

'That doesn't make sense, because the book is too young if your Granddad died thirteen years ago. It's dated 2001. So if it's not yours and it's not Debbie's — and how could it be if she never goes down there? — it must be Bernard's. And there's silverware missing and you can't find the majolica. I don't like the way I'm thinking.'

15

'Oh crumbs,' muttered Luke to Amy as they stood together in the school car park. It was early in the morning, 6.00am, dark and chilly. Cars were driving in and parents were opening car boots, hauling out enormous suitcases. The girls were shivering in bomber jackets and fancy boots. 'Oh crumbs,' he repeated. 'I told them to wear sensible footwear like boots. I meant walking boots, not the latest fashion accessories. And we're only going for a week, not a month.'

The girls flocked over to him, twittering like sparrows. 'Sir, sir, when's the coach coming? It's freezing.'

Amy recognised the voice: Chloe the insolent. And there was her sidekick, Sam. Amy groaned mentally.

The boys clustered in a group, slouching nonchalantly, or playing games of tussle and shoving each other with their shoulders, their laughing voices breaking in the chill morning air.

The coach drew up and the driver loaded the suitcases into the stowage compartments one by one, grumbling that they needn't have packed a kitchen sink each. There was only just enough room for everything.

'I told them to travel light,' grumbled one of the other geography teachers, Simon Long. 'And they were told we're stopping on the coast on the way down, but to look at some of them you'd think they were going to London shopping.'

Before the coach set off, Donna Phelps told the kids exactly what was expected of them and that if they misbehaved their parents would be summoned all the way to west Wales to take them home. Then she and Luke did a head count. Donna sat next to Amy and smiled. 'OK?'

'Looking forward to it, thanks.'

Half a mile down the road, Sam asked at the top of her voice, 'Are we nearly there yet?' and everyone laughed, including Amy.

At first the noise was deafening, with the kids talking excitedly at the top of their voices, but as the journey wore on the early start told and many dropped off to sleep, including Amy. She woke with a start, and hoped she hadn't done anything embarrassing like loll on Donna or dribble in her sleep. She watched as mile after mile was eaten up. As they crossed the Severn Bridge into Wales, those who were still awake gave a cheer, waking everyone else up. Alan Trimble, the head of geography, gave a short talk about the Severn Bore, but Amy heard Chloe whisper, 'He *is* the Severn Bore.'

They bypassed Newport and Cardiff but left the motorway before Bridgend, swung through Ogmore-by-Sea round some very tight bends, and then headed to Southerndown. The coach parked in the car park at the top of the cliff. Alan Trimble handed out work sheets and gave them all safety instructions, issued hard hats, and warned everyone to watch out for falling rocks because the cliffs were very unstable.

Everyone set off in single file down the road. The view was superb, the air clear, the light just perfect for showing off the cliffs. Amy thought it looked as if a giant had built them from blocks and forgotten to cement them together. They didn't look stable and she was glad of the hard hats. Alan Trimble stopped them, delivered a short lecture, then told them to carry on and mind the cars. Soon some of them were complaining that it was a long walk down and why couldn't they have brought the coach down? When someone mentioned that an episode of *Doctor Who* had been filmed there, there was a ripple of excitement, and the pace picked up.

They reached the beach and divided into

groups. Amy was attached to Luke's group and it was nice to be with someone she knew. She felt like a duck in a henhouse and had no idea what was expected of her.

The girls wearing the fancy footwear minced down to the beach looking as if they'd eaten wasps, squealing at the sand, boulders and water.

'Serves them right,' said Luke when Amy joined him. 'They were warned.' They'd also been warned to stay away from the cliffs, but a couple of the boys had to be reminded.

Luke looked alive, burning with excitement as he instructed the kids to look out for fossils, like Gryphaea and corals. 'I prefer Llantwit Major myself, because you're more likely to get ammonites,' he said to Amy, who didn't know what he meant, 'But this isn't bad . . . ahah.' He bent and picked up a lump of pale grey rock with a darker blob in it. 'Gather round — look, I've found a Gryphaea, or devil's toenail.'

'Ewwww, that's gross,' said Chloe.

'Cool,' said Sam, standing too close to Luke, smiling up at him. 'Dunno about devil's toenail; more like my Gran's toenail.'

'Really?' said Luke, moving away slightly. 'Tell her to go to the chiropodist then.'

Chloe and Sam laughed immoderately, but started seriously scrutinising the pebbles and rocks. Then Sam gave out a yell. 'Found one! No, it's more than one. It's an orgy of Gryphaea.' She held it up. Everyone in Luke's group crowded round. It was a group of four or five toenails stuck together. Luke gave Amy an exasperated look at the vulgar comments this provoked. Amy did a quick head count. Eight. Good. Amy had to tell one of the boys off when he threw a lump of seaweed at Sam, and another boy did a rude pantomime with a couple of limpet shells. These kids were nearly adult, Amy realised. Some of them were over 16; old enough to ... She shuddered mentally. *Were we this crass at that age?* Listening to the conversation between the kids, she was rather shocked by the profanity until she recalled a conversation with her mum about her Facebook language; F this, F that. She remembered saying, 'Don't be so old, Mum. Everyone speaks like that nowadays,' and her mum had warned her it was a bad habit she'd need to break if she wanted to become a teacher. Which was true. She imagined telling Chloe to F off, imagined Donna Phelps's reaction and cringed.

Later they walked up to the Glamorgan Heritage Coast Centre for a look around, and ate their picnics before heading back to the coach. The kids complained about the long drag uphill to the car park. Simon Long told them all it served them right for squandering their time on computer games and texting instead of playing out of doors and getting fit. Amy said nothing about her aching legs.

★ ★ ★

Amy had expected that now they were in Wales it would be just a short drive to where they were staying, but it took a good two hours pursuing the sun westwards before they were at last driving down the winding roads towards Little Haven on the west coast of Wales. As they'd driven west the countryside had changed from hummocky mountains to flatter, undulating, rich-looking farmland bisected with hedges. 'It's not what I expected,' she said to Donna. 'I was expecting mountains.'

Donna laughed. 'It's called 'Little England beyond Wales'. The coast is wonderfully rugged, though, as a result of all the uplift and folding. Skerryhaven Field Centre is in some outstanding scenery.'

Amy didn't like to let on that she wasn't quite sure what Donna meant by uplift. It was a word Amy usually associated with lingerie or skin cream.

Skerryhaven Field Centre was about a mile south of Little Haven, with its own small beach. It was a purpose-built facility catering for educational groups. Donna told Amy the school had been going there for about ten years. 'A lot of schools have field trips abroad, and that's nice, but sometimes we overlook the stunning geography on our own doorstep,' she said. 'I love this part of Wales. Well, I love all of Wales except the industrialised parts. And Stan and John always drive the coach for us. It's great. Exhausting, but inspiring.'

★   ★   ★

'I hope you don't mind sharing,' said Donna, pushing the bedroom door open and dropping her case beside a bed. 'At least we have an en suite.'

'I'm just relieved it's not bunk beds and that the beds have quilts. My aunt said it was most likely like a youth hostel with hairy blankets and sleeping bags, and a duty in the morning.' Amy grinned and put her case down next to the other bed.

Donna laughed. 'It's much more modern in youth hostels nowadays. No duties, for a start. A pity, I sometimes think, but they have to compete and modern kids don't like roughing it. Anyway, supper at 6.00pm, and then we have an evening talk about

Southerndown. It's quite an intense week, but it stops the little darlings sloping off to the pub of an evening. Mind you, we do warn the local hostelries to be on the lookout because the children are underage, so all they'd get is a soft drink at best. I come here with my family sometimes. I just love it.'

'I think the kids were more impressed with the *Doctor Who* connection than with the geology,' said Amy with a grin.

★　★　★

Supper was served at a hatch just like school dinners; and like school dinners, the teachers had a segregated dining area, separated from the rest by glass panels, so they could discuss things whilst still keeping an eye on the kids. Once the supper was cleared away, the warden gave everyone a talk on the dos and don'ts and the various items of interest. He reminded everyone to watch the tide, and that the cliffs were dangerous. Then the children looked at the various specimens they'd found, and the photographs of some of the fossils *in situ*. Amy found herself yawning and was glad to go to bed.

16

Breakfast was a self-serve buffet. Amy sat opposite Luke in the teacher's dining area. She still felt shy of the other teachers and it was nice to have a brotherly companion. 'What are we doing today?'

'Local beaches, coastal erosion and coal measures, land use and so on. We'll be walking down into Little Haven and then along the beach to Broad Haven, I'm not sure where after that.'

Alan Trimble added, 'There's a talk first. We make sure we have everyone's phone number and vice versa. Then we head down into Little Haven as a large group to the beach and look at the folding and talk about coal measures as we head towards Broad Haven. We muster in Broad Haven car park at 12.00 noon to talk a bit more geology. Then we take them past the youth hostel along a footpath to Haroldston West. Then back along the coast path. Good views showing the undulating surface ground down by the last ice age. The tides aren't very good for us; it'll be coming in at about 10 o'clock this morning. High tide's at 4.00pm, so we'll have to walk over the top from Broad Haven to Little Haven. It's only about five miles.'

'We don't want to overload them with information. They're only Year Tens and Elevens,' said Donna. 'But I think it's a wonderful opportunity to appreciate some of Britain's best coastal scenery. The views on a clear day are stunning.'

'You sound like an advert for the tourist board,' said Amy.

It was a glorious day for a walk: cool without being cold, almost windless, a vault of blue above with fluffy clouds scudding along. The sea was about as far out as it could go by the time they reached the beach. A stream gushed under the bridge, over the boulders and pebbles, then spread itself out over the sand in shimmering ripples, the wet reflecting the sky and the clouds like quicksilver. The sun, low in the sky, lit up the water with blinding light.

Contrary to Luke's fears, all of the kids were wearing sensible footwear and clothing, and all carried day packs in which they'd put their lunches and A5 clipboards. Some had cameras and binoculars hung round their necks, and they all looked keen. Sam focused her binoculars on Amy, saying in a silly voice, 'It's the lesser spotted Luke-Luke bird. Beautiful plumage.'

Amy chose to ignore it, though she couldn't help frowning.

For the first time in her life Amy looked — really looked — at the cliff face and the rocks when Alan Trimble pointed things out. The rock — coal-measure sandstone according to Alan — was in layers like blankets, but these blankets had been rucked up into loops and curves, or set on edge by some titanic force. The softer rocks had worn away faster, making the beaches and the 'Havens', and a couple of shallow caves in a bay between the two Havens. There was even a tiny patch of coal glistening darkly in the rock face. Luke explained about the last mountain-building period, or orogeny, while the children and Amy listened, entranced.

Of course, it had to be Sam who said, 'Orogeny? So these are orogenous zones, then, sir?' Everyone laughed, even Amy.

They walked north along the beach towards Broad Haven. According to Alan Trimble it had been a coal-mining village, with coal being loaded directly onto the boats from the beach, and then the Victorians had made it a tourist honey pot with bathing huts for the well-to-do.

The tide was advancing rapidly, eating up the slick sand, the waves curling into white horses. The sudsy foam ran up towards them;

some of the girls squealed, the boys yelled, and everyone retreated up the beach. Luke did a rapid head count. All accounted for.

The shops were open, so the kids piled in, coming out with ice creams or chips.

'They smell good,' said Amy. Luke fetched her some while she tried to take photographs of a couple of cheeky jackdaws strutting along a wall. Everyone clustered around, eating and admiring the view.

Broad Haven beach was vast, the sky huge, and the sea a lively slate blue. There were container ships on the horizon — waiting to berth at Milford Haven, Amy supposed — and some islands rising almost sheer from the ocean. Being October, there were only a few other people around.

The party set off for a walk up to Haroldston West. There was a tricky moment locating the footpath to Haroldston Woods. As they entered, Donna said to the children, 'This is private property, and recreational access has been granted in general. Don't do any damage and respect it please. That includes no litter.'

Amy enjoyed the pathway through the woods, and there were attractive ferns on the hillside, which made her wonder if she could plant some in a shady nook at Debbie's. Luke's bouncing steps and grin told her he was enjoying it just as much. Not so some of the kids. One was complaining of blisters already and some were moaning that it was just trees and all uphill.

'There's a church up ahead,' said Chloe. 'You and Mr Armitage could get married there, Miss.'

'Don't be so impertinent,' said Amy. 'I hope you looked the word up when I told you to. We are not going out with each other, and even if we were it's none of your business.'

It was a delightful church, built of local stone and roofed with slate. The bell tower was like a chimney on the end of the church, but with an opening in the middle for the bell, which gleamed dully.

They followed the path round to the road. There was a farm, the church, and a handful of dwellings. 'Is this it? Is this Haroldston West, sir?' asked Chloe of Luke in a plaintive tone. Amy was irritated to see her coquettish body language.

'I don't know,' said Luke, smiling at Chloe. 'Ask Mr Trimble or one of the other teachers. It's my first time.'

Chloe gave a hoot of laughter. 'Field trip virgin.'

'Chloe, that is quite enough of your puerile humour,' snapped Amy. 'And if you don't know what puerile means, look it up.' Chloe gave her a poisonous look but subsided.

'Why is there a church for so few houses?' asked Sam, almost in spite of herself. 'It seems strange. It's very pretty. St Madoc of Ferns. Who was St Madoc, I wonder?'

'We'll go into the churchyard, off the road,' said Donna Phelps when a car had to struggle past the gaggle of children. 'It'll be safer and the church is beautiful and ought to be admired. And remember, boys and girls, this is a sacred building and land, so treat them with respect. We can eat lunch here. But no litter.' She walked over towards a wooden bench in the graveyard and ousted some of the girls who had rushed over to sit down. 'You lot can sit on the grass. Rank has its privilege. Teachers only. Come on, Ms Oldham, and I'm sure Mr Trimble can sit next to us.'

Amy sat down as bidden. Luke seated himself on the sward with Simon Long and the kids.

'Eeouw, it creeps me out a bit,' said one of the other girls, gazing round at the gravestones.

The grass was short and the graveyard well-maintained. The views towards Broad Haven were lovely, across the gentle undulations of the land: some grassland, some woodland, very lush and rural. Broad Haven itself was just visible as a cluster of white dwellings in the fold of the hills.

Amy opened her lunch bag: cheese sandwiches, an apple and a healthy cereal bar. *Yum,* she thought.

'Oh yuck,' said one of the boys. 'Why can't they give us decent food like chocolate and crisps?' He didn't look too chuffed with the juice carton either, but needs must, and he ate it all.

'I'd like to have a look inside the church, but I expect it's locked,' said Amy.

'Me too,' said Sam, who had been wandering around reading the gravestones. 'Are we allowed in the church, please, Ms Phelps?'

'If it's open and if you treat it with respect,' said Donna Phelps.

'Let's see, shall we?' said Amy, somewhat vexed that Sam was accompanying her. Still, it didn't do to make permanent enemies of any of the pupils and maybe Sam was trying to be friendly.

'Please don't laugh, Miss, but my great-great granddad came from west Wales,' confided Sam in a low voice as they went down the path to the entrance. 'I might be looking at relatives' graves for all I know. But I think they lived nearer Haverfordwest. Johnston, not Haroldston. I wish I'd asked

161

Dad more about it before I came. Not that he knows much about it. Dad started researching our family tree, but soon got bored with it. But don't tell anyone, will you please, Miss?'

'Of course I won't laugh, Sam. That's rather romantic, isn't it?'

The church, against Amy's expectation, was open, and they slipped inside. Amy felt a shiver of awe, same as she always felt on entering a church. This one was well-lit with stained-glass windows, a tiled floor, and white stonework.

'It's lovely,' breathed Sam. 'And in the middle of nowhere too. I can't get over that.'

'I expect there are a lot more people around here than you'd think, living in scattered dwellings,' said Amy. 'And there's the farm opposite. I expect they keep a close eye on the place.'

The door opened again and Donna came in. 'There are delightful churches like this all over this region,' she said. 'I find the local history as fascinating as the geology. I came to say five minutes, then we're off.' She gazed around the church for about half a minute before leaving. On the way out she signed the visitors' book and Amy saw her surreptitiously shove a note into the collection box as she left. She and Sam took a last look around and then left, Amy following Sam. They both signed the book too. Sam slipped a coin into the box, which Amy thought touching, and she followed suit. Sam alone didn't seem half so obnoxious as Sam-in-Chloe's-company.

As if to illustrate this thought, Sam paused and said in a low voice, 'I'm sorry I was so cheeky about you and Mr Armitage, Miss. I didn't mean anything by it.'

'Apology accepted, thanks, Sam, but I must say it's pretty wearing.'

'Everyone's got a crush on him. It's kind of fashionable. It's a shame you're not going out together, Miss. You seem right for each other, and that would be soooo romantic.'

By this time they had reached the rest of the party so no more was said as everyone stood, checked for rubbish, then filed out of the churchyard.

Heading back, the group dropped back down into the woods, but took a turn which led them to the road to Broad Haven. They crossed this and took the coastal path back. Every so often Alan Trimble would stop them to point out some geographical feature. It made the enjoyable walk all the more interesting for Amy as much as the children. She found herself and Luke bringing up the rear of the party. On a tricky bit, Luke held his hand out to steady her. His touch sent a bolt of electricity through her.

So Luke was the fashionable crush, then, was he? Hardly surprising since he was so good-looking, young and personable. No wonder everyone fancied him. When Amy was at school the fashionable crush was the English teacher who had the most wonderful brown eyes, soft and poetic. They'd all been in love with him, including some of the boys, and Amy had done English at university because of his influence. The image had been irrevocably tarnished midway through her first year at university when she heard he'd been sent to prison for molesting a couple of boys. Thinking about it, Gareth had been the fashionable crush in that first year at Leicester. He'd had several long-term girlfriends before he'd asked her out. She'd felt flattered; she'd felt special. Now she wondered if she was just another notch on the bedpost. Maybe the best-looking dudes were all the same. A poem started developing in her mind, one about cocksure swains and handsome looks. She dismissed it to the back of her mind, intent on enjoying the day without tainting it with thoughts of no-good men.

The views were wonderful. The air was clear enough to see the islands of Skomer and

Ramsey. There were lots of wild flowers: red campion and yellow tansy, and one or two foxgloves which, to Amy, seemed to be flowering very late. One of the girls pointed this out to Luke.

'It's the maritime influence, and the North Atlantic drift,' explained Luke. 'Keeps the coast mild and relatively frost-free. I'll tell you more when we get back to the centre.' Amy thought he behaved like everyone's favourite elder brother: fun, knowledgeable, but sexually unattainable. Just as well, really, if everyone had a crush on him.

The tide was in by the time they got to Broad Haven so they had to walk over the top via the road. When they got back to Skerryhaven, everyone was sent to their rooms to change footwear, then come to the common room for a drink and a chill-out.

Donna laughed when Amy sat down on her bed and removed her boots with a sigh of relief. 'I could murder a cup of tea,' said Amy, pulling her socks off and rubbing her feet. 'And a shower, but that'll have to wait.'

'We can make tea of coffee any time we want, so long as we clear up after ourselves. We'll make a big pot of tea in case the kids want some, but they seem to prefer spending good money on tooth-rot fizzy drinks. Did you see Tim's face when he pulled out the juice? Anyone would think we were trying to poison him.'

'That reminds me in an oblique way; there's something I must do before I forget.' Amy grabbed a notebook from her bag and started to write. The poem came out as a ballad.

Donna watched her with a bemused expression. 'I've always envied people who can churn a poem out just like that. Mind if I take a look?'

Amy did mind because she never liked to show unfinished poems, but this was the head teacher and she didn't like to gainsay her. 'It needs a lot of work before it's finished,' she said, but she handed it over.

Donna read it through with some sniggers and one or two outright guffaws. 'It's excellent, but my, so cynical for one so young. Is it about Luke? Do you mind me asking what's going on between you?'

'Nothing. Well, not really.' Damn, but what a question. Amy found herself telling Donna about how they met and subsequent events, and about Sam's remarks in the churchyard; about how Luke was the object of all the girls' adoration through no fault of his own.

'They'll grow out of it,' said Donna, though she looked pensive.

'Will they, though? I mean, do we ever?'

said Amy, and she told Donna about Gareth and his idiotic behaviour, and then about her English teacher. 'I thought Gareth was the dog's . . . the bee's knees. I was besotted with him, but now I see what he's really like. As for the teacher, well, I was utterly shocked and appalled. He was so attractive and sexy . . . and evil. The one man who seems both attractive and really nice with it is Luke, and I've blown it there by being an idiot.'

Donna was nodding wisely. 'In my many years as a teacher I've known some bad apples, and you know, every time, there was something I didn't like about them — something I couldn't put my finger on, exactly; something which the CRB checks never highlighted. It's sad but true that teaching is a career which sometimes attracts the wrong sort of people for the wrong sort of reasons . . . and the problem is, you have to wait for something untoward to happen in those circumstances.

'Mind you, in teaching we might have gone too far in our efforts to keep our children safe. I know of one man who lost his career because a boy he'd given detention to made allegations of inappropriate behaviour. Not enough to bring a prosecution against the teacher, but enough to mark his CRB record and wreck his career. I still don't know if the allegation was malicious, but I suspect it was. Such a difficult balance to keep.'

'That's awful,' breathed Amy.

'Indeed. So be very careful to act with absolute propriety at all times with these children, Amy. We in the childcare professions are very vulnerable nowadays, and some of the children know that and use it as a weapon. As for Luke, you have plenty of time to see how the land lies. I would treat him as your elder brother and see how things develop; find out how he is as a character, not as a drop-dead gorgeous bit of manhood.'

'Funny you should say that; I thought he was like everyone's big brother today.'

'He was, wasn't he? Now, how about that cup of tea?'

As Amy stood she found her muscles had stiffened up, in contrast to her spirit, which felt lighter and freer after this strange confessional.

17

Supper was to be served at 7.00pm that night, so those who weren't worn out by the day decided to go into Little Haven to look at the sunset. Alan Trimble, Luke and Amy would go with them, while Donna and Simon stayed behind with those who didn't want to go. Amy was exasperated to see Chloe and Sam hovering around Luke, eyeing him up and cheeking him.

The party wandered down the slipway onto the beach first, the pebbles grinding underfoot. The sun lit up the cliffs to the right, russet and green, while in the distance it picked out the cliffs surrounding St Bride's Bay. A posse of clouds huddled against the horizon. Some of the kids started playing ducks and drakes, yelling when the stones bounced off the water six or seven times, jeering when they just went plop. Luke joined in and Amy watched as he managed a seven-bounce throw. He seemed so natural, so friendly yet not over-friendly with the kids. Just as he was natural and friendly, but not over-friendly with her. She sighed and stared out to sea.

'We'll go up to the point,' said Alan Trimble. 'It's a good viewpoint.' They followed the path up past an inviting-looking pub to the point, a good, safe path with stone walls enclosing them. Amy looked back at Little Haven in the gathering gloom. It looked so quaint with the houses jumbled up. The setting sun lit up the houses further up the valley sides, while those lower down were cooler in the gathering gloom. It all looked so neat, with freshly painted walls of white or blue or pink.

The viewpoint was superb, the cliffs of the bay sweeping round towards St David's Head. The land itself looked as if it has been bitten off at the sea's edge, with high, sheer cliffs. The sun dipped below the cliffs to the southwest. The clouds lit up, then darkened like bruises against the eggshell sky. The kids were oohing and ahhing, taking photos.

'Time to head back,' said Alan.

As they walked down the hill a flock of crows flew over: scores — hundreds — flying, twisting and turning, thick as smoke, cawing raucously. Chloe gave a whimper and grabbed hold of Luke. 'Don't be silly,' he said crossly. 'It's only crows. Pretty spectacular, though.'

They all stopped and watched the aerial display.

'It creeps me out,' whined Chloe. 'It's like that awful film my mum likes. They won't attack us, will they?'

'No, they won't,' said Amy. 'If it's any consolation, it creeps me out a bit too. But it's beautiful to watch.' After a few turns around the bay as a single entity, the crows turned and flew into the trees, thick as leaves on the branches, took off again, then vanished.

'Did you know that a flock of crows is really called a murder of crows?' asked Sam, making savage pecking movements with her hands. 'Mwahahahaha.' Chloe squealed and hid behind Luke.

'I said don't be such a baby,' he said.

Darkness was falling as they walked back over the hill to Skerryhaven, Alan Trimble in the front with a torch to warn oncoming vehicles, though it was still light enough to see by if you were a pedestrian. Luke and Amy brought up the rear, Luke holding another torch.

Amy's skin prickled from his presence. *I wish . . .* she thought. *I really wish . . .*

As they got to the centre's gate and everyone else clattered inside, Luke stopped, so Amy stopped too. He was a dark shadow in the gloom. His whole body spoke of wanting to say something, but being too afraid. 'I wish . . . ' he said. 'I really wish . . . ' He reached out and gently lifted her chin. She moved with him, heart thundering, yearning. He bent and lightly brushed her lips with his. She did nothing to pull away, leaned closer, and turned her head to his. This was right, felt right.

'Oi, Sir. No canoodling,' came Sam's voice, Chloe's irritating giggle following.

Amy and Luke flinched and broke apart with an embarrassed shiver. Both girls were silhouetted in the doorway. Luke muttered something rude, then said, 'Sorry.' Amy wasn't sure if he was apologising for the kiss or the swear words, or both.

Luke avoided her eyes for the rest of the evening.

★　★　★

On Monday they went to the tiny city of St David's, had a wander around the centre, then went for a walk to St David's Head. Alan Trimble wanted to talk about igneous intrusions and wave-cut platforms.

'Oh no,' wailed Chloe as they were walking. 'There are cows ahead. I hate cows.' There were some piebald creatures ahead, but Amy thought they were the wrong shape for cows. Then they got nearer and Amy could see that the beasts were horses.

'Funny-looking cows,' mocked Luke. 'Would you like to milk one of those cows, Chloe?'

Chloe muttered something most unlady-like.

There was a notice explaining that the horses were grazing on the vegetation and maintaining the sward as part of the ecology of the area. They were friendly and came over to the barbed-wire fence to greet the children. The path was narrow at this point, and Amy was anxious for the safety of the kids, particularly as they were inclined to show off, or be more scared of a pony's snort than the drop-down the cliffs.

The scenery was just as spectacular as the previous day, possibly more so, being more rugged. Amy saw a huge boulder just perched on top of some other rocks which had been scoured clean by the last ice sheet. There were even scratch-marks in the rocks from boulders being ground against them. In the sea, the upended rock layers had been worn away. 'It looks like the back of a dragon,' she said out loud.

'Yeah,' agreed Sam. 'You can see where the dragon's tail goes down to the sea.'

Chloe just scowled.

On the way back they dropped down into one of the bays. There were caves. 'I can understand where the myths about dragons living in caves come from,' said Sam. 'Those rocks look just like a dragon has crawled out of the cave and died and got half buried in sand.' Then she spoiled it all by adding, 'Why don't you and Luke go inside for a cuddle, Miss?'

'Mr Armitage to you, not Luke,' rebuked Amy. 'And will you please stop going on like that. I've already said it's very tiresome.'

Sam looked crushed.

★ ★ ★

'I'm getting seriously hacked off with Chloe and Sam,' Amy confided in Luke during a rare moment on their own. 'It's kind of embarrassing, especially as, well, last night . . . ' She looked away, a blush creeping up her neck.

He pulled a wry face. 'They think they're being clever. It's normal with kids that age. It's showing off and one-upmanship with their friends. One of the hazards of teaching, I'm afraid. I tend to ignore it because it stops if you don't rise to the bait too often.' He laughed. 'I considered talking about thrust faults, folded cleavage and slaty cleavage, but decided not to as I think Sam would make capital out of it. As for you and me, I just couldn't find the words, and it seemed the best way of telling you how I felt.' He shook his head. 'I'm confused too. Anyway, best be chaste on a field trip. Anything else is unprofessional. But when we get home, perhaps we can start over, if that's OK with you.'

★   ★   ★

Next day was a trip to Haverfordwest. The kids all tittered over the original meaning of the town's name, 'Ford of the Fat Cows.' They were to do surveys in the morning, meeting outside the records office at the castle at noon to hand their survey sheets to Mr Trimble. They could then go round the museum and the records office if they were interested, or go back into town for a look around. Any problems, the kids were to phone one of the teachers, and they were to remember that the reputation of the school was at stake. They would muster up at the bus station at 5.00pm for the coach pick-up. 'And don't be late,' warned Donna Phelps.

Amy was sure all the kids would turn down the idea of the museum in favour of shopping, but a handful drifted over that way in the company of Donna. Amy saw Chloe and Sam bickering. Sam looked upset, unsure of herself, torn. 'I'm not going,' she said to

Chloe. 'It'll be the same shops as anywhere. I want to look around the records office.'

Amy went over. 'I want to look in the records office. How about you girls?'

'Not likely,' sneered Chloe at the same time as Sam said, 'Yes.'

'Come on then, Sam. See you later, Chloe,' said Amy. Chloe scowled, swivelled on her heel and vanished in the wake of the gaggle of kids going into town.

Luke came over. 'I'm going into town just so that I'm nearby if something untoward happens,' he said. 'But they should be fine. They're nearly grown up after all.' He smiled at Sam. 'Ms Oldham will take care of you, I expect.'

Amy and Sam were greeted warmly by the staff in the records office. Most of the records were now on computer, they were told; what were they after? They needed to register as temporary users if they wanted to look at original documents.

Sam shyly explained that her great-great granddad had lived in Johnston, about the 1880s, but that was all she knew. The archivist showed her how to access the records, and left Amy and Sam to it.

Once again Amy was struck by what a different child Sam was away from the dreadful Chloe. She was more sensitive, very bright, and had an active and empathic imagination. She was soon utterly absorbed by the old records and thought she'd probably found the baptismal record of one of her ancestors from 1877. The archivist came to see how they were getting on, and Sam's eyes lit up excitedly when she conveyed this news.

The archivist smiled. 'I know; I have just the document you might like to look at, but you must be very, very careful with it as it's an original and very old. It's the school log book for that period.' She brought it up and laid it on a cradle of foam to protect the spine. Amy and Sam pored over the venerable document, fascinated by this glimpse into nineteenth-century rural west Wales life.

'It's really cool,' said Sam. 'I feel very privileged. I don't think I'd have been allowed if you weren't with me, Miss Oldham. Thank you.' When they left, Sam also thanked the archivist for all her help.

Chloe was late for the bus.

★ ★ ★

Wednesday was more coastal geography/geology at Marloes Sands. It was a half-mile walk down to the beach. The tide was on the retreat, leaving the sand slick and reflective.

The cliffs, according to Luke, who had spent a month there as a student, spanned the Silurian and Devonian epochs — information which fried Amy's brains. The children seemed excited until she realised they were talking about Silurians — *Doctor Who* monsters. She ran her eyes along the cliffs and saw that the layers of rock had been pushed from horizontal to vertical during the earth's ancient history and acted like a walkable timeline into the past, layer upon layer along the beach. No wonder Luke thought the place amazing. They made their way towards the Old Red Sandstone end.

A flock of birds few down. They were black with bright orange beaks and legs. 'Chough!' said one of the boys excitedly. 'Really rare.'

'Well spotted,' said Donna.

Luke took charge of the class, since this area was his field of expertise. Amy thought he glowed with an inner light. His voice was rich with enthusiasm, but he lost the interest of some of the kids because he went too deeply into the subject.

'I think we'll divide into two groups,' said Alan Trimble. 'Those doing geology GCSE as well as geography GCSE, go with Mr Armitage, Ms Oldham and Mrs Phelps. The rest come with me and Mr Long. Hard hats on, and we'll look for fossils. If you split any rocks, remember to use protective gear. And don't hammer at the cliff face . . . '

This decision split Sam and Chloe up, which pleased Amy. Chloe seemed to be such a bad influence on Sam. Perhaps Sam was trying to impress Chloe by being a pain and coming out with the wisecracks.

The pebbles and boulders changed from grey to red rock as they wandered along, and the tide went right out, leaving dark rocky outcrops poking out of the golden sand, surrounded by pools of seawater. The sea looked rough, the breakers rushing in and curling over, the spume blown about by the wind. Amy tied her hair back because it was annoying her. Luke's hair was ruffled and she imagined combing it out with her fingers. She told her wayward thoughts to behave.

The island of Gateholm was clear, and behind it Skomer was fainter in the haze. Skokholm Island was also just a hazy hump on the horizon. Sam was orientating herself with an OS map. 'I think you can get onto Gateholm Island at low tide,' she said.

'And get stranded,' said Luke dryly.

'It's weird,' said Sam. 'These place names are very Scandinavian. Skomer. Haraldston. Haven, like in Copenhavn.'

'Clever girl,' said Luke with a look of appreciation. 'The Vikings sailed these waters and settled these places.' He told them about the various influxes of peoples over the centuries, people who had made their mark on the land and on the customs. Sam preened and smiled.

Luke continued his lecture as they walked along. Amy remembered to count heads every so often. Children got distracted by a pretty stone or a shell, or stopped to take photographs. The choughs, like jackdaws with orange beaks and feet, flew round the bay, chattering.

Luke looked at his watch. 'Time to head back. The tide's on its way in, and it's a big one.' They were nearly back at the footpath down when Amy's phone rang. She reached for it, but then realised it was Luke's phone she could hear, not hers, though the ringtone was the same. He answered. 'No, she's with you, or she should be ... Oh ... ' He scanned the children's heads. 'No, definitely not with us ... Has anyone seen Chloe?'

Sam got her phone out and dialled. 'Chloe, where are you?' She frowned. 'Can you wave to us?'

Everyone looked around. Amy spotted her sitting like the Little Mermaid on a rocky outcrop. Amy watched a wave break over a similar outcrop further out to sea, the spume rising high from the power of it. Those were large Atlantic waves hammering the shore.

'Oh Lordy. Pass me the phone please, Sam,' said Luke urgently. 'Chloe, you have to get off that rock right now. The tide is coming in fast.'

Chloe stood. Stopped. 'But there's a rock pool this side and it's well deep,' Amy heard her say over the phone. The next wave rushed up and circled the rock.

Luke returned Sam's phone. 'The rest of you, up the beach and make your way along the dry bit to the footpath. Amy, I might need your help.'

With that, Luke ran towards the rock. Amy turned to the kids. 'Go now, do as Luke says. Sam, that includes you.' She ran after Luke, Donna puffing behind her.

'I'm stuck,' wailed Chloe. 'I'll get my feet wet. I can't get down.'

'Don't be silly! You have to; this rock gets covered!' yelled Luke. Still she refused, like a frightened horse at a jump. Luke waded over to the rock. Amy followed him. The tide sucked the sand from under her boots, making her wobble.

'Come here!' said Luke.

'I can't, I can't.'

Amy splashed past Luke and clambered onto the rock. The barnacles scraped at her palms, and a wave nearly took her feet from

181

under her. She stood next to Chloe. 'You have to get off now. Come on, backwards. Luke will guide your feet, and I'll hold your hands. You'll be safe enough. Come on.' She coaxed Chloe until she was within Luke's reach. He grabbed her, put her over his shoulder in a fireman's lift, then took her up the beach. He set her down in a few inches of water and yelled at her to get up that beach now. Donna grabbed Chloe's clothing to steady her and dragged her along out of the surging tide. Chloe was sobbing and whining. Luke waded back towards Amy.

Amy looked down at the roiling water round her feet. She couldn't see the best place to get down, and suddenly understood what Chloe had meant. 'Go down backwards on all fours,' Luke commanded. Amy obeyed, felt him grab her foot and guide it to a foothold. The sea swirled round the rock, over her boots and up to her knees. Luke guided her other foot down, then pulled her from the rock backwards and set her down in the water. It came up to her knees, then swept up to her thighs with the next wave, a cold and vulgar caress. Together they splashed up the beach to where Chloe was standing with the others and Donna Phelps was looking on anxiously. There was a collective cheer from everyone.

'You are without doubt the most idiotic child I have ever met,' said Amy savagely. 'What the heck did you think you were doing?'

'I wanted to come with Luke. Tremble's boring,' said Chloe sullenly. 'But you'd got too far ahead so I thought I'd sit down and wait. Work on my tan.'

Amy envisioned Chloe sitting facing the sun, eyes closed, oblivious. An idiot indeed. 'He's Mr Armitage to you. How dare you behave like a spoiled brat. Look at us.' The damp had crept up to Amy's waist, and Luke's walking trousers were sodden too. 'And it's a long way to the coach.' With a spurt of anger Amy noticed that Chloe was hardly wet at all. Silly, silly girl.

Luke looked furious. He snorted through his nostrils but said nothing, as if he dared not open his mouth for fear of what might come out. Donna Phelps's lips were thin as paper.

A headcount was made, and a rather subdued party walked up to the car park. It was unpleasant squelching along in sodden boots and trousers, but their clothing was specifically designed to take some rough use, and the trousers dried quickly as they walked, leaving salty tidemarks. By the time they reached the car park they were almost dry and so decided to go with everyone to look at Marloes Mere, an area of marshland on the top of the cliff. Amy regretted it because her feet were soon feeling rubbed raw by the soggy boots, and the salt chafed her legs.

★ ★ ★

The first thing Amy did when she got back to the field centre was take a shower. Then she washed her trousers by hand and hung them up to dry in the drying room. She was shivery and cold. Delayed shock, said Donna. After supper Simon Long suggested that she and Luke sneak off to The Ship for a chill-out once the incident forms were filled in. Amy looked askance at him, wondering if everyone was conspiring to get them together on their own.

The question arose as to whether Chloe should be sent home, her parents summoned, but it transpired that hers was a single-parent family and, with two much younger siblings, it might be a hard thing for her mother to fetch her home. 'Besides,' said Donna, 'she's a silly little airhead but hopefully that's taught her a lesson.'

'She wasn't really in any danger, and neither were we, at that point. The biggest danger was wet feet,' said Luke.

'Rubbish. The water was coming in fast, and it was only your quick thinking that meant she didn't have to swim for it. She might easily have drowned — and so might you. But maybe she is best forgiven,' said Alan Trimble. 'And yes, you two ought to go to the pub for a drink and a cuddle. I've seen the sultry looks you've been giving each other all week. Frustrated, that's what you are.'

★　★　★

'I feel a bit dowdy, really,' confessed Amy as she and Luke wandered into the village. 'I travelled light as requested, so I haven't got my best clothes with me. Just walking trousers and these old jeans.'

'You look gorgeous in anything.' Luke wrapped his arm over her shoulders and it felt so right.

The pub was warm and welcoming, all the tables taken by families having a meal out. Amy opted for a pint of Best, same as Luke. Not very ladylike, but who cared? They sat side by side on the bar stools, so close she could feel his body heat on her skin. She looked at his hand on the glass, a strong hand, though finely moulded. He must be very strong to lift that idiot girl over his shoulder like that, and pluck herself from the rock into the surf as he had done. She shuddered at the remembered terror when she thought Chloe was going to drown. Luke was looking pensive, and not very happy.

'Were you scared?' she asked. 'I know you said that we weren't in any danger, but that's not true. The tide was strong, and the sea coming in fast. I saw how the surf broke over those other rocks and it terrified me.'

'I put you in danger,' muttered Luke. 'I told you to come with me. I should never have done that.'

'Don't be so daft. I'd have come with you anyway. And just as well I did because she wasn't going to climb down, was she?'

'Cragfast, in a manner of speaking,' agreed Luke. 'Thing is, Amy, I told you to come with me not for her sake but for mine. I thought I might have to grab her in a compromising way, you know, lay hands on her, and I didn't want any allegations of impropriety. So I wanted you there as chaperone.'

Amy turned this thought over and over in her mind, not quite sure what to make of it. 'Really?' she said.

'You can't be too careful nowadays,' said Luke glumly. 'Oh Amy, suppose you'd drowned? I could never forgive myself. If I lost you I think it would break my heart.' He took a sip of beer then lapsed into silence.

Amy could think of nothing to break the silence so sat in silence too, placing a hand on his, and feeling the tension in it ebb away. As the silence deepened it took on a companionable feel and Amy felt herself start to relax as the pleasant hubbub enveloped them.

A little later Luke said, 'I'm feeling peckish.' His eyes boggled when someone's burger was taken past them.

'Me too,' said Amy. 'Which is awful, considering we're supposed to have had supper.'

'I'll treat you to a burger. Another beer?'

'Coffee for me, please.'

'Actually, I think I'll have a coffee too.'

The meal was enjoyable, but Amy struggled with it in the end. 'I was far too greedy,' she said. 'Eyes bigger than my stomach.'

Luke asked for the bill, and paid absent-mindedly. They were a hundred yards up the road when he stopped. 'I think the bill was wrong,' he said, pulling out the receipt. 'Shine the torch on it for me, please.' He read through. 'Yes, they've not put the coffees on.' He turned back and Amy followed like a puppy. He explained to the landlord, and passed over the extra payment.

'A lot of people would have just not bothered to go back,' said Amy.

'That's their living,' said Luke. 'It would

have been just plain dishonest if I'd done nothing once I'd realised.'

'What if we'd gone home before you twigged?'

'Dunno. I hope I'd send it to them.' Luke shrugged. 'Let's get back.' In the darkness he stopped, pulled her to him and kissed her.

18

Thursday was a coach tour round some of the more interesting geographical locations. Amy wasn't sorry. She'd had enough walking, and was suffering from what she dubbed 'rocks-and-fossil fatigue', and she suspected some of the kids were too. Friday it was a trip to a farm for Land Use, then packing and a barbeque.

On Saturday on the way home they stopped at the Botanic Garden of Wales for a few hours. Amy enjoyed it very much, and thought the whole thing rather well conceived. When they got back to Runworthy it was dark and late, so Donna Phelps gave Amy and Luke a lift home in her car.

As they stood on Amy's doorstep, Luke said, 'I'll take your case upstairs for you,' and he started up the stairs with it before she had time to say no.

She yelled, 'Hi Debbie, we're back,' as Luke pushed her bedroom door open and walked in. She followed him. They both froze.

Luke said, 'Mr Murray!' at the same time as Amy said, 'Uncle Bernard!' A few thunderous heartbeats later she added, 'What are you doing in my room?' He was lolling on her bed, reading one of her books, as if he owned the place.

His face broke into a beam. 'Hello, my darling niece.' He rose and kissed her cheeks. The years fell away, and with it all the hurt and upset he'd caused her aunt was temporarily forgotten. Amy greeted him back, utterly nonplussed. 'I am the prodigal returned,' he added. The men eyed each other up like stiff-legged dogs. 'You must be Luke — I remember you from years ago; bright boy, bright boy.' He held his hand out to Luke, who took it as if it was dirty, and shook it briefly.

'You haven't told us why you're on Amy's bed, Mr Murray.'

'Ah, forgive me. Your aunt said you were due back Sunday. I intended to move out tomorrow morning and stay in The Shoulder of Mutton, but you caught me out by coming home early. I shall move out forthwith.'

'I'll sleep on the sofa,' said Amy, thoughts still churning round looking for some sense to settle on.

'No, no, my dear. It's your bed, and I am merely the repentant husband come back home. My penance is not yet done and I will move out for the time being.'

Debbie joined them. 'Look who's here.'

Amy thought Debbie was sparkling like champagne, happier than she'd been for months. Years even. Amy remembered how much her aunt had loved Uncle Bernard; how devastated she'd been when he left her, abandoned her to go and live in Canada. 'But you left Debbie. You're divorced now,' she said, brain finally starting to work.

Bernard looked shamefaced. 'I know, I know. How wrong I was to do that. But in my defence I have to say I was ill, mentally disordered. I got treatment and now I'm better. I saw sense, and came home.' He beamed a contrite smile at Debbie. She basked in it. 'But to save any embarrassment, I'll see if The Shoulder of Mutton has a room. Can't have Amy sleeping on the floor, now, can we?'

Fortunately the pub did have a room. Uncle Bernard took an overnight bag with him and booked in, but returned to Debbie's for the evening. It seemed he only intended to sleep at the pub, and obviously planned on spending every waking hour in Debbie's company. Amy opened her bedroom windows and changed the sheets. Debbie and Luke gave her a hand. Debbie seemed a little embarrassed. 'I really was expecting you back tomorrow and I've only cooked supper for two,' she said.

'Don't worry, Debbie. I'll cook something for Amy. We have a lot to talk about after the trip anyway.' Luke tugged at Amy's arm. She turned and meekly followed him downstairs. 'Stuff cooking,' he said. 'Let's get a take-away. I'm too tired to cook and so are you.' They walked down to the local Chinese and just ordered the set meal for two. 'What's he doing back here, sniffing round your aunt? I thought he broke her heart, yet here he is like a bad smell. I was gobsmacked when I saw him lolling on your bed. Flaming cheek, I call it.'

'Not really; it's Aunty's house and she thought I was away,' said Amy. Luke was right, though. She felt as if her space had been violated, and wondered if Bernard had been snooping through her possessions. Then she remembered Debbie's glowing expression and felt she could have forgiven Uncle Bernard anything, even murder, if he brought that amount of happiness to her aunt.

As they walked back, Luke said, 'My study or your kitchen? You've got more room.'

'My kitchen, I think.' She was delighted that he had come back round to the idea of being her boyfriend but didn't want to rush things, or find herself under pressure in his room.

'Can I stick my washing in your machine, then, please?'

'Yes, once the sheets are done.'

Amy pulled out a couple of plates and they served up.

'I'm starved,' said Luke.

'Me too.' Amy paused to put some food in her mouth. 'Hmn, this is good.'

'Odd your uncle turning up out of the blue like that,' said Luke in a very low voice.

'Yes. He broke her heart when he left. I hope he doesn't break it again.'

'He'd better not. I really like your aunt.' Luke's hand holding his fork tightened.

'You should have seen the way you reacted when you saw him. Talk about raised hackles. I was surprised; I thought you liked him.' Amy gave a low laugh.

'I did. When I was younger, before we moved away. He made me feel special, bright, clever, important. But you know what? When he tried the same charm on me this evening, it sounded so false, so corny. Maybe I've grown from boy to man in between times, and that makes a difference.' Luke speared a prawn and conveyed it to his mouth. Amy's heart softened as she watched him eat. He kept flicking his hair from his eyes.

'You need a haircut,' she said.

'I know. I'm getting quite shaggy.'

'Weren't the girls awful on the field trip? They all seem to have a crush on you, which makes them act like idiots. That Chloe is dreadful.'

'Oh well, maybe I should just let the hair grow long and straggly, and stop washing and shaving, to put them off.'

'Wouldn't work; you'd still ooze sex appeal.' Amy giggled. 'You could have your pick of the girls.'

'Silly. I couldn't, you know. Illegal.'

'Well, those over sixteen.'

'Still illegal,' said Luke. 'I'd go to prison for abusing a position of trust. Or lose my job and livelihood at the very least. So it's not on.' He stabbed a chunk of water chestnut. 'Even though it's soooo tempting, especially when they throw themselves at you.'

Amy looked up sharply and gaped at him.

He was laughing at her. 'Zwiiizzzzzzzzzzzzzzzz. That's you taking the bait.'

'I could slap you for that.'

'Amy,' he said as he laid down his fork. 'We need to talk. About us.'

'I know.'

'I thought you were amazing the moment I clapped eyes on you . . . '

They heard a sly noise in the hallway. Both froze, eyes wide and staring. Luke stood. Amy followed. Luke yanked open the kitchen door.

Uncle Bernard was there, examining her books. 'Ah, Amy dearest, could I borrow a book to read at the hotel, please? I'm just off now. Your aunt's getting ready for bed. I'll be back in the morning; sleep well.'

He left carrying the book he was holding, without even waiting for her to say yes. Luke stood frowning for a few seconds, then said, 'I think you should talk to your aunt and see what the old rogue's been up to. I'm going to hit the sack because I'm wasted.'

Upstairs, Amy found her aunt in the lounge, sipping a nightcap. Aunty Debbie beamed at her. 'Care to join me?'

'Yes please . . . I'll help myself.' Amy got herself a gin and tonic — a long, dilute one that should last a while.

'Thank you for being so understanding earlier,' said Debbie.

'My flabber was well and truly gasted when I saw Uncle Bernard lying on my bed,' said Amy. 'When did he turn up?'

'Monday. Just knocked on the door, and stood there looking contrite.'

'You're not thinking of having him back, are you, after what he did to you?' Amy tried to keep the dismay from her tone.

Debbie studied the whisky in her glass and swirled it. 'Maybe. I was devastated when he left; couldn't believe it. He made me feel so small. But he's explained why. The business, as you know, was beginning to founder. He tried to keep it from me and got very worried because it was partly his fault; silly ideas. He got severely depressed, felt claustrophobic, and needed some space. Then when he'd gone and I closed the business down, he was humiliated, and still very depressed. Had a breakdown in Canada, took medication, got better, saw sense, and realised he never stopped loving me. He thought he'd come and at least explain. He was shocked and horrified to find me ill with cancer.'

'So he explained. And all is forgiven, just like that?' Amy stared at her drink because she didn't dare look her aunt in the face.

'No, not exactly. He's on probation, as it were. That's why he was sleeping in your bed, not mine, and now at The Shoulder of Mutton.' Debbie took a large sip of whisky and let it sink before saying, 'Bernard did very well in Canada — appears to be rolling in it, so he can afford it. He's bought a small second-hand van as a run-around, rather than a swish new car, so I think he's being a bit more careful with money nowadays. Learned his lesson, I expect.'

Amy thought back to the bookshop business which Bernard had wrecked. Time to change the subject, perhaps. 'I had a business idea, but I don't know how viable it is.' Amy explained some outline ideas to Aunty Debbie, who didn't pooh-pooh them, just looked thoughtful. 'It's probably just daydreams,' finished Amy. 'And I'm not sure how it would fit in with my studies.'

'I'll give it some thought,' said Debbie.

★　★　★

Bernard's presence was like a miasma. When Amy went into the bathroom his shaving stuff was there, and some of his dirty clothing was in the wash bin. There was a faint smell of aftershave; not the subtle and expensive one Luke used sparingly, which she caught on an almost subliminal level, but a cheaper brand which put her in mind of dodgy double-glazing salesmen trying to disguise the fact they smoked. She found it unsettling.

★　★　★

Next morning it was the church bells at 10.00am that roused Amy. She'd slept solidly. She padded through to the kitchen, made herself a mug of tea, and went back to bed. She'd left the bedroom window open despite it being autumn, and it was chilly, but she enjoyed the fresh air.

Uncle Bernard being there changed the whole household dynamics, even if he was 'on probation'. Why was he back? Amy didn't quite buy the change of heart. Her mind went back to her childhood before Uncle Bernard left. He'd been one of her favourite adults, then. Fun, playful, kind and generous. He always had some little trinket for her when she came visiting with her parents. He had little gifts for all of them, she remembered. Enchanting toys, usually, that fitted in your pocket, or were all the rage, status symbols that her mum disparaged. When he left and broke Aunty Debbie's heart he'd broken Amy's heart as well. Mixed up with the sympathy for her aunt had been the feelings of treachery and abandonment for herself. Now she was older, Amy could see that a lot of the hurt had been selfish, and some of it had been sorrow that the little gifts would stop. She must have been fourteen when he left. Surely she hadn't been that crass at that age? But then, teenagers often were selfish and crass, so full of the me-me-me. It had been as if all the emotions and angst for her aunt, for herself, her mother's upset, the whispered, indignant conversations between her mum and dad, had jumbled up and come out as one homogenous lump of pain, now dulled with time.

Now he was back and Amy wasn't quite sure how she felt about it.

She hated the fact he'd been sleeping in her room amongst all her private belongings. If she'd known he was going to stay, she would have put some things out of sight, and prepared the room for a guest.

She recalled the conversation with Luke about the antiques book and the missing silver. It seemed so fanciful, and yet, and yet . . .

She rose and went onto the lounge to see if her aunt was up. She wasn't, but Uncle Bernard was on the sofa, reading a Sunday paper. He beamed, stood and kissed her cheek. 'Good morning, darling. I trust you're well?'

'Yes, thanks. I've just come to see if Aunty Debbie needs a cup of tea.'

'I don't know; I haven't seen her yet. I just let myself in quietly about ten minutes ago. No sign of her yet.'

So he had a front door key, then, and a key to the upstairs flat, if he let himself in. Amy knocked on the door. 'Are you awake, Debbie? Do you want a drink?'

There were sounds of movement. 'That'll be lovely. Tea please.'

'Coming right up,' said Bernard. He sloped

off to the kitchen and Amy was left feeling superfluous.

With a spurt of somewhat unreasonable anger, she followed Bernard into the kitchen. She picked up the mug of tea he'd just made. 'Don't worry, Uncle, you make yourself at home and enjoy your paper. I'll take this into Aunty Debbie. You're not married anymore and it would be . . . ' She groped for a suitable word. 'Unseemly for you to see her in her night attire.' As she said it she thought she sounded faintly ridiculous, as if she'd stepped out of a nineteenth-century novel.

'You've got a very old-fashioned attitude, my girl,' said Bernard gruffly, but then he laughed, as if it was a joke.

Amy walked in and closed the door behind her. Her aunt was sitting up in bed in her nightie and a cardigan. She looked relaxed, radiant, and happy. She smiled and ran her hand over her head. 'It's itching. I think my hair's beginning to grow back.'

Amy took a close look. 'Yes, fine as thistledown, but definitely something there. What are your plans for the day?'

'Bernard's taking me out for Sunday lunch. What about you?'

'I'm going to lie in bed and read. I'm shattered after the week away. I'll tell you about it later.' Amy retreated to bed and started reading one of her MA novels.

★ ★ ★

Amy woke with a start. She'd dozed off and her phone was ringing: a text from Luke. 'Amy, can I wash my gear, pls?' Then she heard him call, 'Amy, my darling . . . '

She went to the window. He smiled up at her. 'Can I put a wash on, please? I forgot last night. We could share a load as it's the same sort of stuff.'

'I'll bring it down.'

'Just put it in a bag and chuck it out the window.'

'Good idea, Romeo.' She opened her case and shoved the dirty washing into a couple of carrier bags and threw it down to Luke. She went downstairs and let him in. 'Beastly Bernard's here,' she said in a warning tone.

'Not now, he isn't. They went out about half an hour ago. I was about to ring the doorbell when they opened the door. He gave me an affable snarl on the way out, and told me you were sleeping.'

Amy laughed. 'You really don't like him, do you?'

'I think the feeling's mutual. Had you any plans for the day? I need to do some chores and shopping. I wondered if I could scrounge a lift.'

'I want some shopping too. Let's drive to the supermarket. And I need a chill-out day, and to do some work. Reading.'

'Reading's work, is it?'

'Sometimes. Just as going for a walk is work for you sometimes. Ugh, I think my trousers are still salty ... hey, you didn't wreck your lovely gold watch in the sea, did you?'

'No, thank goodness,' said Luke. 'I wear an ordinary one for school. That one's far too precious. It belonged to my grandfather. He actually gave it to me on my twenty-first birthday; he always intended it for me and said I might as well have it sooner rather than later. My parents bought me a suit, and he gave me a superb briefcase. That was shortly before he . . . ' A shadow crossed Luke's face. 'After being a scruffy student, I feel like a million dollars when I wear it, and there's the sentimental aspect. I keep the suit for best. It does mean I daren't put weight on, though.' Amy laughed.

Later, when they'd done the shopping, they sat outside in companionable silence. Luke was looking through his photos on his laptop and Amy was reading. She put the book down, sighed, and looked into the distance.

'Worried?' asked Luke.

'Yes. Disturbed, I'd say. Uneasy.'

'Bernard? You're worried he'll want the spare room and you'll get pushed into using the library as a bedsit?'

Amy pulled in a breath. 'Couldn't put my finger on it, but yes, that's part of it, though I think it's more to do with worrying about him breaking Debbie's heart all over again. Besides, I've got plans for the library which don't include it being used as a bedsit. This is only a tentative idea. You know I need a part-time job but can't get one? This idea stems from two things. One's your remark about selling second-hand books, and the other's the two girls who thought I was running a coffee shop. And then you made a remark about setting up a coffee shop. I thought, why not? I could run the two together. People could grab a book off the shelf and settle down with a coffee. If they want the book, they could buy it; if not, put it back. When it's quiet, I could do my studies. And Debbie could help when she's not got any book-keeping work.'

Luke frowned. 'I don't know. I'm sure there's more to running a coffee shop than boiling a kettle, love. And I thought you wanted to be a teacher.'

'I do, but I'm broke at the moment, stone

broke. This would be a way of pruning my books, and making a bit of money. It wouldn't have to be on a large scale.'

'But it's a commitment. It would tie you up all day, every day. I think you need to think very seriously about the potential pitfalls. How will you afford the up-front investments like health inspection and public liability insurance? And you'd need a hygiene certificate, and training?'

'I worked in a pub one summer, between my second and third years at university, and they made sure I was trained. But you're right. We'd need to put in a hand-wash-only sink, and so on.'

'I seem to remember when I was younger that the deli next door used to sell carry-out coffee, but they don't, now. Why don't you have a chat with Alison and see what advice she can give?' He smiled. 'If you turn the library into a café, it can't be made into a bedroom, so you wouldn't be turfed out of the guest bedroom.'

Amy popped next door to see if Alison was able to chat. It was gone 4.00pm so, being Sunday, the deli was closed. Amy returned with Alison, carrying leftover gateau. Amy saw Luke's eyes widen with appreciation, but wasn't sure if it was for the cake or for Alison. She made coffee, served it in the library because the evening had turned chilly, then outlined her ideas.

Alison looked pensive. 'The reason we stopped serving coffee was that it was distracting us from the business of selling foodstuffs. People wanted a place to sit down and drink their coffee, and we haven't got room for that. They'd moan about the lack of facilities, so we stopped altogether. Pity, as there isn't anywhere else much in Runworthy, and people still pop in to buy for something for lunch. It earned some revenue, but not enough to make it worthwhile for us.' Luke nodded with grim satisfaction at this, but Alison carried on. 'That doesn't mean it wouldn't work for you. I like the idea of combining bookshop and café. It would give people a relaxed feeling when drinking coffee, but might reduce your behinds-on-seats turnover substantially.' She looked round the room. 'On bad weather days you'd get what — ten, fifteen people in here at most? And ideally you'd need weatherproof outdoor seating, like aluminium tables. You wouldn't want to have to lug ordinary tables in and out, not in the long term. You need to provide loos, and disabled facilities. And there's insurance. People will sue if they get half a chance, so you must, must, must have insurance. Let's do a SWOT analysis.'

'A what?'

'Strengths, Weaknesses, Opportunities, Threats. List under each heading. Look, I'll show you . . . and then you need a business plan . . . and that needs to be based on fact, not wishful thinking. And what about loos and so on?'

'We have a downstairs loo off the hallway which is pretty decent, and there's the one outside in the wash-house. The wash-house itself could be tidied up and used to store tables for outside. I'd need to get a plumber in for the hand-wash sink in the kitchen, but there's plenty of room for it. Debbie says she knows a good plumber. Actually she seems to know everyone in Runworthy.'

A couple of hours later Alison said, 'You know, I think this idea might have legs, but I don't think you'd make a fortune from it. We could work well together, actually. We sell sandwiches and cake, you sell coffee, and allow people to eat the sandwiches bought in our deli at your tables. You have to decide, I think, whether you want to run a second-hand bookshop which sells coffee, or a coffee shop which sells second-hand books. What did Debbie say?'

'She says she'll give it some thought, but she seemed quite positive. She knows what she's doing and can help with the legalities. I would need to put some money into it, money I haven't really got. And there's a complication . . . ' Amy looked down at the SWOT analysis. It had clarified her thoughts very well, and she was mentally already forming a business plan on the basis of it.

'A complication? Bernard? Yes. I've seen him around, but I didn't like to say anything . . . ' Alison scrutinised Amy's face, presumably trying to determine what Amy thought about the subject.

'Actually,' said Amy, 'I count that as a flipping good reason for starting the coffee shop bookshop.'

'Or the Book Lovers' Coffee Shop,' said Luke. 'To be honest, I'd be tempted to give it a whirl even if it's for a short time. You've got most of what you need here already; it's just a matter of the legalities, and you've said that Debbie is good and knowledgeable about that. And I think it'll take her mind off other things. Therapeutic.'

'Maybe, but I don't want her worn out.'

Once Alison had gone, Luke prowled round the library for a minute or two. 'You'd have to get rid of these boxes; they make the place look untidy.'

'That's some of Debbie's stuff which needs filing,' said Amy. 'She just never got round to sorting it. It was left over from when beastly

Bernard shoved off. Everything was higgledy-piggledy. I mean, look . . . ' She pulled out the old life insurance policy. 'I bet he never knew where he'd put it so if the worst had happened he'd have been searching high and low for it.'

'So it wasn't where you'd expect to find it?'

'Nope. Like lots of other things. I expect this lapsed when he left her.'

Luke held out his hand. 'May I?' There was something in his tone of voice which made Amy hand it over. His eyes widened as he looked at it. 'I wonder . . . '

They heard the front door, and shoved the document back in the box as if it was hot.

19

Amy was waiting for Luke in the empty staff room. She'd sagged into one of the chairs and felt as if her bones had melted. It was gone half past four; the children should have gone home by now. She didn't fancy a gauntlet of bug-eyed kids watching as she and Luke strolled home together.

Luke's face lit up when he saw her. 'Hi, love.'

'You'll have to pull me up. I'm too tired to stand of my own free will,' said Amy. He came over, she gave him both hands, and he pulled her up effortlessly, kissing her a chaste buss on the cheek. They got their coats and started walking home. Amy felt rather than saw Luke's glances at her as they walked along.

'What's up?' he asked eventually. 'You've lost all your bounce.'

'I'm not sure I'm cut out to be a teacher,' said Amy. Once it was out of her mouth she felt tears pricking. 'And all I ever wanted since I was so high was to be a teacher.'

'Chloe and Sam?' His pace matched hers as they walked along. He wrapped an arm around her shoulders. She felt a comforting weight through her coat. It felt right to be entwined like this, far more than it ever had with Gareth, or anyone else for that matter. She felt nurtured, protected.

'That Chloe is a madam,' said Amy. 'You'd think she'd be grateful, but no, she's worse than ever, and she wound Sam up into vicious-lampoon mode, and Sam's good at that when she gets going. But they weren't the worst of it. I was given a class of Year Nines today. Honestly, they were awful. Unteachable, most of them, and they spoil it for those who want to learn. I reckon there were five out of the class who really wanted to study. I was helping out, so there were two of us trying to keep them on the straight and narrow. But it's impossible. They just won't work. It's the least able group. I really felt sorry for the five who wanted to work. I might ask if I can teach them separately. They might not be very bright but they were trying. It's the others that got to me. One boy spent the entire lesson drawing male appendages. He's been given a detention. Ugh, demoralising or what.'

'That's teaching for you nowadays. Sometimes it's a matter of survival, which is why I learned self-defence. A lot do want to learn, and they make it worthwhile. Don't let one bad day put you off.'

Amy sighed and shook her head. 'I just think I'm worn out. That trip took the stuffing out of me. It's Aunty Debbie's op next week, which I'm not looking forward to, and I feel — disorientated now that Uncle B has turned up like that. And I've been thinking about my business idea. I'm wondering if it's going to work, because Aunty Debbie will have to have radiotherapy and I was going to drive her in for that. That takes me away from the café, if I start it, for a month around Christmas-time.'

'You could sell the books you don't want, anyway. On the Internet, perhaps. Or open up as a part-time bookshop at first. Late afternoons to catch the commuters, perhaps, or just over lunch, or all day on the days Debbie doesn't have radiotherapy.'

'I've got this sense of urgency because I want to get my territory established before Uncle B gets too ensconced, you know?'

'I do know, love. He rubs me up the wrong way every time I clap eyes on him . . . and I avoided him most of yesterday.'

By this time they'd reached home. Amy opened the front door. 'Unlocked,' she said. 'That's bad. I must warn Uncle B about not leaving doors unlocked.'

'Too true; don't want strangers wandering in off the streets wanting to buy books.'

She pecked him on the cheek. 'I can make exceptions. Stick the kettle on; I want to dump these in the library. I've got some marking to do.'

'You should have let me carry them.'

'You've got your own, and whatever happened to sex equality?'

'Yes, but still. Actually, can I borrow a book, please? I need to chill out with a thriller.'

'Come and see if I've got anything you fancy.' Amy walked into the library. Uncle Bernard looked round with a start. He'd been standing with his head on one side, looking at her books — her older collectables.

'You've got a fine collection here,' he said. 'You always were a bookworm. Your aunt's sleeping upstairs so I came down here so as not to disturb her.'

'I'm sure you won't disturb her by sitting upstairs and reading. The TV might disturb her, but you could sit and read or something. I want to do some marking in here and I don't want to be disturbed.'

'Well, quite. But I haven't got anything to read so I . . .'

'What happened to the one you took last night? The romance?' asked Luke as he joined Amy.

'Finished it, put it back on the shelf,' said

Bernard. 'This one will do nicely.' He pulled a book off a shelf without even looking at it. 'Toodlepip.' He left the room and they heard his tread on the stairs.

'Gawd, it's like he's been dredged up from a tacky 1940s RAF film,' said Luke. 'It's so affected.'

'He's always talked like that,' said Amy. 'I always thought it was part of his charm when I was a kid.'

Luke said something disparaging.

Amy nodded. 'I think you're right; he'll manipulate Debbie into suggesting I have a bed in here, leaving him the spare room, or worse, jumping into hers. But what's confusing the issue for me is that he seems to be making Debbie very, very happy. Maybe I should move down here and chuck the coffee shop idea.'

'Would you want him in the house twenty-four seven?'

'No.' Amy pondered for a minute. 'And I don't understand why not. He's lovely, really.'

'Forced bonhomie if you ask me.'

'He's making Debbie happy, that's what really matters. I think I'll suggest I cook for myself down here. That way they have their space, and I have mine. I don't think we can resist the inevitable, and perhaps I don't even have the right to try to keep them apart. But I want to keep my bedroom.'

'And I think it's essential for your aunt to have a breathing space at night. Amy, something's worrying me. Something serious. Was your aunt accident prone when Bernard was here? And does she ever suffer from IBS now?'

'Not that I know of, except for the cellar incident. Why?'

Luke shook his head. 'Nothing.'

★   ★   ★

That night, when Bernard had gone back to The Shoulder of Mutton, Amy showed her aunt her SWOT analysis and business plan outline. Debbie was enthusiastic, promised Amy help with the legalities, would ask Kevin the plumber to come as soon as possible, and said Amy should come to the next Chamber of Trade evening. She said she'd get on to it in the morning. 'No time like the present,' she said.

Amy hoped it wasn't because Debbie thought she might not have a future.

★   ★   ★

Amy didn't mention the project to Debbie when Bernard was around, but she sorted her

214

books out. There were a large number that she couldn't bear to part with, old friends, and these she moved upstairs to her bedroom, or put them on the shelves in Luke's bedroom. 'You'll have to pay a tariff to borrow them,' he said.

'What's that?'

He kissed her, a real scorcher. 'That's what.'

'Oh well, in that case I will have to show you what an avid reader I am.'

The books she could bear to part with she labelled up with sensible prices. 'That's odd,' she said. 'I thought I had a couple of old copies of Milly Molly Mandy. They're not very valuable, but they're worth more than the average second-hand book. I don't really want them — I could sell them — but I can't find them. But then, I don't remember seeing them since I unpacked. Maybe they're in one of the boxes in the attic.'

It took a long time to sort the books, partly because Amy checked the usual price online, and partly because she ended up being distracted into reading some of them. Bernard didn't come into the library again, but spent a lot of time with Debbie. The pair went out every day, and Amy was beginning to worry that Aunty Debbie might be overdoing it. She seemed to be running on overdrive, full of sparkle that Amy hoped wouldn't fizzle out.

Luke was a bit distant and preoccupied, and came home late a couple of times. He said he'd stayed late at school, and Amy didn't think to question this in her mind.

★ ★ ★

'I'm going to my cousin's in Stockport for the weekend,' Bernard announced on Friday. 'I haven't seen him for years and I'd like to catch up. Staying a couple of nights with him will save me something at the pub. I'll be back Sunday night to take darling Debbie in for her operation on Monday of course.'

Amy let a breath out as if someone had punched her.

Debbie smiled. 'The operation isn't until Tuesday. I'm first on the list, apparently, but I need to be in by half two on Monday. And since you're doing work experience at the school, Amy love, it makes sense for Bernard to take me in. You could sleep in my bed while I'm in the hospital, Bernard darling. That'll save you a few quid too.'

Amy and Luke exchanged glances but said nothing until later when they knew Bernard had gone and Debbie was upstairs. 'I think I'm jealous, of all things,' Amy confided. 'I assumed I would take her to hospital. That was my job; he's usurped my position. I don't understand why I feel so angry, but I do. He's not even family now, since they divorced, yet he's muscled in and taken over.'

Luke rubbed her back. 'I know, love, I know. It's presumptuous. But if she holds a candle for him I suppose it's only natural.'

'Well, I'm going in on Tuesday as well. There's nothing to stop me.'

'You know, what worries me is the way he's wheedled his way into the household, just as we feared. See, he's sleeping in Debbie's bed now, at least until she's home. Best get this coffee shop off the ground this weekend while his back's turned, or you will find yourself turfed out, or him sleeping in here. Get the bookshop bit up and running. The coffee shop can come later if necessary.'

20

The café bookshop wasn't opened at the weekend, but a large amount of the preparation was done, including the hand-wash-only sink in the downstairs kitchen, which Amy was glad about because its installation wasn't exactly subtle. Luke painted the downstairs loo and the one outside too, and both looked very smart by the time he'd finished them. This activity distracted Debbie from the operation to come, and established the bookshop as a fact, not a 'maybe'.

Gill the Macmillan nurse turned up unexpectedly on the Saturday to see Debbie and wish her luck. Amy was puzzled to see Gill and Luke talking, heads close, in the hallway just before Gill took her leave of them. Amy shrugged. Maybe they were talking about her, worried about her fretting. That might explain the slightly furtive body language. But she was fine really. Worried, of course, but fine. Though she would be happier once Debbie's operation was over. Operations were safe enough nowadays, after all. It was nothing to worry about. Not really.

★ ★ ★

When Bernard returned Sunday night he seemed very pleased with himself, positively preening. Debbie brightened up as soon as he crossed the threshold. Nobody mentioned the second-hand bookshop, though Amy had had a Perspex sign printed up ready to hang on the old sign hook arm. She had decided to open on Wednesday, once Debbie's operation was done. Tuesday would be spent waiting anxiously at the hospital.

Amy gave Debbie a hug before she and Luke set off for school Monday morning. 'I'll come and see you this evening,' Amy promised. She glanced at Bernard, who was hovering possessively. 'And I'll be there for you tomorrow,' she added.

At school Amy asked Donna Phelps if she could change her voluntary hours to a couple of mornings instead of a full day because she intended to open her shop from 2.00p.m. to 7.00p.m. weekdays. She also wanted to warn Donna that things might get complicated round Christmas because of her aunt's radiotherapy. 'Though my aunt would be capable of driving herself in, if push comes to shove,' she added. 'It was the chemo where she couldn't, in case it made her sick.'

The hospital was about twenty miles away. Luke accompanied Amy for moral support. 'You've just missed Bernard,' said Debbie when they arrived on a very pleasant ward. Amy had been expecting to see Debbie in nightwear in bed, but she was outside in a small garden which had been made for the patients and was maintained by volunteers, the League of Friends.

They spent the evening chatting, then left, making sure they used the alcohol hand cleanser both on the way in and out. Some people didn't. 'I hope Aunty Debbie doesn't pick up MRSA or some other ghastly superbug because those people aren't bothered about spreading germs round the hospital,' muttered Amy as she and Luke went back to her car. 'When it says 'everybody, every time,' that's what it means.'

Luke said nothing. Instead he wrapped an arm around her shoulders and squeezed.

★ ★ ★

'No need for you to worry your pretty little head or for you to come in early,' said Bernard on Tuesday morning with a shark's grin. 'I'll give you a tinkle as soon as Debbie's out of theatre.'

Amy was about to remonstrate when it occurred to her that all she would be doing at the hospital was fretting, because Debbie was first on the list and would probably be in theatre when she got there. She'd be better off fretting at home, and making the last minute preparations for her opening tomorrow while Bernard was out of the picture.

When he'd gone she peeped into her aunt's room, and saw that although Bernard had changed the sheets, the old sheets were in a heap in the middle of the floor. Those sheets would need to be clean for when Debbie came out of hospital. She gathered them up and shoved them into the machine. Then she fiddled about with her new toy: a cash register. It was the most basic of basic models, but would at least make the accounts easier and make the place look more professional. She put it away, hiding it in the cellar and pocketing the key because she didn't want Bernard coming across it when he came sniffing round for something to read. *I'll charge him for everything he borrows*, thought Amy. She glanced at the clock. Nearly ten thirty. Aunty Debbie would probably be having her op now.

Both kitchens were sparkling, the soon-to-be-coffee-shop loos clean and inviting, the sheets dry and ironed, and still she hadn't heard anything from the hospital. She hadn't got Bernard's mobile phone number — what an oversight. But then, mobiles had to be turned off in hospital. Surely he should have phoned her by now?

Another hour slid past, and still no news. She decided to phone the hospital and ask for the ward sister. 'I'm sorry,' said the prim voice on the end of the phone. 'We're only allowed to give news to the next of kin.'

'I am her next of kin,' said Amy. 'Well, apart from my mum, but she's in America. I'm Debbie's next of kin here.'

'I'll check her notes,' said the nurse with a doubtful tone. Amy heard the scuffing of shoes, then a clanking as the notes were pulled from the end of the bed. The nurse started to say something, but she heard Aunty Debbie say something. The nurse replied, then Amy heard Debbie's voice.

'Hello, darling. I'm now last on the list, don't ask me why. So I haven't been done yet and I feel like I have a stinky sock in my mouth. I've told the nurse she's allowed to tell you things over the phone, and she'll phone you when I'm in Recovery, so that's OK. There's no visiting until this evening, so

222

I fear Bernard's had a wasted day here. Gotta go now; I can hear the ominous trundle of hospital trolley wheels.'

★ ★ ★

Amy astonished herself by bursting into tears when Luke got back from school. He held her in his arms, 'Oh my God,' he said in a horrified voice.

Amy realised what this must look like. 'It's OK,' she sobbed. 'It's just the stress of waiting, that's all.' She explained about the delay in operating. He sat her down and made her a cup of tea. She was just wondering whether to phone the hospital when the phone went. It was Bernard. 'She's out of theatre and apparently it went very well.' He sounded relieved.

'We'll be over shortly,' said Amy. She put the phone down. 'I should have been phoned by the hospital,' she said. 'They promised.' Ten minutes later the ward sister phoned and told her the same news. 'Thank you, but Mr Murray already told me,' said Amy. 'How come you told him before you told me? I should have thought you should tell me first. It's really too much to hear it second-hand.'

'We always inform the next of kin first. We haven't got time to phone a list of relatives.'

'Well, exactly. I am the next of kin.'

'No. Ms Driscoll put Mr Bernard Murray as next of kin.'

'She can't have done. He's nothing to do with her now. They've been divorced at least four years. He's no relation at all.'

'I'll check the forms,' said the nurse, 'Excuse me, good bye.'

'That man has an outrageous cheek,' Amy exploded as she put the phone down.

Luke looked dubious. 'I don't know, love . . . if that's what Debbie said, that's what they have to go by.'

'But she wouldn't put down her ex-husband as next of kin, when he's only just moved back into her life after abandoning her like that . . . would she?'

Luke just shrugged and looked unhappy.

* * *

Amy forgot her anger with Bernard when she saw him sitting next to Debbie, gazing adoringly. 'She's not very with-it, I'm afraid,' he said as they arrived.

He was right. Debbie was really dopey because she was on a morphine drip. Sometimes she didn't altogether make sense, though she did ask Amy if she would bring her reading glasses the next time Amy came because she'd forgotten to bring them. Amy said she'd be over first thing in the morning.

When they got home she and Luke went into the library for a sit-down and a cuddle (though she supposed she should call it the shop now, not the library).

As they sat down, Luke stood up with a wince of pain, fished his phone out of his pocket, glanced at it, and put it on the table. 'Now where was I?' he said as he sat back down. 'Oh yes.' He started to kiss her, then stopped. 'What's up?'

'Do you mind if we just sit and cuddle and read or something? I'm just not in the mood for kisses.'

* * *

Next morning Amy drove to the hospital in a much better frame of mind. Though she hadn't slept particularly well, she had at least slept. The question of next of kin arose again, and the feeling of hurt returned. How could Aunty Debbie have put Bernard down as NOK when he wasn't anything more than her ex?

Bernard was making his own way over to the hospital later. Amy felt a pang of disquiet at leaving him in the house alone, but at least she should be able to see her aunt on her own. Debbie was sitting up in bed looking very perky, all things considered. She was still hooked up to the morphine but said she needed it less and less. It was self-administered, she said, with a timer to ensure she didn't use it too often. Amy handed Debbie her reading glasses and a magazine she'd picked up from the newsagent on the way in.

'Oh, thank you,' said Debbie. 'I'm bored out of my brains because I can't concentrate on the books I brought with me. A magazine is perfect. How are the preparations for the bookshop going?'

'Ready to open. I need to get back to do the last-minute things and open my door at 2.00pm and watch them all flood in.' Amy laughed. 'I hope . . . ' She paused and bit her lip. 'Aunty, I have to ask because it's bugging me . . . why did you put Bernard down as next of kin when Mum is, and then me?'

'I didn't. I put down Pat. But they said it should be someone easily contactable, so I said you.'

'Oh. But when I called they said that Bernard was listed as next of kin.' Just as Amy was telling Debbie what the nurse had said, Bernard walked in. Amy's heart thudded and she pulled in her breath.

Bernard swept over with an affable smile

and a gust of aftershave. 'Hello, my beloved. And how are we today?'

'We are perplexed, Bernard, because I said Amy was my next of kin when you filled in the form for me because of my glasses being left at home. Yet apparently you put yourself down. That really is too presumptuous.'

Bernard smiled. 'I know, I know, but I did it to protect you, my love, because I was here at the hospital, waiting, and Amy wasn't. I thought they might need some consents in a hurry, and I was worried they wouldn't tell me anything, and I'd promised Amy I'd phone her with news. I did it with the best of intentions. Sorry.'

Debbie looked mollified, but said, 'Well, that will need correcting.'

Amy unclenched her fists and told herself Bernard was just a fool, and there was nothing sinister in what he'd done. She found herself gritting her teeth when she looked at him. 'I'll be back later,' she promised.

★ ★ ★

When she got home Amy was shocked to discover that the front door was unlocked yet again. Anyone could have walked in off the street. Luckily it didn't look as if anyone had, or they'd surely have swiped her phone from the table in the library. She picked it up and slid it safely into her pocket. Blasted Bernard. She plugged the till in and hung the new sign up on the old hook. It had a drawing of an open book where the pages were twisted into a heart shape, with a coffee cup in the heart: 'The Book Lovers' Second Hand Bookshop & Coffee Shop Open'. She covered the 'Private' sign on the railings. And then she waited. She had some assignments to do, and she tried to focus on those, but her brain wasn't behaving itself.

She heard footsteps on the cobbles. A customer? But it was only Bernard. 'What's all this then?' he demanded. 'What's this bookshop coffee shop business? There isn't room.'

'Of course there's room. The front room and the hall, almost the square footage of Driscoll's Bookshop.'

'Murray's Bookshop.'

'Oh, yes, that's right. You changed the name then wrecked the business. I always think of it as Driscoll's, as in successful.'

Bernard went purple. 'You have no right to do this. I had . . . '

'I have every right to do this, and it has nothing to do with you whatsoever. You are a guest in this house, nothing more, and to my mind, not a particularly welcome one — not after the disgusting, shabby way you treated my aunt all those years ago. I don't care if you were ill; you behaved like a complete prat. You had no right to put yourself down as next of kin; that was outrageous. And you have no right to tell me that I can't run a business from what is my home and not yours. Now, please remove yourself out of my shop, either upstairs or out; I don't care which.'

'I'll speak to Debbie about this.'

'Don't you dare, not when she's ill.'

He stomped upstairs.

The anger rattled round Amy's head like static. Her normally diplomatic self had just exploded, and she'd gone too far, let too many secret thoughts out of the bag. But how dare he, how dare he? Surely Aunty wasn't thinking of letting him back into her life permanently? Amy bit her lip. Everything but everything had been so focused on Aunty Debbie's upcoming operation that Amy hadn't given any real thought to the future, vaguely hoping Bernard would disappear sooner or later. The thought that he might become a permanent fixture was appalling.

Her phone went. The hospital? She yanked it out of her pocket and slid it open without looking.

'Hello sexy legs.' It was a young female voice, one she couldn't place but which she thought she knew. 'I long for your hot lips on mine, to be held tightly in your arms again.'

'What? Who's that?'

Whoever it was hung up.

There were three texts for her. She opened them. 'I lv yr sexy bum.', 'UR my hero' and 'CU soon xxxxxxxxxx'. The texts and the phone call were from Chloe.

Chloe? Chloe had a crush on her? That might explain her tiresome behaviour. She stared at the phone, utterly flabbergasted. Then she saw that this wasn't her phone. It looked like hers — was the same model as hers, the same ring tone — but there was something about it . . . She accessed the stored phonebook and flicked down the contacts. There were lots, including hers, Chloe's, and, astonishingly, Gill the Macmillan nurse's. Gill, who had caused Luke's eyes to flick open in appreciation that time in the garden; Gill, whom she had seen in furtive conversation with Luke that time. This was Luke's phone, the one he'd put on the table last night, the one Debbie had mistaken for Amy's all those weeks ago. It was a common enough phone, cheap but good. Lots of people had them. She remembered the time on Marloes Sands when she'd heard it ring and reached for her own. She'd meant to change her ring tone but had forgotten after the excitement of Chloe's rescue. Chloe's rescue — 'My hero'? She put the phone back in her pocket and swallowed hard.

No customers came in, not one. Amy was alone with her thoughts and they weren't good ones.

21

When Luke came home, she was still sitting at her desk with the till, books open, study impossible. 'What's up?' he said. 'No customers? Or Debbie . . . ?' He looked really alarmed.

Amy was about to tell him when she remembered Bernard was in the house, possibly even lurking behind the door to the upstairs flat. She wondered about telling Luke in his room, or the kitchen, but Bernard might come and eavesdrop just like he had before. She was convinced he did this, snooping and sneaking around the place, ear to the door, then innocently looking for a book when discovered. A romance didn't seem his type of reading, yet that was what he'd grabbed off the shelf that first time. Panicked into grabbing the first thing to hand, perhaps.

'Come with me. I have something serious to ask you about.' She led him outside to the back terrace, locking the front door against the unlikely event of a customer. The sun had set and it was nearly dark, so she couldn't see Luke's face. 'First of all, why have you got

Gill's phone number stored in your phone? What is she to you?'

'You've been snooping through my contacts? How rude.'

'It was by accident; I thought it was my phone — same make, as you know, and same ring tone. You haven't answered my question. Are you two-timing me?' Her heart clenched as she waited for his answer.

'Of course not. How could you think that?'

She felt him reach for her in the dark, as if to give her a reassuring hug, but she slid away from his grasp. 'Because of the lustful looks you gave her and because you have her phone number in your phone.'

He pulled in a breath over his teeth, and spoke with a low voice that was barely discernable over the muted noises of the traffic and she had to hold her head near his to hear him. 'This is confidential, and Gill could get into trouble because she's not sure of the ethics. But I told her about the problem with Bernard, and how he seems to be muscling in, and so on. I asked her to advise Debbie to sleep on her own until she's fully recovered. Which isn't strictly ethical, but better for your aunt, I think, and certainly better for you. Happy?' The last word hissed out louder, making her jump.

'No. I'm more concerned about this.' She

took the phone out, read the texts out loud, and told him about the phone call which started it off.

'Chloe sent those texts? Are you sure?' He sounded angry and worried.

'Well, who else would? Gill perhaps? How come Chloe's got your phone number; how come you've got hers?'

'We've both got it, you and I, and we've both got everyone on the field trip, remember? Oh this really is too bad.' His voice diminished as he turned away from her a couple of aggressive steps, then he turned back. 'I'll have a word with Donna Phelps about this and get Chloe to stop it. It's a teenage crush, and it's got worse since we rescued her. And Sam's got cheekier. I'm sick and tired of the pair of them.' He sounded genuine, and Amy believed him utterly.

She felt her legs wobble, fumbled for the seat and sat down. 'Oh thank goodness. I thought, I thought . . . '

'You thought I was dating Gill and having an improper relationship with a pupil? Oh Amy, how could you even think that? It's outrageous.' He spun on his heel and vanished into his flat. He closed the door behind him and she heard the key turn in the lock. Then he drew the curtains. Amy sat in the dark for five heartbeats, then burst into tears.

Later as she lay in bed, hearing the late-night trains grinding though the darkness, Amy turned her thoughts over and over. The bathroom stinking of Bernard's aftershave didn't improve her mood. The smell had even crept through the landing and into her bedroom, despite the wide-open window, or maybe she was hypersensitive to it as she disliked it so much. She shivered and hoped Luke would be more sensible in the morning.

He was. He hugged her, said he was going to sort the Chloe situation out, and said he knew she'd been under a lot of strain with Gareth and her aunt and that had warped her judgement. When she asked him if he would show Donna the texts, he blushed and said he'd deleted them last night in a fit of temper. 'You should still tell Donna about them,' said Amy. 'And the phone call. It's bad, and it upset me a lot.'

Luke looked dubious. 'I don't think so. I've blocked her number and I'll tell her when I see her. If I make it official she may end up suspended, and she's about to do some exams. She's a bit . . . troubled.'

When he came home that afternoon, he told her he'd sorted out the problem, and had discussed it with Donna. Chloe had been spoken to, was being moved to a different class and, incidentally, she would no longer be attending Amy's tutor group. Sam would still be coming, though. Donna had decided to separate Chloe and Sam into different classes altogether.

By the end of Thursday Amy had sold some of her books and Bernard had said nothing more about the bookshop venture. She drove to the hospital see Debbie with a lighter heart.

★ ★ ★

By Friday Debbie was home, and Bernard was once more staying in The Shoulder of Mutton. Amy skipped her own Friday MA tutor group because she wanted a quiet word with Gill. Gill blushed when she affirmed that she had told Debbie to sleep alone, and said that her personal view was that Bernard was a slimeball, but not to repeat it or she'd lose her job. Luke hadn't lied. Amy felt her heart soar. Everything was looking up. She opened shop at 2.00pm with a much more positive frame of mind. The weekend was busy and the till full by the end of Sunday.

22

Amy looked at the rain-drenched figure on the doorstep. 'I see you've opened a bookshop. I'm Lucy. Remember me? We thought it was a coffee shop a few days after the Macmillan Coffee Morning. Are you open? I'd like a look around, please. See if there's anything suitable for Christmas presents.'

Amy held the door open as Lucy pulled the sodden pushchair inside. 'You're soaking,' Amy said, rather unnecessarily. 'Come into the kitchen where it's warmer. We've lit the range.' Lucy complied and pushed her hood back. 'Let me take your coat and hang it on the back of a chair by the range,' added Amy. No way did she want the girl dripping all over her stock. The coat wasn't fully done up over Lucy's now very prominent bump.

'I fibbed a bit,' Lucy confessed. 'I missed my bus and was looking for an open shop to shelter in, but they're all shutting and it's dark and horrible out there, and the next bus isn't until 6.40. But now I'm here, I'll take a look if I may.' It was half past five and teeming down spears of freezing rain.

'Would you like a cup of tea to warm you up? On the house.'

'Would I ever,' said Lucy, her face breaking out into a grateful smile.

Amy made some tea and found some juice for Josh, who was snugly cocooned in a plastic bubble, which Lucy undid now they were indoors.

'Come though to the bookshop,' said Amy. Lucy looked at the books as she sipped her tea. Amy told her of her plans and asked if she thought they would work.

'It'll be wicked,' said Lucy. 'I'll stop by every Tuesday with Emily. And when Josh is at playgroup, I'll stop by because there's no point in going home. And I'll tell my friends to come and buy books and drink coffee and stuff.' Lucy bought several books, some of them hardback non-fiction books which Amy had picked up from a jumble sale for next to nothing at the end of the sale. Amy got a reasonable price and Lucy seemed delighted because they were good as new.

After she'd closed Amy got the coffee things ready for the next day. People were dropping in by word of mouth, and the coffee side of things was beginning to prove profitable. Things were definitely looking up.

'Hi there,' said Amy as PC Bishop the neighbourhood police officer came through the front shop door. 'Is there another spate of purse-dipping?' Her greeting smile faded when the saw PC Bishop's expression.

'Would you mind closing the shop for a few minutes?'

Amy's heart clenched. Her face must have reflected this because PC Bishop added, 'I just need a word.'

Amy locked the door then went into the front room and slipped the 'open' sign to 'closed'.

'Some serious allegations have been made,' said PC Bishop. 'I'm asking you as a witness. Did Luke Armitage receive some odd phone calls recently?'

'Yes,' said Amy, frowning, and explained. 'Will I have to make a statement or something?'

PC Bishop looked torn. 'Maybe,' she said. 'At the moment, although some allegations have been made, I'm trying to keep it low-key until I have more evidence of wrongdoing. Thanks very much for your help.' When PC Bishop left, Amy flicked the sign to 'open' again and wondered what on earth all that was about. Surely a few saucy texts and a funny phone call weren't a police matter? Unless Chloe had done this to a lot of people, perhaps?

★ ★ ★

'I've had one hell of a day, thanks to you,' said Luke poking his head round the door as he came home that evening. 'I'll tell you exactly what I mean when you've shut up shop. Honestly Amy, I expected better from someone who's supposed to love me.' He shut the front door with a bang and stomped round the back to his flat.

'Well boo you,' she muttered under her breath. 'That's so rude. Suppose I'd got a customer browsing in the front room?' She tried to ignore what he'd said, but it was worse than an unscratchable itch.

★ ★ ★

At two minutes to seven Luke came back round. 'Well? Don't you want to hear how you very nearly wrecked my career?'

Amy locked the door and turned the sign to 'closed'. 'I'm not sure I do if you're going to speak to me like that, but since I haven't the vaguest clue what you're talking about, you'd better tell me. I had PC Bishop round earlier wanting to know about the texts Chloe sent you. I thought Chloe was in trouble or something. Not you.' She went to put a hand on his arm, but he shrugged her off.

'Of course it's to do with Chloe. Someone alleged to PC Bishop that I was having an improper relationship with Chloe. Lucky for me PC Bishop isn't the type to arrest first and ask questions later, and very luckily the allegations were made in person to PC Bishop and not through the official channels or I would have been up the creek and out of a job. She came to speak to Donna Phelps, to see if there was any other evidence before taking the matter further. I gather Donna said that I'd already spoken to her about Chloe, and that she didn't think anything was going on; or if there was, it was what amounts to stalking on Chloe's side, but that's been resolved. Then I was called to the office and I had to answer some rather pointed questions, like why had I deleted the texts. So I explained exactly what happened. Then Sam burst into the office and said it was all her fault. Donna flipped, but Sam held her ground and said she'd suggested the texts to Chloe as a passing joke not actually expecting her to do it, and she never suggested a saucy phone call.

'I gather that the sequence of events was

that PC Bishop questioned Chloe before I was spoken to. Chloe denied sending the texts — denied everything — which made it look even worse, like she was covering up for me or something, which was idiotic because we know she'd sent them and had admitted as much when I first reported it to Donna. Chloe was told to stay in isolation under the watchful eye of the secretary, but she ran off and told Sam, sort of laughing hysterically about it, and crying in the next breath, according to Sam. Sam was appalled; she's got more brains than Chloe, and she thought I was about to be arrested. Maybe I was. But as it was, her bursting in like that meant that Sam's version was believed. So PC Bishop said she felt there was no substance to the allegations.'

'That's awful. Good job you'd already spoken to Donna about this. But why's it 'all my fault'? I could hardly lie to PC Bishop and say the texts didn't happen, and actually that corroborated what you and Sam said.'

'Who made the allegations of an improper relationship, an abuse of a position of trust, in the first place? That's what I want to know.'

'Me too. Chloe?'

'I don't buy that. It doesn't make sense. Why make the allegations, then deny the texts having admitted to them before?' Luke was studying her face with a strange, almost hungry expression.

'She got scared when they were taken seriously? She's pretty mixed up, that kid. Did you ask PC Bishop?' Amy couldn't think of anyone who would know about the texts apart from Chloe or Sam.

'Yes — 'not at liberty to say, but no, it wasn't Chloe.' There are only two others who knew: Donna, and you. Donna would not have involved the police early on because she knows what it means. That leaves you.'

'I didn't make any allegations.'

'You didn't believe me about the texts at first, practically accused me of being a paedophile, then seemed to believe me. I bet you were planning to tell PC Bishop even then. You lied to me and you betrayed me. I can't have a relationship with someone who doesn't trust me. Your paranoia is wearing me down. That's it; we're finished. I shall be moving out as soon as is practicable.'

'No. I swear. I didn't. It must have been Chloe stirring things up. Attention-seeking, that's what.'

'I don't believe you.'

'Well, thanks. You're prating on about trust and in the next sentence you're calling me a liar. How dare you.'

'Exactly; that's why this must end. I love

243

you, or I thought I did, but maybe it's all a sham.' Luke's lower lip trembled. He turned away.

'It's not. I love you and I believed you. I never said anything to the police. Why won't you believe me?'

'Because it doesn't make sense. I'll start packing right now, and move back to Mum and Dad's until I find somewhere else to live . . . '

'No. Please no.' Amy's voice caught. 'Even if you don't believe me, please don't move out. If you do, there's no reason why I shouldn't move downstairs, which would leave the bedroom spare, and Bernard could move in permanently, and I don't trust him, I don't trust him one bit. And Aunty needs the rent money and I bet Bernard won't pay any.'

'OK, I'll stay for your aunt's sake, but the relationship's over as far as I'm concerned. I'll pass the time of day if we meet and so on, be civilised . . . ' He turned, unlocked the door and went outside, but not before Amy had seen tears dewing his eyelashes. She locked the door behind him, the room dissolved in front of her and she fled to her bedroom.

23

Later, in the weary aftermath that comes after a good cry and a troubled night's sleep, Amy realised that Chloe could have told anyone about her silly texts, any of her friends, to share the laugh, to big herself up. And any of those friends could have told a parent, who could have seen things very differently and thought it a matter for the police; and PC Bishop as neighbourhood officer was well known, the ideal person to have a quiet, unofficial word with . . .

If she had been thinking straight she would have thought of this last night. If Luke had been thinking straight, he would never have blamed her. In the cool of morning she had a long think about herself, a long think about Luke, and whether her distrust was spoiling any chance of a good relationship. She sat up. 'I ought to do a SWOT analysis on him,' she said aloud. She grabbed a sheet of paper and wrote:

Strengths.
After the dodgy start he seems honest,
evidenced by the way he went back when

the bill was wrong at the pub.

He's utterly gorgeous.

He's only ever acted honourably.

He's not pushing himself on me and seems to respect me. Unlike Gareth.

Weaknesses

He's a man and men are untrustworthy. No, that's not entirely fair. OK: Men are only after sex.

He didn't reply to my texts and his excuse was a bit feeble.

Opportunities

He's here, in a separate flat, but not far away. That's almost too good an opportunity. I expect that's why I haven't dared go into the flat now it's his space, and we have to meet on my territory or neutral territory. Fear — that's a weakness. I'm afraid to give my heart after Gareth, that's what it is. But that's a weakness on my part, not Luke's. And now I'm getting muddled because I've written this under the wrong heading.

Threats.

Bernard. Now why did B immediately spring to mind? Surely Gareth is a threat? Maybe not, not anymore. He was. He was the biggest threat, but only because I'm allowing it. I need to be stronger. Take more risks.

Gill, gorgeous Gill. She's a threat. But again, it's me that's turning her into a threat because of my suspicious mind, and my mind is suspicious because of Gareth, and Gareth's only a threat because I allow it. So if Gareth isn't a threat, Gill isn't a threat. I have to learn to trust people again. So it's logical that I should trust Luke and risk falling in love with him.

Oh, it seems awful to use a SWOT analysis on a relationship. Love should be the province of the heart, not the head. My heart has been saying for a long time what my head is now telling me.

I love him.

* * *

When she went into the upstairs kitchen to make a cup of tea, Bernard was rifling through the fridge. He brought out a carton of orange juice, one of those she took with her on school days. He'd previously been told they were reserved for that, so that she didn't run out unexpectedly, but he seemed to have forgotten. He grinned at her. 'Good morning, Precious.' He seemed sleekly self-satisfied.

'Morning Bernard.'

'Uncle Bernard to you.'

'Not now. Now you're just plain Bernard.'

The upstairs kitchen was too small for the both of them so Amy went downstairs, made herself a coffee and went outside to contemplate the view. She heard the French windows open and turned to see Luke in his dressing gown and pyjamas coming out onto the terrace.

'Morning, darling.' His face fell. 'Morning, ex-darling.' His hair was standing on end and she yearned to smooth it down. His cheeks pale and there were bags under his red eyes.

'I've been thinking,' said Amy, and she told him those thoughts (but not the SWOT analysis — that was plain embarrassing).

She felt a stab of fury when he looked dubious and said, 'Um,' in a non-committal way.

'Whatever happened to innocent until proven guilty?' she snapped, picked up her mug and walked down the garden path. The fallen leaves were yellow and russet, speckling the garden, and there was a distinct chill in the air. When she turned back Luke had disappeared.

★ ★ ★

It was late afternoon when Amy's phone went. It was Luke. 'Can you come and see me at the park? I think we need to talk, and to coin a phrase, 'walls have ears'.'

'Luke, I have a shop to run now. I can't just shut it and rush off.'

'Debbie can mind the shop if she's feeling up to it. Or even Bernard, if it comes to that.'

'I am not having him anywhere near my business. But I'll ask Debbie. I'll call you back.'

★ ★ ★

'This is ridiculous,' said Amy, shivering as Luke approached the bench she was sitting on. The sun was setting and the air was chilly. 'I can't stay long. Debbie is keeping shop, but I don't want to tire her out.'

Luke sat down beside her, close, but not close enough. 'I know. Thanks for coming. I wanted to chat to you without Bernard being able to overhear, for definite.'

'And you think this is any better? It's getting dark. Anyone could sneak up on us. Aren't you getting a bit paranoid?'

'Yes. Just like you.' He swallowed. 'I think I've been a bit of a fool, Amy. I jumped to conclusions. You're right, that girl could have told any of her friends. And I've been thinking too. Maybe Bernard overheard and thought it a good way to get rid of me.'

'But we made sure he was nowhere near.'

'True. I must be wrong about that, then.' Luke shrugged and Amy felt his hand tentatively take hers. 'I'm so sorry I acted like that. I was really frightened for my job. If I'd been arrested, been formally investigated, I could kiss my career goodbye, even if the claims were unsubstantiated, because that investigation would be on my CRB record.'

'But that's not fair if you're exonerated. How come?'

'Two applicants for a job, one has a clean CRB record, the other has been arrested on suspicion of improper behaviour. Everything else equal, who are you going to employ? And there are good reasons for keeping such arrests on record, now, because predators do pick jobs where they get access to children, and people know there's something not quite right about them but don't have proof. Children need protection, but it's tough if there's a false allegation.'

Amy thought back to the field trip when Donna had told her about the teacher who had lost his career due to a possibly malicious allegation, and thought back to the way Luke had glowed with enthusiasm and knowledge, lighting up those around him, kindling the interest of the children. He was a born teacher. 'Well, I was just as bad, thinking for even one minute you were having an illegal relationship with . . . that girl. I don't think I've been very sensible or thinking straight lately. And Bernard is a real thorn in the flesh. I feel so stressed out just now.'

'What does Bernard do for a living? He always seems to have loads of money.'

'Successful investments, he says. I don't know.' Amy's fingers closed round Luke's, the warmth of them sending shivers through her. 'I love you and I was devastated when you said you were going. Quite apart from anything else, I feel a bit marginalized and beleaguered with Bernard there. He's taking over and Debbie seems to have forgiven the terrible way he treated her. I can see why too. There are times when I think back very fondly to when I was small and he was my beloved uncle. Sometimes it's like nothing's changed, and I find myself liking him a lot, then he does something selfish or gets on my nerves. He was furious about the bookshop, and that makes me think we're right about him having a hidden agenda. I . . . I'm frightened.'

'You know what I think?' said Luke in a contemplative tone. 'I think we should still look as if we're a bit frosty with each other

251

and you should pretend to be taken in by him. I think we're fighting a guerrilla war here.'

'I'm not sure I could do that, not when all I want to do when I'm with you is hold hands, hug, kiss. And I think we might be getting a bit paranoid. Maybe Bernard is OK, maybe he *was* ill, maybe his coming back is the best thing that happened to Aunty Debbie. I don't want to ruin her happiness.'

'True. Let's get back and relieve your aunty from her bookshop duties. I'm beginning to freeze solid here.' Luke stood, pulled her to her feet, kissed her ardently, and they turned for home.

★　★　★

When they got back to the bookshop, Debbie gave them a relieved smile. 'It's been so busy I've had to rope Bernard in. I think you might need to employ someone, just for the busy periods like Saturdays. Apparently Bob Brown the stationmaster is suggesting to people to come here if they've a long wait for a train, hence the sudden influx. People love sitting down for a coffee and a read.' The hallway lights lit her from behind, her new hair a faint nimbus, making her seem slightly otherworldly.

'I hope we can afford it.' Amy took her coat off and went to wash her hands. 'If we're not careful we'll end up spending more on wages than we bring in from books and beverages.'

Later, when they'd closed, she was eating supper with Luke. 'What is the arrangement with Debbie? Do you mind me asking?' he said.

'As owner of the property I should pay her a rent but she's a 50% shareholder so theoretically we share the work and the profit. She's right about help just now, while she's still undergoing treatment, and she says she's going to advertise for a Saturday helper. I think we can afford it, especially if we take on a young person. Debbie will sort that while I think about how to replenish the shelves without paying out more than we earn from selling the books. I'm going to look through the paper because people often sell a box of books quite cheaply, and car boot fairs ditto, especially at the end of the day. Alison's pleased because their sales of sandwiches at lunchtime are up, too. It's looking good, but it's early days yet.'

* * *

Amy and Luke were at a car boot fair when Debbie hired a Saturday helper. When Amy saw whom Aunty Debbie had employed she felt the blood drain from her face, and Luke looked as if he'd been slapped. Sam blenched when she saw them. 'I didn't know it was your shop, Miss Oldham,' she said. Her eyes flicked to Luke. 'Does this mean I don't get the job after all?'

'Nothing to do with me,' said Luke, and he stalked off to his rooms.

'I'm not friends with Chloe anymore, Miss,' Sam added in a whisper. 'And I need this job.'

'I don't see that we can go back on our word,' said Amy. 'But working here shouldn't be the subject of gossiping with your friends.'

'I don't have any friends, Miss — only Chloe, and we're not friends now, not after . . . They all think I'm a geek.' Sam said this straightforwardly and without a trace of self-pity. Amy thought back to the field trip and to the tutorials. It was true; nobody but Chloe showed Sam any interest. Amy had an enormous rush of sympathy for the child. She was bright, very bright, and that tended to isolate her from the other children. That could ruin her self-esteem. She needed this job, and not just for the money.

'Let me show you around, teach you the hygiene rules, and show you what needs doing.'

Once Sam had got into the swing of what was needed, Amy was able to forget any previous history between them. Sam was biddable, hard-working, well-mannered and intelligent. No wonder Debbie had given her the job.

Luke wasn't so easy to convince. 'Is your aunt having a subtle go at me? Rubbing my nose into my recent brush with the law by deliberately giving the job to that girl?' he ground out between his teeth. 'Because if she is, she's succeeding.' He was pale, trembling even.

'Now who's being paranoid?' said Amy. 'Of course not. It's a coincidence. Debbie doesn't know about the Chloe situation — it's confidential — so how could she possibly know how awkward it is to employ Sam? She did it unknowingly, and you're being oversensitive. And we can't tell her even now, can we? Because it's still confidential.'

Luke let his breath out in a huge gust, and Amy saw his expression turn from tense anger to calmer acceptance. 'You're right, I am a fool,' he said.

★ ★ ★

Over the next couple of weeks Amy was busy with the shop's paperwork and pricing up

255

books when she wasn't busy with her MA studies, and Luke was busy marking and preparing for lessons. They sat in the library-cum-coffee shop on the green sofa, after the shop had closed, out of the way of Bernard. Even though it was now busy during the day, it felt like Amy's private space in the evening.

Bernard seemed to vanish every weekend, visiting his cousin in Stockport, which was a relief as far as Amy was concerned. Saturdays were the busiest days and Debbie was doing quite a bit of work, mainly working on the till where she could sit down all the time. Sam served the coffee, which Amy insisted on making.

Gill came in for coffee sometimes and bought the occasional book, as well as visiting Debbie as her Macmillan nurse. Customers often donated books they no longer wanted. Amy's Friday morning tutor group decamped to her shop and they had their session before the shop opened at 2.00pm. The shop was profitable enough to cover Sam's wages as well as give Amy and Debbie a healthy profit.

Mid-December, Debbie started her radio-therapy three times a week, and she insisted that Bernard take her in. Amy was torn, feeling both that she was letting her aunt down, and relieved that she didn't have to give up so much of her time. Though the treatment only took a couple of minutes, they had to be there for quite a large part of the day — time when she could be working or studying.

★ ★ ★

'Bernard, that's my café coffee, not household coffee, and café milk. You know you're not supposed to use it. The stuff you can use is upstairs in Aunty Debbie's kitchen. You could even consider buying some of your own coffee, perhaps.' Amy thought she sounded shrewish, but this wasn't the first time she'd found Bernard pilfering company coffee.

'Young Luke nicks it; why shouldn't I?'

Luke abruptly entered the kitchen through the back door. 'I heard that. I do not. How can I? You take that back.' He glared at Bernard.

'You just remember your place, young man. You're the lodger, nothing more.' Bernard blithely walked out with a steaming mug of coffee.

'Honestly, Amy, I think you should lock the kitchen door,' muttered Luke. ''Remember my place' indeed.'

'Good idea,' said Amy. 'I keep losing little things and it's getting annoying.'

Amy, lying in bed reading, heard Debbie's squeal all the way from the lounge, then Debbie knocked on her bedroom door and burst in. 'Your mum's emailed. They'll be over for a week at Christmas and need us to put them up. I'm so excited.'

Amy's heart soared. 'Brilliant. But where are we going to put them?'

Debbie thought for a minute. 'Isn't it about time you shared Luke's bed?' she said with a mischievous gleam in her eye.

'Aunty Debbie, that's an outrageous suggestion. We've only been going out for a few weeks.' As she said this Amy wondered if it was such an outrageous suggestion. The thought of sharing Luke's bed was actually a very nice one, one which sent her heart thundering and the blood rushing to her cheeks.

'But if you did, Pat and Tom could sleep in your room, and the twins could camp in the lounge.'

'Or the cellar,' said Amy with a wicked grin.

'Or the attic. We could make one of the attic rooms habitable perhaps, by moving some of the clutter into the cellar or cramming it into the other attic room.'

Amy laughed. 'Horsehair mattress and all. But there's only one bed.'

'Becky can have that, and Ben can have an airbed. Oh, how wonderful, a full house for Christmas.'

'And where am I going to sleep? I'm not quite ready for Luke's bed yet.'

'The green settee in the library — I mean bookshop, perhaps? Or you have the horsehair bed and the twins can camp out on the floor. That's the best idea . . . you can have fun as siblings together.'

24

It was half past nine in the morning, the Saturday before Christmas. Amy was in her bedroom making her bed when she heard a noise in her room. Puzzled, she turned and looked. Nothing. She heard the French windows swing open and Luke say, 'Sam, what on earth are you doing, knocking on my doors like that and capering round like a mad thing? Don't you realise my space is private?'

'I know, but I had to talk to you and ask your advice. It's important.' The words were so clear that Sam and Luke could have been standing in Amy's bedroom. The window was open because Amy always opened her window wide to air the room first thing. Amy went over and listened as Sam continued, 'That man Bernard, who's always with Mrs Driscoll; I'm not sure he's quite what he says he is. He doesn't know me well, and I was out with my mum in the supermarket café, eating a meal, and I heard his voice . . . He was sitting at a table with a coffee, on the phone to someone called Alma, and he's all lovey-dovey with her

— says it won't be long, to have patience, and he loves her, stuff like that. It's like he's talking to a girlfriend ... at his age. But when I've seen him with Mrs Driscoll he's all over her like a rash. And it seems really odd, but I didn't like to tell Amy about it because she's her aunty and it's not like it's my business or anything. But I thought someone should know. What do you think I should do?'

Amy leaned out of the window. 'Do me a favour you two ... whisper something to each other.'

Luke and Sam jumped as if she'd hit them. Luke said, 'OK,' leaned towards Sam and said, 'You did the right thing.'

'Good,' replied Sam. Amy heard everything clearly, including Sam describing Bernard as a scumbag. 'I'm coming down,' said Amy with an anxious glance at the clock.

When she'd joined then she said, 'Sam, you were right to tell us, but don't mention it to Debbie, please. And please keep your ears open for anything like that. It's much appreciated but utterly confidential. We might tell you more when Mr Armitage and I have discussed it. But now we need to open up shop.'

Later Amy told Luke about the window. 'I should have remembered,' she said. 'It's like an amphitheatre. Anyone standing in my room would overhear anything said in a normal voice on the terrace.'

'But who would be in your room? That's private.'

'Debbie might, I suppose, though she tends to respect my space. But you know Bernard's dreadful aftershave? It was only faint, but I noticed it in my room the evening we discussed Chloe on the terrace. I thought it had just seeped in, he uses so much of it, and the bathroom reeks of it. Now I think Bernard was snooping in my room, overheard the conversation about Chloe and reported you to the police as a means of getting rid of you, just as you suspected.'

* * *

On Sunday Luke helped get the attic room ready for Amy and the twins. Some stuff was carried all the way down the stairs to the cellar, and the attic room was aired and made habitable. 'That's odd,' said Amy. 'Where are the Tiffany lamps?'

'I swear they were up here,' said Debbie. 'They were in that old display cabinet because they're valuable, and now they've gone. I think we've had a sneaky burglary; I think I'll talk to PC Bishop.'

She went to email the police officer — residents often emailed their neighbourhood constable with information or for advice. Amy and Luke turned to each other and mouthed, 'Bernard?'

When PC Bishop came round they couldn't tell her when the lamps had last been seen. And that yes, sometimes the front door wasn't locked. PC Bishop said she'd send a scenes of crime officer round to see if there were fingerprints on the display cabinet and that she'd give them a crime number to put on the insurance claim. 'Mind you,' she added as a Parthian shot, 'they might be reluctant to pay up if the premises were insecure.'

'Well really,' snapped Debbie when PC Bishop had gone, 'If they don't I shall be furious, as I've shelled out loads to them over the years and never claimed anything. They should cover lapses of remembering to lock the doors as well as break-in burglaries. Insurance companies! Bah!'

★   ★   ★

Luke dumped the scuttle of coal next to the range. Amy was getting the cups ready for the café. 'Mind you don't make too much dust,' she said.

'Did you move the old struts?' asked Luke. 'The ones which were part of the old banister and broke that time? There were in a heap near the steps down into the cellar, remember?'

'No. Why would I?'

'I thought maybe you'd brought them up for kindling.'

'Good idea, but no.'

'Odd — I swear they were there yesterday, but you know how it is with things; you don't notice something when it's there, just when it's gone. And then you can't remember when you last saw it. Not enough to swear by, anyway.'

Amy followed Luke back down into the cellar. 'Maybe someone's just had a tidy-up.'

'If so, it must be Bernard . . . Now why would he suddenly want to get rid of the struts he weakened that time? Evidence, perhaps? There were some screws on the floor too. I can't find those either.' He snooped around, then suddenly brightened. 'He missed the strut I put to one side absentmindedly when I first came down here. I'm taking this into safe-keeping in my rooms.' He held up the two bits of wood like a prize exhibit.

★　★　★

Amy knocked on Luke's French windows. 'Tell me I'm not going mad,' she said. 'Come and have a look at this, please?' She led him all the way up to the attic. 'You remember these boxes of clutter that were in the front room?' She indicated the boxes of half-sorted study junk. 'When I was getting the bookshop ready in a hurry, we decided to shove these boxes up here for Debbie to sort at her leisure. Remember what was on the top of this box?'

Luke's eyes flicked wide. 'The old policy insuring Debbie's life, the one with the enormous payout?'

'Yeah. I suddenly remembered it when Debbie said 'insurance' in that angry tone. I thought I'd see if there was any way I could check if it's still active, after what young Sam said, because I'm getting very suspicious . . . but it's gone.'

'Maybe your aunt has tidied it away or thrown it.'

'Maybe, but why just tidy the one thing and leave the rest of the box unsorted? Maybe Bernard took it.'

'What do you mean about suspicious?' Luke leaned closer to her. 'Because I've always had a bad feeling about that accident in the cellar. If Debbie had been killed then, Bernard would have been rolling in it. And do you know if your aunt's stomach problems were properly diagnosed, or did the GP just say it was IBS?'

Amy frowned for a good couple of minutes, searching her memories. 'I don't know about the IBS, to be honest, though I don't remember anything about her going into hospital for tests. I do remember Mum moaning to Dad about useless GPs though, because he'd just told her to eat more wholemeal bread, and it didn't help. And, now you mention it, I seem to remember Mum saying that Debbie should have had a proper investigation. But it's too long ago to be sure. It's only snippets that I overheard.'

'Do you remember when the stomach troubles started?'

'Not really.'

'Before or after the cellar incident?'

'After, I think, because apparently the doctor had told her that stress could bring on symptoms of IBS. I think he was a useless GP and I'm so glad he's retired and Debbie has a less misogynist one.'

'And as soon as Bernard shoved off, the symptoms disappeared?'

'Not exactly, I don't think. Shortly afterwards, but that might be because she was more upset about him running away and the IBS faded away.'

Luke shook his head. 'With something like IBS you'd expect it to get worse with such a stressful situation, not better, surely?'

'What are you saying, Luke? Surely you don't think B was giving her a slow poison?' As she said it, Amy began to wonder. Maybe Luke was right. But surely nobody was stupid enough to try and poison Debbie; it would obviously be murder and he would be a prime suspect.

'I don't know. I doubt it. I just think it's a bit odd, that's all, especially the cellar incident. How come she tripped in the first place?'

'Bernard couldn't have pushed her, because he was away.'

'How convenient. It wouldn't take much to make the steps slippery; a bit of sand, perhaps. A thread of cotton across the top step.'

'But that would have been found.'

'Not if Bernard had come back to find the tragedy, too late for Debbie. He'd have removed any evidence before phoning for an ambulance — except that Debbie didn't die, and Alison's mum found her in time. And now Bernard's back. You don't suppose . . . '

'I don't know. But unless the life policy is still active, he's not likely to gain anything if Debbie dies, because the house isn't willed to him as far as I know . . . I think it would go to Mum. Besides, it's not easy to murder someone and get away with it, is it? Tell me I'm just being silly.'

'You're not being silly but I really don't see what we can do about it. It's not as if we have concrete evidence, is it?'

25

'They're here!' squealed Amy as the taxi drew up and her family spilled onto the street. Luke helped with the luggage. The café wasn't very busy just then so Amy left Sam in sole charge for twenty minutes while she greeted her family upstairs. Blissfully, Bernard was absent, visiting his cousin, though he would be back in the evening.

'How was your journey?' asked Debbie.

'Traffic was bad and we're all exhausted. Wish we could have come yesterday and not be so jetlagged for Christmas Day,' said Amy's mother, Pat.

Tom, Amy's father, gave Amy a hug. 'How's my eldest daughter?'

The twins Ben and Becky, stood by nonchalantly, pretending they weren't that bothered, that they were cool about it all. Amy looked at them with sudden shyness. They'd grown in the last few months; changed subtly. It might be down to the clothes they were wearing or the slight change in mannerisms. *We mustn't grow away from each other*, Amy thought with a sudden panic, giving them both a hug. But even that was wrong; six months ago she'd have greeted Ben with a mock wrestling match. 'Cool,' she said, for lack of anything better to say. Then she added, 'I'd better get back to the café. No, we don't need you, Debbie, thanks. Luke's helping now he's brought the cases up.'

In a lull in the café, Luke asked, 'Are you sure I should stay to Christmas dinner? Don't you want to be just family? I'm getting pangs of conscience over Mum and Dad, though they're off to my gran's for Christmas Day.'

'You'll be going home for Boxing Day, so it's not as if they won't see you, and I'd like you here, especially if beastly Bernard is going to be here. Besides, I want you to meet my family properly and it's not easy to do that with them across the pond.'

'OK, so long as you're sure. But I'll leave you to your family this evening.'

★ ★ ★

'He's really hot,' said Becky into the darkness.

'Have you had sex with him yet?' asked Ben.

'Mind your own business, but no,' said Amy. 'For goodness sake, go to sleep.' The old bed wasn't uncomfortable, surprisingly enough. She'd bought a memory-foam mattress topper quite reasonably, put it in a duvet cover, and was lying on that under another duvet. The horsehair mattress itself she'd covered with an anti-dust mite cover and it kept rustling. Ben and Becky were on airbeds in sleeping bags. The years melted away and it was as if they were in their early teens again.

Next morning they found Christmas stockings hanging on the attic door. They opened them together, then the twins went back to sleep. Luke texted, 'Happy Xmas. Can I come in for coffee, pls', so Amy sneaked downstairs and let him in. He looked altogether scrumptious. Amy greeted him with a hug and a kiss. 'Happy Christmas.'

'Happy Christmas. Was the Christmas stocking your idea?' His eyes were dancing with laughter. 'It was hanging on the French windows.'

'You got one too? Must be Debbie, then. Just the sort of thing she'd do.'

'I'm touched. What's the timetable for today? I mean, what's happening?'

'Aunty will be up soon to get the turkey on. The men go and dig up leeks and parsnips, pick spouts and so on, and get the table ready while the women sort the food out. Church for those who want to. Back for pressies, then dinner about 2 o'clock. Actually, I think I'll nip up and put the turkey in the oven, since it's bigger than usual. And I think we'll peel the veg down here to keep out of people's way.'

★ ★ ★

Amy was thrilled with her presents that her parents had brought back from America. They hadn't brought Luke anything, being unaware he would be there, but Debbie had, and of course Amy had, so he wasn't missed out. He had brought small gifts for everyone, even Bernard, for whom he had bought a small bottle of some decent aftershave. ('Ulterior motive in that,' he'd told Amy with a wink when he bought it.)

The turkey was perfect, the ham was delicious, the various types of stuffing worked well, and the vegetables were a feast in themselves. Bernard moaned that being a diabetic he had to be careful, and made Becky squirm when he talked about injecting himself with insulin. 'Eww, that's gross,' she said. Amy silently agreed.

Bernard had provided the wine, and had chosen well, and everyone was feeling replete and contented when Debbie said, 'By the way, Bernard and I are going to get

272

remarried. We realise we still love each other.'

'Yes,' agreed Bernard. 'I was a fool and I've seen the error of my ways.'

'When?' squeaked Amy. The blood was pounding in her head, mixing horribly with the wine. She grabbed the table to steady herself.

'Early in the new year, not sure of the date yet,' said Debbie. 'We have to sort the legalities.'

'We've had a little chat,' said Bernard, 'and we think it would be better if you stayed in the attic room, Amy; make it your own. Then I can move into the spare room until the wedding — observe the proprieties, don't you think?'

'No,' said Luke. 'That's not fair on Amy. That's her bedroom. You sleep in the attic. Or better still, stay in The Shoulder of Mutton.'

'How dare you? It's not your place to dictate,' thundered Bernard.

'Bernard can't afford to stay there any longer,' reasoned Debbie.

'You've got a damned cheek,' said Amy's father. The twins studied their plates and exchanged glances with each other.

'It's all right, Luke; we'll discuss it later,' said Amy, giving him a frown.

'It's not all right. You'll have to go downstairs to the bathroom for a start, and why should you be ousted from your room like that?'

'You are a very rude and impertinent young man,' said Amy's mother. 'It's nothing to do with you.'

Luke swallowed. 'Yes, you're right. What happens to the girl I love dearly has nothing whatsoever to do with me. Letting her family push her around like some bit of excess baggage is none of my business. Now, if you'll excuse me, I think I've intruded enough on your family togetherness.' He wiped his mouth on his napkin, stood, and left the room.

Amy stood as if to go after him. 'Don't you dare,' snarled her father. 'He's shown his colours all right. Callow young oaf.'

The rest of the meal carried on round Amy as if she were in a bubble of isolation. Everyone carried on as if nothing had happened, but Amy knew if she defied her father, it would make the situation worse, far worse.

She managed to escape during coffee, though, and shot down the stairs to Luke's flat. She knocked on the French windows. 'Luke, it's me.' No reply, so she phoned him. 'Luke, I need to talk. I want to have a good cry, and if Dad sees me he'll have a go at me.'

Luke unlocked the door and pulled her in. 'Sorry, I was well out of order. I don't know what came over me; I'm not normally so bad-mannered. I'd even started to apologise, but all that anger and frustration welled up inside me and it came out all wrong, worse than all wrong.'

'Do you really love me?'

'You know I do.' He gave her an ardent kiss to prove it.

'Well, in that case, please try to get on with my family. Dad can be very autocratic and tends to treat me as if I'm still a kid. He and Bernard always got on well, and I even remember him saying to Mum that Bernard probably walked out because Debbie can be a bit hard-hearted.'

'What a preposterous thing to say. Your aunt's lovely.'

'Where business is concerned she can be pretty ruthless, though. Well, not ruthless so much as frighteningly realistic. You need to be, in business. Pity she's not so sensible when it comes to men.'

'I'll pour us a drink, unless you'd rather have coffee,' said Luke. 'Gosh, you're cold.'

'I think I'd rather have a coffee, to be honest. I think I've had enough to drink. Oh Luke, she's going to marry him and we suspect he might be a crook — or worse, a potential murderer. I wish we'd told her of our suspicions before. Now it'll look like we're just trying to stop the marriage for selfish reasons. And I don't think Mum will listen either, not now.'

'I think you're going to have to say something. Why don't you corner your mum and tell her?' He handed her a coffee. 'I hate the idea of you sleeping on that manky old mattress up in the attic while that slimeball uses your room.'

'It's only until the wedding. Oh Luke.' She blinked the tears back.

'Shh, shh now. We'll just have to see if we can find some proof about Alma and see if we can find the missing Tiffany Lamps for sale somewhere. We could start by looking online.'

'I wonder,' said Amy slowly. 'I wonder if his trips to see his Stockport cousin have anything to do with this. And I tell you what: I don't think it's the first time he's nicked stuff.' Amy reminded him about the missing silverware. 'Aunty Debbie just thought she'd put it somewhere else. I'm now pretty sure he nicked that and sold it before he abandoned her.'

'And what about those books you mentioned? Milly Molly Mandy? Maybe . . . Right, I think we try and trace his cousin — find out about him, and see if there's any reference to Bernard on the internet. Time to start playing sneaky.'

★ ★ ★

On Boxing Day, Luke went to stay with his parents for a few days, and Amy's mum and Bernard took Debbie for her radiotherapy, and then went shopping for a wedding outfit for her. Amy started to move her belongings up to the attic room. Her father, after telling her what an unsuitable young man Luke was, snoozed in the armchair in the lounge while the twins surfed online and talked with their friends using Amy's computer.

Amy seemed to be missing one or two items, but she couldn't think what. Her grandmother's rings that she'd inherited had definitely vanished. That upset her because of the sentimental value.

★ ★ ★

Amy's mum paused in her inspection of the garden. Even though it was winter there was quite a bit of interest from old seed heads and grasses. 'I'm glad Luke's gone home because I want to have a serious talk with you, my girl.'

'Well, that's good, because I need to have a serious talk with you. About Bernard. I think he's a crook. Lots of things have disappeared since he arrived out of the blue, including the

Tiffany lamps, which together are worth about £30,000. They vanished when he arrived. As have my rings, and various other odds and ends. Just disappeared. I've caught Bernard sneaking round the house, even in my bedroom. Odd how he just turned up like that, out of the blue, not even a letter from him.'

'We bumped into him in the States. Didn't he say?'

'No.' Amy's mind whirred. 'Did you by any chance tell him about Debbie's cancer?'

'Of course we did. He said how sorry he was to hear that and how he'd always regretted walking out like that. Asked after her, so we told him.'

'So, after all these years he suddenly turns up here all smarmy and apologetic when he learns that Aunty Debbie has a serious illness which might be terminal? Bloodsucker.'

'Amy, that's disgusting.'

'It is disgusting. Of him. Have you forgotten how awful it was when he left Debbie in the lurch like that? And now he comes back like the prodigal son. I never did understand that story. I always felt sorry for the elder brother who worked hard and was diddled. Luke doesn't trust him.'

'Oddly enough Debbie said the same thing to me. About things disappearing. Only the

278

culprit, she thinks, is Luke. She told me how you caught him trespassing that first day, and how things have vanished since then. She told me he's been horrible to Bernard. You both have. Luke's a bad influence on you and I hope you're not thinking of doing anything stupid like marry him.'

'Luke's lovely. Yes, he put his foot in it on Christmas Day, but he was only protecting my interests.'

'Oh was he? Or had he figured that with you living up there it would be harder to pilfer any more stuff? Honestly Amy, I credited you with more common sense, especially after the Gareth fiasco. Your aunt and I have been discussing this and have decided that Luke must move out by the end of January. She's going to give him notice. Then you can have the ground floor as originally planned and Bernard and Debbie can have the upstairs flat, which will give them the privacy they deserve.'

'But Bernard might be worse than a thief,' said Amy, and she explained about the struts and Luke's suspicions.

'Don't be so bloody preposterous,' said her mum. 'These struts disappeared after Luke made you think the whole thing very suspicious, eh? What's to stop him being the one to have brought them up and shoving them on the range, especially as it seems to be his job to bring the coal up? I think he's charmed you out of your common sense, just like Gareth did, then brainwashed you into suspecting Bernard. I know Bernard of old, and though he can be a bit clumsy at times, he means well. Your first introduction to Luke was him inside the house, uninvited, with a book in his hands.'

Amy started thinking, really thinking. With her mum telling her these things, she saw things with a different light. Hadn't she thought Luke a burglar when she caught him in the house with an unlikely story about thinking the bookshop still open? Hadn't he bristled when Bernard turned up? Hadn't he badmouthed Bernard since then, turning Amy from him? Maybe there *was* an ulterior motive. Stuff had disappeared after setting up the coffee morning, which had allowed Luke to poke round the place, seeing what was worth pinching. Luke could have nicked the stuff as easily as Bernard. On the other hand, he didn't have a car, so it would be hard for him to transport items like Tiffany lamps once he stole them, whereas Bernard had that tatty old van and could easily hide booty in that. And when exactly had the silverware vanished?

But what about those dodgy texts from

Chloe, and the fact Luke had Gill's number? He'd had glib explanations for that, and, for that matter, he might have warned Chloe off after thinking he might be found out, rather than because he was innocent. What was to stop him being a handsome bad guy? Bernard was handsome, and she thought him a bad guy. Her old English teacher was handsome, and utterly evil. And what about Gareth? She hadn't shown much discernment there, had she? Maybe she'd picked the wrong person as villain. Maybe her parents and aunt were right.

In the midst of all these suspicions she never got round to asking her mum if Debbie had been properly diagnosed with IBS.

26

Luke swallowed twice when given his notice. 'Could you at least make that half term, please, which would give me more time to find somewhere else and give me time to move my stuff?'

Debbie nodded and said, 'Very well then,' at the same time as Bernard said, 'No.'

'Half term it is, then,' said Debbie, shooting a look at Bernard.

Luke vanished into his flat and Amy didn't dare follow because her father was frowning at her. Instead she went into her bookshop, ostensibly to sort out the shelves while it was closed, but really to get away from the family, who were packing. It seemed awful to be avoiding them when they were only there for a brief time, but the atmosphere was so hostile she couldn't think straight.

When she realised she wasn't doing anything useful, she made a coffee and curled up on the green sofa with her laptop. On her Facebook page Luke had left a message: 'Please come round. I need to talk.'

'When Mum & Dad have gone,' she replied. It was only half the truth. She wanted to think about what her mum had said. She tried thinking back to when she first noticed the silver was missing. Luke was on the scene by then but there was no way he would have had enough time to go down into the cellar and pilfer the silver, hide it and take it away. Bernard, on the other hand, had had months if not years to pilfer the silver and the majolica, and that book they'd found in the cellar must have been his, so he would have known what was valuable.

Luke didn't have access to the main part of the house, whereas Bernard had free rein over every part, and was there at times when both she and Luke were at school. Debbie still spent a lot of time resting. It would be far easier for Bernard to pinch anything and hide it in that van of his.

Bernard had an annoying habit of making free with her coffee. Luke had gone back to pay for coffees that had been overlooked when they were in west Wales. Bernard was always snooping through her things. The Milly Molly Mandy books had never resurfaced.

How come Bernard was apparently so wealthy when previously he'd been such a dork with money? Was it all a lie?

And who the heck was this Alma?

Amy started browsing, looking for the

items she knew were missing, but she drew a blank.

★ ★ ★

A mantle of melancholy settled over Amy as her family put their cases into the taxi. She was expecting a last-minute lecture from her father about Luke, but in the end he just hugged her and told her to take care, and not to do anything he wouldn't do.

'Look after Aunty Debbie for me,' said her mum quietly as they embraced.

'I will, I promise.'

She hugged the twins goodbye and this time it felt right, as if they'd grown up in the space of a week. Perhaps they wondered when they'd see her next.

With a final round of hugs with Debbie and Bernard, they were in the taxi and driving away. Amy found her face was wet. She knew they meant well, but the rancour had soured the holidays, and she felt that everything had changed, shifted, so that she was no longer so secure in their love, so sure of their support.

Debbie buried her face in Bernard's shoulder. Her own were shaking. Bernard held her close and murmured comforting platitudes at her.

Amy slipped away quietly. She couldn't face anyone, not even Luke. Not yet.

★ ★ ★

Luke was in his rooms looking at flat lettings online when Amy went round. Her eyes were sore and she felt like a well-wrung dishcloth.

Luke said nothing but gazed at her as if to determine whose side she was on. She fell into his arms. 'It's not fair,' she said, eyes welling up. 'It's not fair.'

'It'll work out all right in the end, you'll see,' said Luke, kissing her forehead, holding her tight to him. 'We'll just have to go with the flow. There's nothing else we can do.'

'If I'm to have these rooms, what's to stop you staying with me?' said Amy impulsively.

'Pride. And actually, I don't think your Aunt will be too pleased. Besides, if Bernard and I are under the same roof, sooner or later murder will be done.'

'Luke, I'm frightened . . . ' She told him that, far from turning up as the unknowing prodigal, unaware of Debbie's illness as he'd implied, Bernard had been fully cognisant of the situation. 'I think he's marrying her for the house. I think he thinks she's going to die.'

'He's a fool then. She's not going to die; the doctors are delighted with her response to the chemo.'

'But he didn't know that when he came over. At first the news was a bit . . . well, iffy, though nobody liked to say it.'

'But it depends on her will, if he inherits or not.'

'Which will be annulled when she marries again and has to be redrawn, or he inherits automatically, I think. I don't know for sure.'

'But she's not likely to die. Not now. And you've said yourself how she's so much happier now he's back.'

'Yes, but he's a con man. He's good at manipulating people.'

Luke stared blankly at the computer screen for a couple of minutes before saying, 'I think . . . I think we should tell Gill about all this. She's sensible, and she's good at keeping things confidential. Why don't you say you feel unsettled by everything and can she offer you some counselling, and then tell her in confidence?'

Amy was about to say no, but changed her mind. 'Maybe I could see her when Bernard has taken Debbie to radiotherapy — it's her last week, thank goodness. Maybe you and I could see her together. She might think I've gone nuts otherwise.'

Gill listened gravely to everything Amy and Luke had to say, but then she shook her head sadly. 'Ethically speaking, there's nothing I can do about this. This is so difficult because I can see exactly what you're driving at, but it's way outside my brief to interfere. All I can do is advise Debbie to take things slowly for at least a couple of weeks after the radiotherapy has ended. This is advice I have already given her because the side-effects from radiotherapy actually continue to get worse before they get better after the last treatment. So for her sake I can advise she gets all the rest she can, no excitement. But that only gives you a breathing space. Maybe you can find evidence of wrongdoing in the meantime, but it would have to be pretty convincing to persuade Debbie. Another thing; just how reliable is this young lady and her talk of Alma?'

Amy and Luke exchanged a glance of consternation. Good thought — was Sam reliable?

'I know you're worried, but . . . well, I couldn't be involved.' Gill paused as if thinking hard, then added, 'Not really. It's not ethical.'

'I understand,' said Amy. *But it's for Aunty*

Debbie's sake; she's being taken in by a con man! she felt like screaming. 'Aunty's very vulnerable at the moment,' she added, 'despite her verve and good spirits. I think she'll be glad when the treatment is over and she can get on with her life. She says she's stopped looking in the mirror because that's not her . . . ' Amy shocked herself by starting to cry.

'I know,' said Gill soothingly. 'It's a tough six months or so — tough on everyone, not just the patient, though of course it's the patient who feels it most. I'm glad you've spoken to me, because you need help and support too. Do you think you're jealous of Bernard? Is that part of the problem, partly the reason why you find it hard to accept this marriage?'

'I resented him barging in like that, and yes, he sort of took over everything. He deprived me of my caring role, but that's not the reason I'm worried. Or at least, I don't think that's the reason.'

Gill looked at her with wise eyes and said nothing.

27

'Aaaagh, I don't believe it,' said Amy staring at the blank blue screen of her computer. It was Saturday, halfway through January, and it was very quiet in the café, so quiet that Debbie was working on some book-keeping upstairs and Amy was trying to get on with some MA work. Bernard was visiting his cousin.

Amy was tired because she'd not been sleeping well; the attic was chilly and creaky, with strange scurrying noises. She hated it, despite trying to imagine stories about Between-Maids or Maids-of-all-work. She hated the thought of moving into the ground-floor rooms even more because of what it meant to Luke. She was behind with her studies. It was hard to concentrate.

Debbie, when asked when the wedding would be, had just given an enigmatic smile and said they'd find out when the time came. And now Amy's computer had seized up. She felt like throwing it across the room.

'What's up?' asked Sam.

Amy was very restrained in her language as she told Sam. 'BSOD.'

'Mind if I take a look?' said Sam.

'Be my guest,' said Amy. 'I'm beginning to hate that heap of junk.'

Five minutes later the computer was up and running again. 'I think it's that upgrade that's causing the problem. You've got a software conflict. I think I've sorted it. And, please tell me you back up your work . . . '

'Why, have I lost stuff?' asked Amy in a panic.

'Not yet, but suppose your hard drive went wrong . . . '

'Oh, well; I'm not sure how to do it.'

'Right, well that's another thing to sort out, isn't it? You must back your work up.' Sam went on to make some recommendations.

Amy felt quite told off by this sixteen-year-old. 'Thanks. I'm impressed. Maybe you should get a job at a computer shop.'

'I tried,' Sam said frankly. 'I want to do computer forensics as a career. But there weren't any jobs going, so I applied for this one.' She looked grave. 'I know it's been a bit awkward, with — you know, but I really like working here. I'll be sad to leave.'

'Leave?'

'Mr Murray told me he was taking over in the café and that my services were no longer required.'

'No. No, I'm not having this. No way. How

dare he! He can't. The business is nothing to do with him.'

'Is it true he's going to marry Mrs Driscoll?' Sam fiddled with the mouse but clicked nothing.

'Sam, how far can I trust you, really trust you to keep very quiet about things?'

'Utterly, Miss. I learned my lesson and I feel I owe you. You took me on trust despite what happened and you treat me like an adult — like a sister, even, so yeah . . . ' Sam seemed to run out of words. Her flushed face said the rest, though. 'I'd like to help.'

'OK, yes, Mrs Driscoll is going to marry Bernard, and I am dead against it because of the sort of thing you've just told me. Bernard does not have any say in the café because it's a limited company and only Mrs Driscoll and I are directors. He's got nothing to do with it and he had no right to give you notice, so you keep your job, OK?' Amy watched Sam's face relax slightly, but the troubled expression remained, and now Sam's eyes were full of questions, so Amy continued. 'He's got nothing to do with the café yet, but I fear that if they get married it won't be long before he's interfering with everything, including this. How dare he. I don't trust him, so what I need to know is who this Alma is. I'd also like to trace a couple of Tiffany lamps and

291

various other items which have vanished from the house. I need an address for his cousin in Stockport, who I suspect might be linked to these items disappearing. And I need to obtain these in an above-board and not illegal manner, and at the same time run a café bookshop, and do my MA. Do you think you can help in any way? I can't lead you astray, but I'm not sure I'm using the computer search engines in the best way possible. I must stress that any help you can give me must be legal.'

'Oh I'm good at that,' said Sam, eyes gleaming. 'It sounds like fun.'

'Right, campaign meeting with Mr Armitage after the café closes. We'll tell you what we know and what we're afraid of.'

*   *   *

'Are you sure that was wise?' said Luke once the 'campaign briefing' was over and Sam had gone home.

'Yes. I really like her. I feel so sorry for her because she's very bright, highly intelligent, and the girl has style, real style. That marks her out as weird and geeky and a right old Billy-No-Mates. So she sort of got picked up by Chloe the airhead, also a Billy-No-Mates because she's got a cruel streak and hurts people. So Sam tries to impress everyone, including Chloe, by being tiresomely witty. Now she's not under Chloe's influence the real Sam is shining through, and I can see a girl of ardent loyalty and a fair amount of common sense. After all, she put her place in the school on the line by bursting into Donna's office like that and confessing to what she'd done. So yes, treated the right way, I trust her. Besides, if Bernard marries Aunty Debbie, he'll get rid of Sam. I also think he'll get rid of me. He's already succeeded in ousting you. Talking of which, have you found anywhere else yet?'

Luke scowled. 'No. Looks like back to Mum and Dad's.'

Amy slid her arm around him and hugged, as he looked so despondent. 'Cheer up; it can't be that bad.'

'You haven't met my dad,' he quipped. 'Seriously, though; I love my parents, but it's hard. They have their routines and foibles, and I have mine. Dad even told me off once for folding the inner bag of the cereal packet the wrong way.'

★　★　★

The days slipped past with no progress in the 'campaign.' Amy continued to look online,

293

scanning the auction house lists for Tiffany lamps and for the items she thought were missing; her rings in particular rankled. But she found nothing.

One good thing to be cheerful about was that Debbie had got over the worst of the radiotherapy, and was looking better than she had for months. Looking at her with her cute curly hair, at first glance you would never know she'd had breast cancer. And she seemed happy, so happy. Amy cringed because she feared that happiness was all a sham; and worse, Amy would be the one to burst the bubble.

Luke kept out of Debbie and Bernard's way.

★ ★ ★

Amy glared at Bernard. 'I don't want you helping, thank you very much. I have all the help I need in Sam,' she said through a stiff jaw.

'I gave that girl her marching orders.' Bernard frowned. 'Some things need to change round here.'

'Yes, like you shoving back off to Canada would be a good idea. You're not to interfere with my business. I like Sam, and she's working for me, not you. You had no right to try to sack her, none whatsoever. You've got a damned cheek. You can't even remember to use the right sink to wash your hands. You're a liability and you're not to interfere.'

'We'll see about that, young woman. Your aunty is in love with me and when we're married things will change round here.' He turned on his heel and went upstairs.

Sam watched, cowering in the kitchen. 'Shall I leave? Would it make your life easier?'

'No, please don't, Sam. I know it's a bit hard, but I feel beleaguered and I need all the friends I can get.'

Impulsively, Sam gave Amy a hug.

Later, Amy tried to get Debbie on her own so she could complain, but Bernard was always with her. Besides, once the anger had left her, Amy was filled with dread at confronting her aunt. Perhaps she should call a Board Meeting between the two of them, and put this issue on a formal footing. But that idea filled her with dismay.

* * *

The last Friday in January, Luke came in through the front door just as Amy was shutting up shop. 'I've got Gill on my mobile. She wants to speak to you,' said Luke. 'Your phone went to voicemail.'

Amy dried her hands swiftly and took the phone. 'Hello.'

'Hiya, I just thought you might like to know the library is selling off its withdrawn books. I know you're always on the lookout for stock, but some of them look useful for you personally. There are some nice non-fiction books too, very reasonably priced. I thought you had the idea of leaving books on the outdoor tables to encourage browsing; you won't want your best books for that.'

'Oh thanks. I'll come over right now.' Amy changed to sensible shoes and a warm coat, then grabbed her purse. 'It's ridiculous,' she laughed. 'Last summer I was thinking off culling my books.'

'You did,' said Luke. 'You just replaced them, that's all.'

'Coming?'

'No. I have a mountain of marking to do, and I'm shattered already. Sorry. If you buy loads, phone me and I'll come and help lug them home.' He did look tired, with dark bags beneath his red-rimmed eyes.

'Drat it, I can't find my library card,' said Amy as she sorted though her purse.

'You don't need it if you're buying, not borrowing.'

Just as Amy was leaving, Sam met her on the threshold. 'I've just emailed you, but I think I need to tell you things in person.'

'Eek, I'm just off to the library.'

Luke's phone went. He listened, then said, 'Gill says Bernard is in the library using one of the computers.'

'Why? Why would he do that when he can use Debbie's?' asked Amy.

'Why indeed?' said Luke. 'Makes you wonder, doesn't it?'

'I'm going to have a look while I'm there, and see if I can find out why,' said Amy.

'I'm coming too,' said Sam with a defiant jut of her chin.

Amy looked at her watch. 'The library closes soon; we haven't got very long. Let's see if we can find out what Bernard is up to.'

As they were walking rapidly up the street, Amy paused, 'Bother. He'll spot us if we get too close, and stop whatever he's doing.'

Sam pulled a pashmina from her pocket and looked at her dim reflection in a shop window as she wound it into graceful folds around her head, until only her face was showing. 'I bet he won't recognise me unless I actually speak. He's hardly spoken to me except to tell me I'm fired. He's not normally there on a Saturday . . . and that's something I need to tell you about.'

'Later please, Sam. Later.' They got to the

library. 'You go in first.'

Sam did as she was bidden. Bernard was sitting at the computer desks, luckily with his back to them. Gill appeared beside Amy. 'I was just mooching over the books when he drifted in. He faffed around with the computer for a bit, then asked one of the librarians for assistance. Probably doesn't know how to log on.'

'I don't understand how he can log on at all,' whispered Amy. 'He needs a library card for that. Otherwise anyone could walk in off the street and view something totally unsuitable without trace. He can't have a card because he's not really resident.'

'Maybe he's lied to get one,' Amy said.

As they were watching, Sam drifted up to Bernard silently, paused for a moment or two, sat down beside him at the next computer and logged on.

'Perhaps we should sneak up behind him,' said Gill.

'Not yet. Leave it to Sam.'

'Sam?'

'She's just sat down next to him.'

'That's Sam? Good grief, I didn't recognise her.'

'Good.'

They lurked behind some of the bookshelves. 'I feel like I'm in some second-rate spy movie,' said Gill. 'What's he up to now?'

Amy pulled a book off and peeped through. 'Still on the computer. We're getting some funny looks from the librarian.'

'Sit down and start reading then. It's because we're snooping and looking suspicious. She probably thinks we're going to nick some books.' They sat down in some comfy chairs which were angled so that they were mostly hidden but Bernard was just visible to them.

'I'm leading you astray.' Amy laughed.

'Yes, you are. I think it might be time for someone else to take over as Debbie's Macmillan nurse. I'm getting too personally involved. I really shouldn't be doing this. I'll get struck off.'

'Seriously? Oh Gill, I never realised.'

'Well, not yet, because I haven't done anything to compromise my professionalism. But it's not ideal. Mind you, it's getting to the stage when your aunt won't need me.'

Amy found herself grinning at this. 'True. Makes me believe in miracles.'

'Bother. I think he's spotted us. Shh, he's standing up. He's off. He looks a bit furtive,' said Gill.

'Maybe he thinks we haven't seen him.'

'Probably. Under normal circumstances the natural thing to do is go and greet someone you know, and we didn't. Ergo, we haven't noticed him.'

They waited until Bernard had left the building, then went over to Sam. Sam had deftly switched chairs and was sitting opposite the terminal Bernard had been using. 'He was using your card to log on,' said Sam to Amy. 'He had it next to him on the desk, but he's taken it with him.'

'The rat. What was he doing?'

'Emailing, then browsing. I noted the sites down. I hope he didn't notice. He seemed spooked and left in a hurry.'

'I think he spotted us,' said Gill.

Sam grinned. 'He was so spooked he forgot to log off. Which means I can look at what he's been up to.'

'Good,' said Gill. 'But look, we must make an exact note of every site and every move. This might be evidence, and we need to preserve it as best we can.'

Amy gave Gill a strange look. 'OK, Sam, where did he visit?'

They went backwards though his browsing session, through a couple of quality auction house sites, one of which dealt with fine art antiques, including Tiffany lamps. 'That's them,' said Amy. 'Those are Aunty's lamps, I swear it.'

Sam looked very excited at this. The

previous page Bernard had settled on was jewellery. Rings. 'They look like mine,' said Amy. Back further over several items. 'They look familiar, but I can't swear to it. Ah, that teapot, that looks like one of ours. I never knew it was that valuable,' she added, looking at the reserve price. 'I nearly dropped it once. Oh gosh.'

'He's got two windows open,' said Sam, bringing the next window up. It was his email account, still live, still accessible. 'What an idiot he is,' said Sam. 'Maybe he thinks shrinking it down is the same as closing it down.'

'Can we print these?' said Amy.

'Yes,' said Sam. 'As long as it's for our own studies. Copyright and all that. We have to pay for each sheet.'

'Print that inbox page please, Sam,' Amy said. There were emails from a KelvinMBBM-FineArtsAntiques@ and from AlmaABPettifer. Then Sam clicked on the sent box, and printed the contents of that page.

'Look at his contact list next,' urged Gill.

'Should we be doing this? It's illegal, surely?' Amy bit her lip.

'Don't know,' grunted Gill. 'You're only looking at what someone using your login details has left visible. You have every right to see where he's been, I think. He could have committed fraud or downloaded something untoward. Morally I think you have every right. Legally, I don't know, but who cares? He's a criminal and your Aunt's happiness and property are at risk.'

He had half a dozen people in his email address book. Sam said, 'This is great, and I'll tell you why later. Time's running out. I want that last email he sent. You'll see why.' She opened it.

Amy read it. 'Print it out,' she said in a chilled voice. 'Let's print it out several times so we don't lose it.'

'I'm going to re-send it to my address then wipe all obvious trace of doing that,' said Sam.

'Send it to my address, too, to be sure,' said Gill, and she gave it to her. Sam did so, then opened the next one he'd sent.

The librarian came over. 'Last five minutes please, ladies. We like people to log off half an hour before closing time, and settle up any printing costs.'

'OK, thanks,' said Amy. The librarian drifted off, and Amy said, 'Just print as much as you can. We'll read it later.'

'OK, and I'll do a screen dump and print of each of the sites he visited, and I'll email those to you too,' said Sam.

'Ladies, your time is up,' said the librarian.

'Look, this is urgent, desperately important,' begged Amy. 'It's . . . '

'A matter of life and death,' said Gill.

The librarian laughed. 'Just a few minutes more, then; I must insist.' She walked off but kept giving them chivvying looks.

'I think I've got all I can that's reasonable,' said Sam a minute later. Amy paid for the printouts, and they escaped into the cold night air. Amy shivered, but it wasn't the external cold which caused it. She felt all iced up inside, because she knew she had the evidence of wrongdoing that would hopefully put Bernard in prison. But in the process she would be breaking Aunty Debbie's heart all over again.

28

Amy and the others let themselves in quietly. 'I'm so cold,' moaned Amy. 'I need to think this through. What on earth am I going to say to Debbie? I think I might wait until Bernard has gone to bed, and then speak to her.'

'Let's talk this over first and get your mind straight, otherwise she might not believe you despite the emails. After all, she might think they're some sort of elaborate plot of yours and that you are the author of the emails,' said Gill.

'Besides,' piped up Sam, 'I sent you an important email. It's got some links to some interesting sites which I think you should look at before you talk to Mrs Driscoll. And I ought to be getting home soon or my parents will worry.'

'Oh Sam, sorry, yes. Do you want to give them a call and tell them you're OK?'

Amy went round and tapped on Luke's French windows. There was no answer. Her heart clenched. She knocked again; still no reply. She tried the door handle carefully. Unlocked. She looked inside and turned the light on. He was asleep over his marking. He woke suddenly, looked like a rabbit in headlights for a moment, then found himself. 'Oh crumbs. I've not been sleeping well,' he said. 'I've been worrying about you and me. And bother; I've drooled on someone's homework. What's up? You look shattered.'

'Come and see.'

Luke followed her round to the old kitchen. Amy fetched her laptop, logged on and picked up Sam's email. When she clicked on the links she found herself at the same internet sites Bernard had been visiting.

'Those rings have only just come up for sale. And the lamps haven't been offered before while I've been looking,' said Sam. 'But I concentrated on places near Stockport. Oh, and the cousin is a member of various internet forums discussing antiques and stuff. And I know his address. And no, I didn't hack into anything, or do anything illegal, if that's what you're wondering.'

'So it looks like proof that Bernard's the thief and takes the stuff up to his cousin to sell,' said Luke. 'But is that enough to show Debbie that he's no good? It might not be; she seems to have been very forgiving in the past.'

'My dad's on his way,' said Gill. 'I just phoned him.'

'What? Why?' Amy blinked at her.

'I think he needs to see this. He's a detective inspector with the police. He'll know what to do. This looks like serious fraud and worse. Besides,' she said with a sympathetic glance at Amy, 'I think it might be better if you don't confront Debbie. It might be better to keep what we've found a secret from her. If Bernard is arrested in relation to some stolen property, then it's not your fault, is it? You did report the lamps as stolen, didn't you?'

'Yes, and the rings. But not the other stuff we've found on the internet. I hadn't really missed them, only in the 'where've I put that so-and-so?' sense.'

'Is it really a matter for the police?' asked Luke. He still had the cute, bewildered half-asleep look.

'Read the email please, Luke, and you tell me,' Gill said.

My beloved Alma,

Not long now, my love. She's marrying me soon — we've got the Certificate of No Impediment and it's all systems go. Pat told me Debbie's cancer was very serious, but unfortunately her treatment seems to be successful so far, the quacks being very pleased with the chemo, so it's Plan B. I'll have to pick my moment carefully, especially if she makes any move to write another will, because I had a look at her current will and it favours Pat and her children, and I can't risk her writing another in their favour. (You do know that any previous wills are annulled on marriage in England, don't you, and that as her husband I inherit if there's no will? I don't know whether that's true in Canada, so I just thought I'd mention it, my love.)

The life insurance will come in very handy. I found the documents when I was having a good look round . . . It was worth keeping up those payments after all. How would you fancy living in a Georgian house in a quaint English town? Anyways, my love, I have plenty of insulin put by. Accidents are too chancy, as I know from past experience.

I know the cash is running out, but you have to speculate to accumulate. I'm hoping for a cash injection soon, which is better than an insulin injection, ha ha.

I'll phone you when I'm a married man.
All my love,
Bernie.

Luke raked his head in the way Amy loved best. 'I suppose the cash injection is the proceeds from the sale of the Tiffany lamps and rings. This is a conspiracy to murder, isn't it? Or am I reading too much into the 'pick my moment', 'Plan B' and talk of wills?'

'He's a fool if he thinks he'd get away with murder using insulin,' said Gill. 'There would be a post-mortem because it would be an unexplained death, and low blood sugar would be found. Besides, he's a bit screwed up on the rules of intestacy, I think, unless he owns the house as a joint tenant, and I presume he doesn't.'

'I'm not sure,' said Amy. 'I think it's Aunty's house outright. It was her dad's. It's been in the family for years. But whatever, being caught after the event wouldn't help Debbie, would it? What a fool Bernard is.'

'What a criminal,' said Gill.

There was a tap on the door which nearly stopped Amy's heart.

'Here's my dad,' said Gill.

Luke let him in and Gill introduced him as DI Toby Hutchings. Amy thought he was very hot, considering his age — distinguished-looking, with an air of decisive authority.

He said, 'Please call me Toby.' When they showed him what they'd found, he looked very thoughtful. 'I think there's enough to arrest him over the stolen lamps, but that would take time because we'll want to get a search warrant for his cousin's address, and stop the sale of the lamps and so on. I'm not sure this email is enough to arrest him for conspiracy to murder, and if I only arrest him for theft and fraud, chances are he'd be bailed pending further enquiries. Your aunt could still marry him.'

'Oh she wouldn't marry him after this,' said Amy.

'Are you sure?' asked Luke. 'Six months ago if I'd asked you if she'd remarry Bernard you'd have said there was more chance of mice eating the moon.'

Amy opened her mouth to protest, but said nothing. Debbie always was a bit daft over Bernard, or she would never have let him back into her life.

Luke picked up the email again and read it. 'I wonder . . . 'Accidents are chancy'? Amy, can you tell Toby why Debbie won't go into the cellar?'

Amy explained, then said, 'Let's show you what we found, Toby. But we'll have to be quiet. If Bernard comes snooping he'll know something's up.'

'If he comes snooping, I'll arrest him,' said Toby.

Gill took one look into the black maw of the cellar and said, 'I'll keep watch up here.'

Luke went to his rooms to fetch the broken strut he'd hidden, while Amy found the cable of the lamp they'd left down there and plugged it in. Toby pulled in a breath when he saw the mannequin, but he walked carefully down the steps. Luke and Amy followed.

'When we first came down here there was a pile of struts from where the banister and handrail was mended by Bernard. They disappeared one day when Amy and I were in school and Bernard had free run of the place. But he missed one which I'd picked up to look at and absent-mindedly put to one side. When I found it I hid it in my room. Look.' Luke held up the broken strut with what amounted to perforations where Bernard 'had tried to strengthen them'.

Toby took the strut pieces, studied them carefully, then shook his head. 'This could be the work of a helpful fool,' he said, 'not an attempt at murder. Even if we arrested him, without more evidence we'd have to let him go.'

'You don't think it's suspicious that they vanished, like Bernard was covering his old tracks?' said Amy.

'I think it's suspicious, but I'm not sure it's suspicious enough.'

'I wonder,' said Luke, fiddling with the short screw he'd picked up and placed in the jam jar on the old cane table months before. 'I should have done this ages ago.' He went to the toolbox and found a suitable screwdriver. The new struts were four inches wide and strong, with three evenly spaced screws holding them to the edge of the steps. No way would that wood splinter or snap if weight were put on it, but if Debbie refused to set foot into the cellar after her near miss, there was no reason for it not to be made safe after a murder attempt had failed. Uncle Bernard wouldn't want to repeat the accident himself.

Luke undid the screws holding one of the new struts. When he'd taken the strut off he looked closely at the brickwork where the wood had been screwed on. 'Look. There are three evenly spaced holes in the brickwork, fitting the new strut. No signs that any previous holes have been filled in, just small pits in the brickwork where the drill overshot the end of the wood of the original slat when it was drilled out *in situ* — no rawplugs, no nothing.' He offered the old bits of wood up to the middle hole. 'It looks to me as if the extra holes were only drilled into the wood, not deeply into the wall, and these very short screws put into the wood to make it look as if it was fastened to the brickwork with three screws, not one. That looks like deliberate sabotage to me. Lazy, though.' The short screw was too short to engage with the wall.

'Very lazy. I think that's enough for me to arrest him. I wish all criminals were this stupid. If he'd succeeded, and your poor aunt had broken her neck, did he really think he'd get away with it?' Toby turned businesslike. 'Right, this is now a crime scene, and I need to get several things in motion. First, though, I'll request some help to invite a certain gentleman to the station. He might put up a bit of a fight.'

★　★　★

They stayed in the downstairs kitchen until some more police officers arrived, a man and a woman in uniform. 'Will you show us which room Bernard is sleeping in, please, Amy? Actually, could you go into the living room to see if he's there? If he isn't we'll assume he's gone to bed. Then lock yourself in the bathroom until after the arrest, when you'll need to comfort your aunt, no doubt,' said Toby.

The lounge, dining room and kitchen were all empty. Bernard and Debbie must have both gone to bed. Amy hid in the bathroom and waited for the rumpus. Her heart hammered painfully and she could hardly breathe.

Then came a tap in the door. 'Could you

come out please, Amy? They're not here. They've gone.'

Amy unlocked the door.

'There's a note in the lady's bedroom,' said the female officer. 'It's addressed to Amy.' Amy went through into her aunt's room. The bed was neatly made. In the middle of it was the letter. She tore it open.

My darling Amy,

By the time you read this I will be well on the way to becoming Mrs Bernard Murray for the second time. I now know that Bernard never really stopped loving me. It was his depression that made him abandon me like that. It grieves me that you cannot see this in the same light. I think it's jealousy that makes you blind, and fear that he may oust you from your business, the café. Well, be assured that your home is here, and the business is for you to run as you see fit. Bernard is wealthy enough to support me. We will live in the upstairs flat, and now that Luke has been given his notice, you will have the entire run of the ground floor. That Luke is a real distraction to you, and probably a thief besides, and you will be better off without him.

We have deliberately decided not to get

married in the local registry office because I wouldn't put it past that Luke, or even you, to burst in and make a fuss. Neither do I feel that you would be welcome as guests anyway, since you have made no secret of your antagonistic feelings towards Bernard. This saddens me, but I think, once the wedding is a fait accompli, *you will get used to the idea.*

Much love, Debbie.

'Oh well, if they've gone, sir, can we . . . ?'

'Yes. Thanks. I appreciate your help,' said Toby absently. The officers vanished downstairs. Luke, Gill and Sam came up. 'They've gone, then?' asked Luke. Amy nodded.

Toby held his hand out for the note. 'This *is* your aunt's handwriting, isn't it?'

Amy looked up sharply. 'Yes.'

'Right, I think we have enough to issue a warrant for his arrest, but we might not find him in time to prevent the marriage. I'll do all we can to locate him. Do you happen to know his car number plate, or have you got any photographs of him?'

'I've no photos, sorry. Aunty might have, but I don't suppose she's printed any.'

'Pity. Leave it with me. Can I take all these printouts, please? I don't think there's much more you can do here, Gill. Shall I drop you off at home on the way to the nick?'

'Good idea, Dad.'

When they'd gone, Amy, Luke and Sam went down to the downstairs kitchen again.

'So when did Debbie and Bernard go?' said Amy. 'We saw Bernard in the library a couple of hours ago. He must have sneaked back and they left while we were faffing around in the library.'

'Or he met Debbie somewhere else. I expect they thought you might try to stop them if they went off together. So perhaps he went off with the van already packed with their suitcases, parked up, sent his emails, then waited for Debbie to join him.'

'Look at the time,' exclaimed Amy. 'Sam, your parents will flip. We should have suggested Gill's dad take you home too.'

'No they won't. I've phoned them again and told them I'm safe and will take a taxi home when I'm ready. They trust me to be sensible. Please don't send me home now.'

'But there's nothing we can do now except pray the police find Bernard in time,' objected Amy.

'Yes there is,' said Sam. 'For one thing, you could look in your aunt's computer for photos of Bernard, email them to Gill and she can give them to her dad.'

'Oh, I'm not sure I like that idea,' said

Amy. 'It's private.'

'Better that than let Bernard murder Debbie,' said Luke. 'I'm sorry, love, but I think needs must. Sam won't look at anything personal, will you?'

'I expect her photos will be easy to find,' said Sam. 'People usually have a folder called 'Pictures' or 'Photos'.'

'You two do that,' said Luke. 'I'm going to do a search for a list of registry offices on my laptop. In the morning we'll phone each one and ask if their wedding is booked there.'

Sam easily located the photographs. 'Your aunt ought to have this password protected,' she said disapprovingly. 'Anyone could access her accounts. Still, worked out OK for us.'

'And now, Miss, I'm running you home,' said Amy, 'even if it is just down the road.'

29

Amy was woken from a bad night's sleep by the persistent ringing of the doorbell. It was gone eight o'clock. 'Oh gosh, I meant to get up two hours ago,' she moaned, looking accusingly at her alarm clock. She must have turned it off in her sleep.

She went downstairs. 'Sam, why are you here so early?'

Luke appeared. 'What's up?'

Sam was hopping from leg to leg. 'I've been thinking. And I've got more stuff like Alma's home phone number from the internet. But more importantly, they might not be getting married at a registry office.'

Amy gasped. 'Bother. You're right. We just assumed. It could be any approved premises. And the police are busy. With the best will in the world, they might not have enough manpower to find out which registry office — and even then, they might draw a blank if it's in a hotel or something.'

'I'm sure Gill's dad is putting one hundred percent effort in,' said Luke.

'I've had an idea,' said Sam. 'I know Bernard used the library computers to send the email to Alma. He couldn't afford anyone to see that email. But surely if they were looking for somewhere to get married they'd look together, online? If so, we might be able to trace their recent browsing.'

'It's worth a try,' said Amy. They went upstairs to the lounge and Amy logged on to Debbie's computer while Luke sorted out some breakfast and desperately needed coffee.

Amy and Sam found a hotel website which was licensed for weddings in a town about two hours away. Amy was all for jumping in the car there and then, but Luke said, 'Phone Gill's dad; tell him.'

Toby phoned back to say he'd checked and there was no wedding between Bernard Murray and Debbie Driscoll booked at that venue . . . could they look again? He'd be over shortly.

By the time Toby had joined them they ended up with a list of possible places that Debbie had browsed over. 'I've put an ANPR tag on the vehicle,' he said. 'But I've got no other help at the moment, so this is useful work. We need the venue.'

'I could look at her emails, see if there's a booking receipt,' suggested Sam.

'Great,' said Amy.

'This looks promising,' said Sam, scanning

Debbie's inbox. 'It's from a hotel. Shall I open it?'

'Yes please.'

'Bingo,' said Toby. It was a small, twee hotel in a woodland glade just an hour's drive away. The payment was for an overnight stay for four people, breakfast, and the ceremony at ten o'clock. When Sam looked at the website it said it was ideal for quiet, private weddings in a romantic setting, and gave a map, which Sam printed out.

'What now?' said Amy. 'I want to rush over and stop her.'

'Right,' said Toby. 'I think you need to be there if possible, to pick up the emotional fall-out. I'll go in my job car, because I can blue light it, if necessary. I'll also see if I can get some assistance, but that might not be possible. You follow in your car, Amy, as fast as you can safely. It's not as if her life is in immediate danger, so no reason to break your own neck over it.'

The cold, fresh wind of common sense blew over Amy. 'But we must find it before they leave for their honeymoon,' she added with another stab of fear. 'They're only booked in for last night. As soon as she's married him she's in danger, especially as he now knows her prognosis is good and she's not likely to die of cancer. He might bump her off as soon as practicable to stop her writing another will.'

'Right, let's go,' said Toby. 'Not you, Sam. Sorry. It's too dangerous.'

Sam's face fell and she looked about to burst into tears. 'Please,' she appealed to Amy.

'Toby's right,' said Amy. 'Besides, it's going to be emotionally very unpleasant and I'm not sure Debbie would want you there because she'd be embarrassed later. But can you please look after the café for me? We're due to open soon.'

'Oh gosh, of course, yes. I'll do my best.'

'If it's too much, just close for the day and put a note re personal circumstances.' Amy gave the girl a hug.

★ ★ ★

'We're lost. Oh, why don't you have a Sat Nav?' said Luke as they drove down the single-lane track through the woods. 'This can't be right.'

'Phone Toby,' said Amy, bouncing the car over a pothole and grimacing. 'See if he's found it yet.'

Luke did so. 'He says it's the right road, keep going, we can't be far behind him. And a squad car is on its way.'

320

Abruptly, they came across Toby's car parked in a passing place. He was walking back to the car down a path through the woods. 'It's a couple of hundred yards up that way. I didn't like to drive any closer in case I spooked him. The van's there, so I presume they're getting ready for the wedding.'

Amy looked at her watch. 'It's nearly ten o'clock. We should go and stop this.'

'And I want to get my man,' said Toby. 'I wish we had time to wait for backup.'

'If they see a police car, Bernard will guess,' Amy said. 'You, on the other hand, might just look like you're lost, or a hotel guest. And we might just look like anxious relatives.'

'OK, we'll wander up on foot,' said Toby. 'There's plenty of cover, with rhododendron bushes lining the last bit.'

They walked quietly up to the building. Sure enough, Bernard's white van was there, as well as several other vehicles. Amy and Luke followed Toby round to the back door. There were sounds of someone moving around in the kitchen. Toby knocked on the door with his knuckles. A rather flustered-looking woman in a pinny answered the door and boggled at his warrant card. She let them into the kitchen, where she had obviously just finished serving breakfast. 'Is there a Bernard Murray staying here?' asked Toby.

She nodded. 'They're having a pre-wedding meeting with the registrar.' She glanced at the clock. 'The wedding's about to start. Is there a problem?'

'Yes. Show us through please.'

The woman silently showed them through the most romantic and charming hallway to a small room where Bernard, Debbie, a couple of Debbie's friends and someone Amy guessed was the registrar were standing. Debbie's face was a mixture of guilt, incredulity and pleasure. Bernard looked thunderous. Toby walked straight up to him. 'Bernard Murray, I'm arre . . . '

Bernard grabbed Debbie's upper arms and shoved her roughly at Toby, who caught her, then struggled to keep his feet as Bernard barged past them both. Bernard aimed a punch at Luke, who ducked, and with a slick movement, brought Bernard down onto his front, one arm behind his back.

'Amy, take,' said Toby, passing Debbie into Amy's arms before dropping to his knees beside the prone Bernard, and slapping handcuffs on him. 'Bernard Murray, I'm arresting you on suspicion of theft, fraud, conspiracy to commit fraud, attempted murder and conspiracy to commit murder. You do not have to say anything, but it may harm your defence . . . '

The rest was drowned out by a heart-rending wail from Debbie. If Amy hadn't been holding her, Debbie would probably have fainted. 'I don't believe it,' said Debbie, finding one of the seats. 'Whose murder?'

'Yours, Aunty. Sorry,' said Amy, blinking back the tears.

'Don't listen to them,' Bernard raved into the carpet. 'It's lies, I tell you, lies.'

'Come back into the dining room,' suggested the registrar. 'This is most irregular.'

The two friends of Debbie's were standing, mouths agape, exchanging aghast looks. 'Can someone tell us what's going on?' said one of them.

'The wedding's off, I'm afraid,' said Amy.

They helped Debbie into the dining room. Amy could feel Debbie trembling as she held her arm. Amy's heart was still thundering in her ears. Two police officers arrived and Toby handed Bernard over to them.

'Don't listen, it's lies, it's that Luke. He stole the lamps and things. He's framing me.' Bernard's raging protests diminished as he was placed in the police car, then were cut off as the door was closed. The car drove off.

'Perhaps you would like to tell me what this is all about,' said Debbie icily, having regained her composure. 'Amy, love, this really is too bad.'

'I'm sorry Aunty, but it had to be done. Your life was in danger,' Amy sniffed. 'We intercepted this email.' She handed it over.

Debbie read it and turned pale. 'Who's Alma?'

'Phone her yourself,' said Amy. 'Ask her. We found her number.'

'I'd rather you didn't do that,' said Toby. 'Takes two to make a conspiracy, and my counterparts in Canada are about to ask this Alma some rather searching questions.'

Debbie's icy hauteur collapsed in a welter of tears. 'I love him. Loved him. He made me feel special again, made me feel like a sexy woman despite all that's happened to me. I feel so ugly now.' She groped in vain for a tissue.

Toby supplied a serviette. 'You are an attractive woman, no question of that,' he said gallantly. 'You surely don't need a criminal with an ulterior motive to tell you that.'

'Really?'

'Well, I think so. Truly I do.'

Amy noticed with astonishment that the detective was blushing faintly. Not just a gallant remark, then, but an honest one. She saw an admiring light in his eyes.

'But my hair . . . ' said Debbie, putting a

hand to her unruly mop.

'I know it's curly and a bit wayward now, but I find that rather fetching. And it will grow straight again, just as you've grown to like it curly, I expect.' Toby's eyes looked inward momentarily, as if revisiting the past.

'I've had an awful shock,' said Debbie. 'I've been a bit of a fool.'

'I'm afraid I'll need to ask you some questions, and you'll need to make a statement. In fact, you all will need to make statements.'

The registrar cleared her throat. 'I've been asked to remind you that another wedding party is due to arrive at noon. It's just that your cars are in the way and it's all a bit . . . difficult.'

'We'll leave now. I'd like to seize Bernard's luggage as evidence, please, Ms Driscoll. And yours, unless you have something you need desperately, like medicine.'

'No, no, of course,' said Debbie quietly.

'And it may be best if I take you back to the police station immediately, rather than let Luke and Amy talk to you . . . it might contaminate your evidence. Will you be all right with that? It's rather tough on you, I'm afraid.'

'Actually, I think I should prefer that. I need to have some quiet thinking time

— coming-to-terms time,' said Debbie, tears coursing down her cheeks.

★ ★ ★

Back home, Sam looked at Amy with a question mark on her face.

'Got there in time,' said Amy. 'How's the café?'

'Manic. People have been great, though, being patient. And one of your regulars, Lucy, said she'd help keep the tables cleared and clean.'

'Oh what a star,' said Amy. 'Is she still here?'

'Yes I am,' said Lucy from behind her. 'And it's a pleasure. I brought some books I've decided to throw out, and found Sam here was struggling a bit, so offered to help. I hope you don't mind. It was easy because Josh is at home with his dad.'

'Mind? You've been so kind,' said Amy. She sagged down on the seat by the till.

'I'll get you a coffee,' said Luke.

'Please. I feel like I have scrambled egg for brains.'

★ ★ ★

Later, when the café closed, Amy gave Sam a précis of what had happened.

'So is Ms Driscoll still with the police? Was she arrested too?'

'Good lord, no. She's the victim,' said Amy. 'I wonder if Alma's a victim too.'

'No,' said Sam decisively. 'If someone told you he was contemplating murder, wouldn't you do something about it?'

'Of course.' Then Amy wondered, *But what if it was Luke?* 'I hope so. I don't suppose we know for sure until faced with the dilemma. Bernard is very glib-tongued, very convincing. He even had me fooled for some of the time. Now, I'm going for a lie down before I fall down.'

She woke to Luke's knocking on the door. 'Debbie's home. Toby brought her. She'd like to see you. Us.'

Amy sat up abruptly, with a sick lurch of her heart. It was no good; this had to be faced.

Debbie was in her lounge, sitting stiffly upright in her armchair. 'Sit down, all of you, please.' Her lips were crimped. She looked brittle. Toby took the other armchair, and Luke and Amy sat on the settee. Amy's hand sought Luke's. He squeezed.

'I've been an utter fool,' began Debbie. 'Bernard let me down once before. Badly. Nobody knows just how badly. At the time I discovered some serious discrepancies in the company accounts; a lot of money was missing. They looked like errors, which I made good from my savings, but it wasn't enough. That ruined the bookshop, and hastened its closure. Not that I think it could have continued with competition from the internet. Lord knows why I covered up for him — he always was a bit of a spiv, as my dad would say. I defied Dad and married Bernard, and look where it landed me. No children and a broken heart. Twice over, now. I thought he was just a charming but incompetent man, and I loved him. But now I know the extent of his evil. Those Tiffany lamps for sale online are definitely mine; I identified them. And those rings do look like yours, Amy. We can't have them back yet because they're exhibits in his trial. We also can't talk about this anymore because it's *sub judice* . . . isn't that right, Toby?'

Toby nodded.

Debbie continued. 'Luke, I have wronged you. I thought badly of you when you saw through Bernard, and only ever sought to protect Amy's interests. And mine, come to think of it. Will you forgive me? Will you stay? Please.'

'Oh yes, please. I'd love to. I want . . . I need . . . ' Luke covered his face briefly. 'I think you might need some help round the house, for a start, especially for the upcoming season. And . . . and moral support. I'm good for that too.'

'Just so long as you don't talk about the case,' said Toby. 'I will need to see you both, and young Sam for statements, but that can wait until tomorrow as you all look exhausted. Now, I think I must leave you. I have a mountain of paperwork to do.'

'I'll see you out,' said Luke.

'What a nice man Toby is,' said Debbie when she heard the front door close. 'Such a gentleman. Such an air of quiet authority. You feel safe with him, don't you?'

'Aunty, I have to advise you against forming romantic attachments on the rebound,' said Amy with a gleam in her eye. Then she winced because it seemed so tactless, but Debbie didn't take offence.

Debbie smiled ruefully. 'So true, Amy love. And I'm not ready for that, not nearly ready. He tells me he has a year and a half to go . . . '

'Sounds like someone serving a prison sentence,' said Amy with a subdued smile.

'I know,' said Debbie, her laugher laced with an edge of hysteria. 'I meant before he retires. He's charming. We had a long chat about inconsequential things on the way home. He's made me feel a lot better about everything; less of a fool.'

They heard Luke's tread on the stairs. He came back into the lounge. 'How are you bearing up, Debbie? We feel so dreadful about all this.'

'Oddly enough, I don't feel too bad,' said Debbie. 'I am upset, naturally, and I feel like a complete idiot, but not as bad as I'd expect, which surprises me. I'm more angry with myself for being a fool, than heartbroken over Bernard. It's as if I've been inoculated against him after the first time. If anything, it's cured me of him completely. In my heart I never did quite let go of him first time around.'

Amy looked for something distracting to say but could only come up with, 'That was a lovely hotel you stayed at.'

'When we get married I'd like to have it in a place like that,' said Luke.

Amy gaped. 'Is that an assumption, or a proposal?'

Luke blushed. 'I think it's a sort of Freudian slip. Shows what's going on in my mind. Sorry, Amy my love. I've been too afraid to talk about the future, and everything's too emotional at the moment, but when everything has calmed down, I intend to ask you to marry me — No.' He pressed two fingers against her lips. 'It's too soon, and you've been through too much to even think about it yet, so I won't ask just now. But I love you, Amy. I want you to know that.'

'I know you do. I know it in my heart of hearts,' said Amy. 'I love you too.' She pulled his head down towards hers, and they kissed.

We do hope that you have enjoyed reading this large print book.

Did you know that all of our titles are available for purchase?

We publish a wide range of high quality large print books including:
Romances, Mysteries, Classics
General Fiction
Non Fiction and Westerns

Special interest titles available in large print are:
The Little Oxford Dictionary
Music Book
Song Book
Hymn Book
Service Book

Also available from us courtesy of Oxford University Press:
Young Readers' Dictionary
(large print edition)
Young Readers' Thesaurus
(large print edition)

For further information or a free brochure, please contact us at:
Ulverscroft Large Print Books Ltd.,
The Green, Bradgate Road, Anstey,
Leicester, LE7 7FU, England.
Tel: (00 44) 0116 236 4325
Fax: (00 44) 0116 234 0205

Other titles published by Ulverscroft:

A LIFE LESS LONELY

Jill Barry

A quiet English town is home to Dr Andrea Palmer, young widow of a military hero and mum to little Josh. Focused upon her son and vulnerable mother, she has no thoughts of finding romance. Events conspire to change that, but she wonders how many times a broken heart can mend . . . Keir is the self-styled bad boy of the consultants' dining room. He dislikes his eligible bachelor tag and anticipates meeting Andrea only because her qualifications perfectly equip her to co-present his findings. When Andrea and Keir meet, each feels a frisson. But flirtatious nurse Moira has other ideas, and is determined to have Keir for herself . . .

SOMEDAY WE'LL TELL EACH OTHER EVERYTHING

Daniela Krien

It is the summer of 1990. The Berlin Wall has collapsed, and Germany is preparing for reunification. Away from this upheaval, young Maria moves in with her boyfriend on his family's farm in the sleepy countryside of the East. A chance encounter with an enigmatic older man ignites an improbable affair. Henner is damaged and unpredictable, yet Maria is uncontrollably drawn to him. As the summer progresses, keeping their passion a secret becomes ever more difficult. A bold and powerful love story ensues, where violence and desire are inextricably entwined, painting a portrait of a community in flux.